Praise for

Perfect Timing

Before He Cheats…an interesting take on the relationship between a submissive and his master…a story where the main characters had to overcome a lot of inner struggles to have more understanding for one another and it was a good read. ~ *Whipped Cream*

If you like stories about men falling in love despite themselves, if a D/s relationship with a curious and totally inexperienced submissive partner fascinate you, and if very hot sex scenes that are tender at the same time are your thing, I am pretty sure you will like While Under the Influence. ~ *Queer Magazine Online*

Total-E-Bound Publishing books by Kim Dare:

Pack Discipline:
The Mark of an Alpha
The Strength of a Gamma
The Duty of a Beta
The Love of a Mate

Perfect Timing:
You First
Silent Night
Time to Do
The Three Minute Man
Bi Now, Gay Later
The Stroke of Twelve
Before He Cheats
While Under the Influence

Collared:
Turquoise and Leather
Imperial Topaz

G-A-Y:
Gaydar
Gay Like You
Gay Until Graduation
Gay Since Today
Gay Pride
Gay for Pay
Gay Divorcee
Gay Man Seeks Same
Gay Friendly
Gay Best Friend
Gayday! Gayday!
Gayish

Anthologies:
Threefold: Trust, Love, Submit
Night of the Senses: Whispers
Caught in the Middle: Between Tooth and Paw
Friction: Yes!

Gaymes: Elliot's War

Seasonal Collections:
Christmas Spirits: The Gift
My Secret Valentine: Secret Service
Summer Seductions: In the Heat of the Moment
Mistletoe and Submission

PERFECT TIMING
Volume Four

Before He Cheats

While Under the Influence

KIM DARE

Perfect Timing Volume Four
ISBN # 978-0-85715-781-2
©Copyright Kim Dare 2011
Cover Art by April Martinez ©Copyright 2012
Interior text design by Claire Siemaszkiewicz
Total-E-Bound Publishing

Published in 2012 by Total-E-Bound Publishing, Think Tank, Ruston Way, Lincoln, LN6 7FL, United Kingdom.

Total-E-Bound Publishing is an imprint of Total-E-Ntwined Limited.

BEFORE HE
CHEATS

Dedication

To not being afraid to fight for what you want.

Chapter One

Monday

"My, my! Does Rupert have you house-trained already? He doesn't usually trust his toys with a key until their spirit's been completely broken."

Leon Powell frowned as he glanced over his shoulder. "What did you —?" He quickly cut himself off when he saw who stood at the bottom of the steps leading to Rupert's front door.

Somehow James Campbell was still able to look down his nose at Leon, even while standing a good three feet below him.

Leon opened his mouth, but hurriedly closed it again, before he ended up something he shouldn't. Heaving his heavy backpack into a more comfortable position on his shoulder, he took a deep breath.

Be polite, he reminded himself. Rupert does business with the guy. It would probably be a really bad idea to call him an arrogant pillock and slam the door in his face.

"I'm sorry," Leon said in his best 'I'm dealing with a professor I need a good grade from' voice. "I don't think Rupert's home right now, but when he gets back I'll make sure he knows you called."

Turning his back on James, Leon once more offered his key up to the lock on Rupert's front door.

Toy… Broken… Trained? James' words niggled at the back of his mind, but Leon did his best to push them away as he opened the door and stepped inside. He had plenty to think about after a day full of lectures and workshops. He didn't need anything else messing with his brain.

Crouching down to pick up the day's post, Leon only just stopped his backpack sliding off his shoulder and scattering a dozen thick text books across the elaborately tiled entrance hall.

Suddenly, the front door jerked towards him, almost knocking him off his feet. Leon looked up just in time to see James stride past him in a blur of expensive tailoring, as if he were no more important than the damn doormat.

"Rupert's—" Leon begun again.

"I'll wait."

Before Leon could say another word, James had marched straight into Rupert's study, as if he was the only one who actually had a right to be there. Leon's fist tightened around his keys as he pushed the jagged bits of metal into his jeans pocket. He was the one with the keys. *He* was the one who Rupert actually wanted to find waiting for him when he came home.

Quickly slamming the front door, Leon tossed the mail on the hall table and rushed after James.

Backpack hurriedly tossed into its habitual resting place beside the big leather sofa, Leon shoved his hands into his pockets. A moment later, he pulled them back out and made a conscious effort not to look like a nervous little school boy as he watched James run a critical eye over the various books and ornaments on Rupert's shelves.

Leon barely held back a sigh when he realised there really wasn't any polite way to get rid of the man. "Would you like something to drink?"

"Doesn't Rupert prefer his boys to kneel when asking their betters if they can be of service?" James asked, as he draped himself languidly into one of the high backed chairs flanking the fireplace.

"Boys?" Leon repeated, blankly. As in boys *plural*?

James' laughter was like fingernails on a chalkboard. "Don't tell me Rupert has you thinking you're the only submissive in his stable."

Submissives and stables and everything else be dammed. The only fact that really registered in Leon's mind was the possibility of his boyfriend screwing other guys. A strong hand clamped around his heart and squeezed several beats out of it.

For just one brief moment, Leon was too shocked to try to school his features into displaying anything other than his honest reaction. Sod's law that he had to meet James' eyes during those same few seconds.

"Child, Rupert's one of the most highly respected dominants in the city," James said. "You didn't really think you'd have him all to yourself?"

Leon just stared at him unable to bring a single word to his lips as he slowly lowered himself onto the sofa. It was either that or collapse to the floor as his knees buckled beneath him.

James laughed again. "I should have guessed that you were *very* new." He paused for a moment to look Leon up and down. "The first cheque obviously hasn't even cleared yet."

At least that was an insult Leon understood. His gaze automatically followed the same path James' had traced, taking in all the same details that James had no doubt been so quick to note.

Battered running shoes—complete with dozens of scuffs from all those times where he'd stopped his bike on the gravel outside his hall of residence and hadn't had time to bother with complicated things like brakes. Jeans that weren't any particular make and that were already shabby at the edges. And, last but not least, a long-sleeved and slightly paint-stained hoodie that screamed his status as a lowly art history student.

Resisting the urge to straighten up, or even push his hair out of his eyes when the overly long blond strands slipped forward to obscure his vision, Leon held James' gaze as if his life depended on it. "I'm not after Rupert's money."

James chuckled politely, as if Leon had just told an amusing anecdote at one of those fancy dinner parties Rupert had occasionally dragged him to. "Let me guess," he drawled. "You're just using him for sex— very *Pretty Woman*. Julia Roberts gets all the good lines, doesn't she?"

"I'm not a prostitute," Leon snapped.

James smiled the same fake smile so many of Rupert's friends pinned to their lips whenever they didn't want to waste a real smile on someone like him.

Leon frowned as he dropped his gaze to stare at the coffee table in the middle of the room, wondering at what precise point in the last six months he'd started thinking of himself as 'someone like him'?

Maybe it wasn't their fault, Leon told himself as he folded his arms across his body and tried his best to be charitable when he wasn't really in the mood. Rupert was rich, after all. Stupidly, impossibly rich in the way Leon had thought people only were in the movies.

Rupert had his own business, three sports cars, this stunning town house, another place in the country and a slew of gold diggers of both genders throwing themselves at him at every opportunity. And Leon had…well, half a dorm room, a rusty mountain bike, an insufficient scholarship and three quarters of his master's degree left to complete.

Of course people thought he was after Rupert's money! The important thing was Rupert knew he wasn't and he knew he wasn't, Leon told himself. James wasn't important—he was just a necessary evil.

"Rupert's meeting probably ran late," Leon muttered, in a half-hearted attempt to remain polite.

James didn't even bother to indicate he'd heard anyone speak. Silence fell over the room. Leon turned his attention to trying to rub away the smudge of oil paint he'd acquired on the pad of his thumb during one of his practical workshops. As he scrubbed at it, his mind wandered towards the topic of his latest project.

He jumped when the phone on Rupert's desk suddenly rang.

"That's probably his now," Leon said, not quite able to hide his relief as he pulled himself to his feet and quickly strode across the room. Stopping next to the desk, he waited patiently for the answering machine to pick up, just in case it wasn't actually Rupert calling to tell him he'd be home late.

Even if James was looking at him as if he was crazy, Leon was cheerfully willing to be damned before picking up the phone and finding out it was anyone else.

What the hell would he say? 'Hi, I'm sorry Rupert isn't here to take your call, but I'm his much-younger and completely skint student boyfriend, and I'll be happy to take a message for you'?

Finally, the answering machine picked up.

"Hi, Rupert, it's Gerald," the contraption reported to the world in general. "Sorry I missed you last weekend but it turns out I'm going to be in town this Friday after all. Give me a call if you're up for some fun. I've got a new flogger that I'm dying to try out!" The rich male voice left a number and hung up.

Leon was pretty sure he hadn't displayed any visible reaction until James' grating laughter filled the air again. "Oh, dear. It seems I was right. You've got some competition!"

Unable to think of a damn thing to say, Leon stayed mute for a full half a minute, just staring down at the phone. Eventually, as the silence dragged on and Leon's heart rate threatened to reach a critical tipping point, he had to say something, anything, to break it.

"He's probably just a friend." Even Leon wasn't sure who he was trying to convince. The voice had sounded *very* friendly.

"He sounded more like one of Rupert's submissives to me. And a sub whose much closer to his usual calibre of lover too. I'll bet you can't take one of Rupert's floggings half as well as he can…"

"No," Leon said, with every ounce of confidence he could muster. The guy had said 'last weekend' and no matter how kinky they both might be, he couldn't have had a date with Rupert then.

They'd spent every minute of the previous weekend together—just as they'd planned to for as long as Leon could remember. And Rupert had never even mentioned the possibility of him needing to cancel or having any other engagements. And, anyway, Leon told himself firmly, Rupert wasn't the type to cheat. For several seconds, Leon watched the little light on the answering machine blink off and on, announcing that there was one message waiting to be listened to. Rupert wasn't that type at all.

"You're sure?" James pushed.

"Yes." Leon was sure. He trusted Rupert, and he was going to keep on trusting him, even if an evil little voice in the back of his mind chose that moment to remind him that possibility of Rupert being more interested in double choc chip with extra sprinkles, rather than simple vanilla, had occurred to him more than a few times before.

"So, Rupert's told you that you're to be his only submissive?"

The question hit the air just as Leon forced himself to tear his eyes away from the blinking light and turn back to his guest. For just the briefest moment, his guard failed him. Something of his horror at the idea must have shown in his eyes.

"Oh, I see. How very quaint!" James laughed. "But, really, child, you surely can't expect Rupert to understand your—shall we say, rather less than sophisticated?—ideas. If he hasn't raised the matter of exclusivity, anybody who is anybody would realise he has every right to play with Gerald, or any other sub who catches his eye."

Leon looked down at his hand. His knuckles were white. His fingers were starting to cramp, but he couldn't quite convince himself to unfurl his fist.

Of course they were exclusive! A moment ago there'd been no question in his mind about that fact.

"You know, it's quite usual for dominants to take several lovers at the same time. And Rupert has never been short of offers."

James rose unhurriedly from the chair and crossed the room to stand directly in front of Leon. He stroked his fingers across Leon's cheek before Leon had a chance to pull away.

"You're such a silly little thing, but don't feel too bad. Keep your jealousy under wraps and Rupert might yet keep you around for a while longer. Do remember to tell him that I dropped by, won't you?" James offered Leon another obviously fake smile, turned and walked out of the study as if he didn't have a care in the world.

A few moments later, Leon heard the front door close behind him. He waited for the house to take on the safe, comfortable aura it usually possessed. No luck. It still felt like ghosts were tap-dancing up and down his spine.

Rubbing irritably at the back of his neck, Leon stood right in the middle of Rupert's study. Every conversation he'd ever had with the older man rushed through his head, as he searched for a conversation that he was sure had to have taken place.

Nothing.

Mentally scrolling through every curse word he knew, Leon turned back to the desk and studied the flashing light some more. It announced there was only one message waiting to be replayed.

Don't be jealous. Leon shook his head. Bloody stupid advice. He and Rupert were...

Spinning away from the desk, Leon pushed his hand through his hair and tried to think clearly. But, what the hell did he actually know about how two guys acted when they were...dating? Leon rolled his eyes at himself. He didn't even know if that was the right bloody word for what he and his first ever boyfriend were doing.

With a girl it would have been so easy. Leon had no doubt that if a guy and a girl got to the stage where they spent all their free time together, left half their wardrobes at the other person's house and the guy couldn't even remember the last time he'd slept at his own place, a certain amount of seriousness was implied.

Of course, none of his relationships with women had been conducted with a pink, leather-clad elephant in the room — that thing they both knew was there but neither had actually mentioned aloud to the other. Leon's teeth nipped at his bottom lip. He glanced over his shoulder and stared at the flashing light again.

They should talk about Gerald's call. When Rupert got home, Leon had no doubt he should calmly ask the other man exactly where he stood. He'd be sensible and mature and he'd make it clear to his boyfriend that he wanted them to be exclusive from that moment on. Maybe he'd even gather enough courage to ask Rupert exactly what he was into when it came to leather and…

Leon took a deep breath.

Yeah, like that was really going to happen. No, the best thing to do would be to make sure that when he finally acquired the balls to ask Rupert for them to be exclusive, he would be very inclined to say yes.

Leon nodded to himself. If there was one thing he really was certain of, it was that Rupert wasn't someone who anybody with half a brain gave up without a fight. His finger hovered over the buttons on the answering machine before he snatched it away.

Turning to pace the room, he considered his options. He'd been brought up to fight fair, but suddenly, the taking part didn't mean jack. Leon strode quickly back to Rupert's desk and carefully erased the message.

He was just going to buy himself some time, that was all. If the guy wasn't interested enough in Rupert to phone back then he didn't deserve a chance with him anyway.

* * * *

By the time Leon finally heard Rupert's key in the lock, he had a plan. It was a good plan. He was proud of it. It would work. Okay, Leon silently admitted to himself, maybe it wasn't exactly *guaranteed* to work, but it was still a good plan. Well, maybe it wasn't the best plan ever, but it was the only one he bloody well had.

He might not have screwed his way through half the aristocracy the way everyone else in Rupert's life had, but he wasn't a closeted virgin any more either.

"Hello? Leon? Are you home?"

By the time Leon plucked up the courage to step out of the study, Rupert was standing by the hallway table sorting through his mail.

Leon squared his shoulders. There was no time like the present, best to start as he meant to go on, and all that bull.

Rupert glanced up. He smiled when he saw Leon lurking in the study doorway.

As he looked back at the envelopes in his hand, Leon took a step towards him, then several more in quick succession.

"Did you have a good—?"

Quickly covering Rupert's mouth with his own, Leon licked the rest of the question from his boyfriend's lips as he sought to deepen the kiss.

Rupert was tall. Leon had to go up on his toes to bring his mouth to the right height. Curling his hands into fists against Rupert's jacket, he tugged at the expensive fabric, trying to pull the larger man down for easier access.

Several aeons passed. Rupert remained perfectly still, frozen in place, unrelenting to his lover's pleas. Leon's confidence faltered. Damn, but this really was a stupid idea. The guy had just come in from work. Why the hell would he want some idiot throwing himself at him before he'd even had time to take his coat off?

All his courage bleeding away in a swirling red mass of pain, Leon took half a step back, ready to stutter out an apology. Just in time, he heard the letters in Rupert's hand tumble to the floor. He slid his arms around Leon, pulling him closer as he seemed to catch up with current events and decide he liked being welcomed home that way.

Relief pounding through him, Leon arched into his lover's touch. Slipping his hands past Rupert's jacket, he shoved the perfectly cut material aside, only to realise that Rupert's shirt was still in his way.

Letting out a frustrated groan, Leon tugged at the buttons, desperate to feel skin under his palms, to feel the strength in Rupert's muscles as they wrapped around him and reassured him that, despite all evidence to the contrary, everything really was okay.

Rupert threaded his fingers into Leon's hair, tugging pointedly at the strands until Leon got the hint and tilted his head to the exact angle his lover desired.

Leon pressed their bodies even more firmly together as Rupert deftly took over the kiss.

The moment he felt Rupert's burgeoning erection rub against him through their clothes, Leon rocked his hips, thrusting clumsily against the other man, while Rupert expertly moulded their lips together.

Rupert dropped one of his hands to Leon's arse. Within seconds he'd taken control of that movement too, guiding Leon into just the right rhythm, just the right everything.

No! That couldn't be allowed to happen. If all Leon did was follow Rupert's lead, he'd be far too easily replaced by any obedient little twink from those clubs Rupert kept hinting they should visit.

Moving his hands to the taller man's shoulders, Leon tried to push him back towards the hallway table. For several moments, Rupert kept them both perfectly balanced and completely stationary.

Leon murmured his frustration into the kiss. Finally, Rupert seemed to register the intent behind Leon's wriggling. He took a step back. Keeping Leon close and maintaining the rocking rhythm of their hips, Rupert danced them backwards with perfect co-ordination, until he collided abruptly with the table's edge.

Rupert jerked his hands away from Leon's body. Reaching back, he caught hold of the dark mahogany to steady himself. That momentary distraction was all Leon needed. Dropping to his knees, he scrambled for Rupert's belt.

"What—?" Rupert swung his hands forwards and wrapped them around Leon's wrists, stopping all work upon his belt.

With his eyes heavy-lidded with desire and his lips parted suck in deep lungfuls of air, Leon had never seen the older man look more perfect. It had never felt more vital to keep Rupert in his life forever either. Keeping their eyes locked together, he leaned in and pressed a kiss against his lover's straining fly.

Rupert frowned slightly, apparently still somewhat behind on current events.

Carefully extracting his hands from Rupert's loosening hold, Leon lost all interest in fumbling with a belt. Dipping his head, he kissed Rupert's trousers instead, nuzzling enthusiastically at his hard-on through the expensive fabric.

Glancing up, Leon murmured his appreciation as he flicked out his tongue to taste the material between them. He trailed his mouth up and down the line of Rupert's erection, letting the dark blue fabric catch at his lips and pull them apart.

Suddenly finding himself running the show for once, Leon wasn't about to waste what might be his best opportunity yet to show Rupert how right it was for them to stay together, just the two of them, forever.

Trying desperately to keep his movements calm and self-assured, Leon worked a line of teasing kisses back to where Rupert's hands rested on his belt. Delving past the older man's fingers with his tongue, Leon narrowed his gaze as he tried to work out if it would be possible for him to undo the other man's zip using nothing more than his lips and teeth.

He didn't get the chance to try. Leon's mouth hadn't even found the buckle before Rupert had undone it for him. Dragging his zip down, the older man pushed all the material impatiently out of the way, completely baring his crotch.

For a second, Leon thought Rupert was going pull him closer, but he didn't. He moved his hands back to rest on the table on either side of his hips instead, as if making a point of giving Leon free rein to do whatever he wanted.

A touch of heat rushed to Leon's cheeks as he realised Rupert was probably already well aware of how much he loved going down on him. He obviously knew his boyfriend didn't need any encouragement to dip his head towards his cock.

Not about to shatter a very accurate understanding of his preferences, Leon leant forward until his lips hovered just on the verge of enveloping the tip of Rupert's shaft in a warm, moist cocoon.

Stretching the moment out, Leon lapped up a drop of pre-cum as it gathered in expectation. Lifting his eyes slightly, he fixed the gaze on one of the buttons of Rupert's half-open shirt. As he watched, it stilled. Rupert was holding his breath.

Success rushed through Leon in a huge wave that almost managed to wash away all his nerves. In that moment, when Rupert was too focussed on him to spare a thought for anything else, even for breathing, it was easy to believe the other man cared for him — maybe even that he cared almost as much as Leon had grown to love him over the last few months.

Lifting his gaze further, Leon eagerly watched Rupert's eyes follow his every movement as he finally leant forward that last inch and took his lover's cock into his mouth.

Setting his hands on Rupert's sides to steady himself, Leon felt him shift beneath his grasp as he started breathing again. Very slowly, Leon took Rupert's shaft deeper, sucking gently around him as his tongue caressed the vein on the underside of his erection.

Pulling back, Leon pressed a quick kiss to the head, promising to return soon. Dipping his head, he ran his tongue over the neatly trimmed hairs that covered Rupert's sac as he lapped at his lover's balls. A moment later, he found the right angle. Parting his lips wider Leon took each one into his mouth in turn.

Murmuring his pleasure, he let the vibrations build, so Rupert would know how much he loved the taste of him. Leon was almost sure he felt the sac tighten, pulling Rupert's testicles up to his body even as he held them on his tongue.

Another rush of pleasure spread through Leon's veins as he sensed his lover's delight with his actions. He smiled to himself as he let the other man's balls slip delicately from between his lips and turned his attention back to Rupert's cock.

Taking the long, thick shaft deep into his mouth, Leon abandoned all attempts at teasing. He'd learnt a lot about what could make Rupert come over the past weeks and right then he was determined to use every trick he knew.

Bobbing his head more quickly, Leon sucked Rupert's cock even further into his mouth, desperately trying to move his head as rapidly as he moved his own hand when he was jacking himself off.

Rupert didn't thrust to complement his rhythm. He remained perfectly still, obviously completely in control of every inch of his body until, finally, he reached out and touched Leon's shoulder, politely warning him he was about to come.

Leon retreated just far enough to make sure he caught the full taste on his tongue. Rupert's hips jerked forward the tiniest fraction of an inch. Hot, salty cum spilled into Leon's mouth. Swallowing down everything the older man was willing to offer him, Leon whimpered his enjoyment of every drop he received.

Even when Rupert retrieved his hand, Leon was in no rush to relinquish his moment of success. Leon stayed exactly where he was, allowing his lover's cock to soften between his lips.

In those seconds, everything was so simple, so perfect, but all too soon reality tapped him on the shoulder. Far too late, Leon realised his actions might be considered somewhat strange. It wasn't beyond the bounds of possibilities that Rupert might ask him what the hell was going on. Suddenly, Leon's confidence in the supreme wisdom of his plan faltered.

When Rupert finally nudged him to get up, Leon released Rupert's cock, but he wasn't at all inclined to stand and look him in the eye. Staying on his knees felt like a much better idea, although Leon hadn't actually realised just how hard or cold the mosaic tiles would be until he was down there.

Rupert Hargreaves reached down, wrapped his hand around Leon's arm, and helped his young lover to his feet.

Apparently still in no rush to meet his eyes, the boy kept his head bowed as he brushed specks of non-existent dust from his knees. Rupert smiled down at the top of his lover's head as he absentmindedly did up his fly and straightened his own clothes.

Finally, Rupert's patience was rewarded. Leon lifted his gaze a little, but it still only reached halfway up Rupert's chest before making a hasty retreat towards the floor.

Tucking a knuckle under Leon's chin, Rupert made a point of being as gentle as he knew how when he slowly brought his lover's gaze all the way up to his face.

"I'm sorry about your shirt," Leon blurted out.

Rupert chuckled as he glanced down and saw that several of the buttons were now conspicuously absent. When he looked up again, he saw the worry in Leon's expression. The boy really thought he gave a damn about his shirt?

"That was one hell of a welcome home, sweetheart." Slipping his fingers through the belt loops on Leon's jeans, Rupert pulled him in for another kiss — a sweeter, gentler greeting.

He felt a little of the tension in Leon's muscles drain away as their lips lingered together, but it rushed back the very moment the kiss ended. A tiny frown creased the skin between Rupert's dark brows. That wouldn't do at all.

"Who was your last lecture of the day about?" he asked.

Leon blinked. "Casper David Fredrich?" he hazarded cautiously, as if he thought it might be some sort of trick question.

"If this is the mood he puts you in, I've just decided what I'm going to buy for myself next Christmas," Rupert said, careful to keep his tone perfectly serious. "Where do you think we should hang one of his paintings?"

He was just able to catch sight of Leon's smile before the boy dipped his head to hide his blush.

"Maybe we could move it from room to room," Rupert mused. "Take it on a complete tour of the house."

Leon shook his head at his teasing, but the smile was still there when he looked up. A couple of nibbles on his bottom lip, and he even found his voice. "Did you have a good day?"

"Until a few minutes ago it was nothing special," Rupert admitted. "Since then — bloody amazing." His fingers were still hooked through Leon's belt loops. He tugged him closer as he dropped his voice to a whisper. "The more important question is—how would you like me to improve your day? Any preferences, sweetheart?"

Leon merely shrugged, apparently more than happy for Rupert to make all the decisions—for his lover to do whatever the hell he wanted with him. The idea sent another shot of pleasure racing down Rupert's spine. If it had been physically possible he was sure he'd have been as hard as rock again. Damn, but Leon really was one hell of a natural submissive. A little bit of training and he'd be glorious...

Rupert turned away. He strode into his study and across to his desk without another word. Led by a belt loop, Leon had little choice but to follow.

The denim tugged against Rupert's fingers for a moment. Looking over his shoulder, Rupert followed Leon's gaze to the answering machine, but the steady light merely informed him there were no messages waiting for him.

Dismissing the contraption from his mind, Rupert sat on the well-padded chair behind his desk, a tug on Leon's belt loops easily brought the younger man to stand between him and the desk.

Rupert rolled the chair forward, well-oiled wheels not making a sound on the thick carpet. Leon had little choice but to step back or get run over. He jumped as he backed into the desk, as if he'd somehow managed to forget the huge piece of furniture was there.

Rupert kept rolling forward until Leon scrambled up to sit on the desk top. Rupert advanced even further then, until Leon spread his legs wide to make room for the chair between them.

Finally satisfied with their new positions, Rupert leant back, extended his legs comfortably beneath the desk, and simply gave himself a few moments to admire the man before him. Even when Leon's nerves got the better of him and he began to fidget in a way that would have annoyed Rupert in any other submissive, he was undeniably gorgeous.

"It never ceases to amaze me how someone so beautiful can be so self-conscious," Rupert murmured.

Leon shook his head. If he was trying not to blush he was remarkably unsuccessful. Rupert held back a sigh. When Leon looked at him with that particular light in his eyes, it was all he could do to keep his inclination for dominance even partially in check.

Rupert took a deep breath and let it out very slowly. No rushing the boy. He'd promised himself that at the start and he wasn't going to go back on his word now.

"Take your clothes off, Leon," Rupert said. He almost managed to make it sound like a suggestion rather than a demand. "Let me see you properly."

Leon hesitated, as if Rupert hadn't seen him naked a hundred times before.

"Shirt first." There was far less evidence of a suggestion left in his words that time, but at least the straight-forward order prompted Leon into action.

He quickly pulled the scruffy hoodie over his head and dropped it off the back of the desk, revealing a slim torso with some nicely developing lines of muscle.

"Shoes next."

Leaning forward, Leon lifted one foot and yanked at his tangled laces. Nerves and knots weren't a good mix. Quickly giving up, Leon forced his foot out of his trainer without undoing the tangle and tugged off his sock.

He didn't seem sure what to do with his bare foot. Catching hold of his ankle, Rupert guided it to rest on the leather seat just outside his thigh.

His other trainer quickly tossed behind him, Leon placed his left foot on Rupert's other side and looked for his next order. Rupert made him wait for several minutes as he ran his eyes over the skin already on display for him. A visible shiver ran down the younger man's spine as he was thoroughly inspected.

"Jeans," Rupert finally ordered.

Leon leant back a few inches and managed to undo the top button of his fly without too much fumbling, then the next and the next. He didn't hesitate until he ran out of buttons.

"Place your hands on the desk behind you."

As he obeyed, Rupert hooked his fingers in the waist band of both Leon's jeans and his boxers.

"Up."

Bracing himself on the desk top, his feet wedged against Rupert's chair, Leon obediently lifted his hips. It only took Rupert a moment to have both garments around Leon's ankles.

"Down."

Leon did as he was told. The moment he'd kicked his jeans off his feet, he discarded them in the same general direction as his shirt. He managed a whole five seconds of stillness before he found it necessary to start fidgeting again. Reaching up, Leon pushed his hand through his hair, brushing the scruffy blond strands back from his face.

Rupert raised an eyebrow at him moving without his permission. Leon slowly lowered his hand back to his side. A few seconds later both hands rested exactly where Rupert had specified just a few minutes before, on the desk behind him.

Rupert nodded his approval. One hell of a natural submissive…

By the time he lifted his gaze back to Leon's face, the younger man's eyes were closed while he struggled for self-control. Rupert smiled to himself. Perfect.

Leon received no warning before he leant forward and took the boy's shaft between his lips. Leon bucked against the desk. His eyes sprung open as he yelped in surprise. Rupert looked up and met Leon's gaze as he pulled back until his lips teased the very tip of his cock.

The boy bit down on his bottom lip very prettily as he scrambled for control, but as Rupert dipped his head lower over his lap once more, he was well aware that there was already very little control left in Leon.

Pushing away his desire to watch his lover squirm, Rupert forced himself not to tease too much. He didn't make Leon wait too long before he took his shaft all the way to the base. Short blond hairs tickled his lips as he let the tip of Leon's cock slip into his throat in the way he knew he loved so much.

Leon screamed as he came, as if he couldn't quite resist the urge to tell the whole world how much he loved being allowed to spill into his lover's mouth that way. His hips jerked, rapid little movements that Rupert was easily able to ride out as he pulled back to taste him properly.

Gradually, Leon's hips fell still. The only movement in the room was the rapid rising and falling of his chest as he tried to catch his breath. Rupert leant back in his chair, his fingers steepled in front of him once more.

As he slowly opened his eyes, Leon offered Rupert a slightly embarrassed smile. "I think we can consider my day remarkably improved," he whispered.

Rupert nodded, just once, a curt little motion. His hands itched to reach out, wrap themselves around Leon's wrists and hold him in place for as long as he wished. His mouth wanted nothing more than to form words he'd never allowed himself to say in Leon's presence—words like 'dominance' and 'submission' and 'mine'.

Forcing down every instinct he possessed, Rupert returned Leon's smile and rolled his chair back, silently granting Leon permission to get off his desk and retrieve his clothes.

Leon padded barefoot around the room and found his jeans, but he didn't bother with anything else right then. As he pulled the denim on and did up the buttons, Leon's gaze fell on the answering machine again.

"James Campbell called to see you before you got home," he mentioned, a few seconds later.

Rupert's shoulders tensed at the name. "What did he want?"

Leon shrugged. "He didn't say, just told me to tell you that he dropped by."

"That's all?" Rupert pushed, sure that James wouldn't have missed an opportunity to screw things up for him if he got the chance.

Leon nodded. He was a bloody terrible liar.

Their eyes met. Rupert raised one eyebrow.

Leon sighed as he seemed to realise he wasn't going to get away with brushing the topic aside like that. "Are all your ex-boyfriends such complete bastards?" he finally asked.

A man he'd screwed and whipped a few times hardly qualified as a boyfriend in Rupert's view, but that didn't seem to be the moment to point that out. "Is he giving you a hard time?"

Leon shrugged again. "No more than he probably gives everyone."

"Anything I need to worry about?" Rupert asked, studying him very carefully through narrowed eyes.

Leon blinked, as if he thought *Rupert* was the one acting strangely out of character that day. "I think I'm past the age where I need someone to defend me from the school bully."

"A pity," Rupert murmured as he relaxed a little. "I quite like the idea of riding in on a white charger."

"And I'm the damsel in distress?" Leon asked.

No, pet, you're the submissive. Somehow, Rupert kept the words back as he strolled around the desk and slipped a comfortable arm around Leon's shoulders. Pressing a kiss onto the younger man's temple, he reminded himself that he had no right to say the would-be submissive was already under his protection.

No, in his infinite wisdom, he was being patient. Rupert held back a sigh. Patience really wasn't his strongest attribute.

* * * *

Attempts to allow things to progress at Leon's preferred speed were all well and good, but they didn't change the fact that, by the time Rupert closed his bedroom door behind them that night, he still hadn't managed to shake off the idea something was very wrong in his young lover's world.

"Does it bother you that I stay over here all the time?" Leon asked, suddenly.

Rupert turned and looked across the room. Leon's back was to him. It was impossible to see his expression. His only clue to the submissive's state of mind was the way Leon fiddled nervously with the coins on the dresser.

No, I want you here all the time. You belong here, with your master.

Rupert mentally shook his head and tried to find words that were more suitable for the occasion. "I'm sure your room-mate is a wonderful guy, but perhaps we'd better wait until he's away for a few days before you invite me to stay at your place," he said, taking great care with each word he chose.

Rupert placed his hand on Leon's shoulder as he reached his side. Leon turned to face him. Rupert frowned slightly as he tried to read his expression and failed. "Does it bother you that much that you always come to me?"

"I didn't mean…" Leon looked down. "No, it doesn't bother me at all. You're right. We'd hardly fit comfortably in my single, would we?" His chuckle sounded incredibly forced.

"Leon?" Rupert asked, his frown deepening rapidly. "Why do I get the feeling we're having two different conversations?"

Leon shrugged. "Maybe I meant more — would you prefer it if I didn't stay the night after we…?"

Tension flooded into Rupert's spine. "You mean — do I want to throw you out as soon as we zip up?" he checked. It was impossible for him to hide how unimpressed he was with the question.

Leon shook his head, rapidly backtracking. "I didn't mean that either. It's just that we never really spoke about it. I just assumed…"

"You assumed I wanted you in my bed all night rather than just for however long it takes for us to have sex? You were right," Rupert informed him. "I have no interest in treating you like some sort of rent boy, sweetheart."

Leon nodded. He met Rupert's eyes for another brief moment and smiled. "Sorry, I'm just being an idiot," he said, and promptly disappeared to take his turn in the en-suite.

Rupert watched him go in silence, wondering what the hell he'd done to make Leon believe he thought so little of him.

As they both settled into Rupert's bed a few minutes later, the same thoughts were still running around inside his head. Spooning close behind him, Rupert made more effort than ever to ensure that Leon was completely comfortable there.

He held back a frustrated growl as he felt Leon slip quickly into slumber. Obviously he'd have to wait even longer than he anticipated before he mentioned the possibility embarking on anything other than an entirely vanilla relationship.

Chapter Two

Tuesday

"Do you want to go out tonight?" Leon did his best to keep his voice completely relaxed, as if it didn't really matter to him one way or the other. He was pretty sure he only actually succeeded in making himself sound like he had a sore throat.

Rupert glanced up from his newspaper. He didn't appear particularly suspicious of the suggestion. He even smiled when he saw Leon hovering around the threshold of his living room.

"We can if you like," Rupert offered, setting his paper to one side. "Any special occasion?"

Leon scraped his teeth against his bottom lip as he bit back the truth. "Not really. I'm, um…I'm going to go shower and change and, um…stuff."

It was all Leon could do not to take the stairs two at a time as he beat a hasty retreat. Reaching Rupert's bedroom, he strode quickly to the wardrobe that had been cleared for him to use and jerked it open before he could change his mind.

The trousers Rupert had bought for him were tucked away at the very back, behind all his normal gear. Soft leather caressed his fingertips as he dragged them out from their hiding place and scurried into the bathroom.

Leon quickly locked the door behind him, hung the trousers on the hook on the back of it and took a deep breath.

One thing at a time. Perhaps if he broke it all down into small, simple steps then the panic rushing through him would subside. A shower—he could do that.

The warm water cascading over his skin should have helped him relax, but by the time he stepped out from under the spray, Leon still wasn't sure if he was ready for those trousers. If he tilted his head to one side and considered them from just the right angle, he could almost convince himself that it didn't matter that they were made from leather rather than denim, they were still basically jeans. More importantly, they were jeans that Rupert had liked enough to buy him six weeks ago, and which he'd never even put on.

What makes you think they're a present for you? Rupert had chuckled then, a rich beautiful sound Leon loved so much. *I'll be the one admiring the view whenever you wear them.*

A few minutes later, as Leon struggled to wriggle into them, he was more than ready to give up pretending they were anything like the scruffy denim he usually hid behind. For one thing, there was generally room beneath his jeans for some sort of underwear.

As he wiped the steam off the mirror with a corner of his towel, Leon caught sight of his leather-clad reflection for the first time. His eyes opened very wide as he silently examined the picture he presented.

Slowly turning away from the glass, he peered over his shoulder. It looked like someone had sprayed the black coating straight onto his skin. He might as well have been naked.

He turned around once more. They were so tight he could see the outline of his cock through them, and he wasn't even hard. If he got an erection he was either going to tear a seam or castrate himself with his own blood supply. There was no way in hell he could leave the house looking like—

Leon jumped as the door handle rattled.

"Leon?"

"I'm getting changed," Leon called back through the woodwork. Looking over his reflection one more time, he nibbled at the edge of his finger nail.

Damn, but he looked like one hell of an idiot...

"Suddenly you're bashful?" Rupert asked from the other side of the door.

"I'll be out in a minute," Leon offered.

It was so easy to imagine Rupert standing in the bedroom, shrugging and shaking his head, unable to see what the fuss was about, but for some reason willing to humour his lover anyway.

Finally Leon managed to focus on those parts of his reflection that weren't clad in leather. He was used to looking in the mirror when he shaved every morning. After that, it was inevitably more luck than judgement. But, as he realised that he might well be weighed up against other candidates for Rupert's attention, he couldn't help but wonder how he might compare to the man's other lovers.

Squaring his shoulders, Leon forced himself to take stock as objectively as possible.

Blond hair which was supposed to be cut short and kept out of the way, except he never remembered to go and get the damn stuff cut. Blue eyes, which he guessed were okay.

As he lowered his gaze, Leon could pick out some reasonable lines of muscle across his torso. His finger nail sneaked back to his mouth and suffered even further from his nerves. He certainly wasn't as well developed as Rupert, but those of his former lovers he'd met hadn't been muscle-men either.

Fair to middling, Leon decided. He probably wasn't going to win too many points on looks, but with a bit of luck he wasn't going to lose hundreds either. Leon glanced towards the door. Hiding in the bathroom like a little girl was one thing that definitely wasn't going to win him any prizes.

Leon took a deep breath, unlocked the bathroom door, and stepped out of the en suite before he could change his mind.

Rupert stood on the other side of the room with his back to him, staring into a wardrobe, studying his own choices for the evening. "You didn't say where you wanted to go," he said, without turning around.

"I thought we might go to that club you mentioned before."

Rupert glanced over his shoulder. His gaze slowly traced its way up and down Leon's body. He turned around to face Leon properly. "Yes, we should definitely go to Blacks," he agreed.

Leon wished he could put his hands in his pockets to stop himself fidgeting, but there weren't any pockets, and there wasn't room in those trousers for anything that wasn't already tucked away behind his fly anyway.

Leon shuffled his bare feet against the bedroom carpet, but it wasn't long before he couldn't stand the silent appraisal for another moment. "I can get changed if…"

Leon shook his head at his own stupidity. He'd been right. This was a mistake. He looked like an idiot— like someone who was pretending to be part of a world he had no business in.

"Changed?" Rupert didn't sound familiar with the concept. Suddenly he regained his focus. "No."

Leon pushed a hand through his hair as it began to dry and flop forward. "I've got a pair of new-ish black jeans here somewhere." He turned towards his wardrobe.

"No!" That was definitely an order.

Leon stopped. "I just thought…" He trailed off again as Rupert began to circle him.

Frowning slightly, Leon turned to follow his progress.

"Stay still."

Leon obediently froze as Rupert slowly walked all the way around him several times.

It shouldn't have been possible for Leon to feel even more naked than he did when he wasn't actually wearing any clothes. His bare feet wriggled against the carpet once more.

Finally returning to face Leon, Rupert looked him up and down one last time. "Glorious."

Leon wasn't even sure if Rupert knew he'd said the word out loud.

Swallowing down his nerves, Leon cleared his throat. "You said you'd like me to wear them sometime."

"I have very good taste," Rupert agreed. He didn't lift his attention from the leather as he said it. It was several seconds before he met Leon's gaze. "And not just in clothes. You look amazing, sweetheart."

A chaste little kiss, barely more than a brush of their lips, shouldn't have made Leon feel much better about the world, but it did. He let out a breath he hadn't even realised he'd been holding.

Leon nodded. It seemed like the right thing to do, even if he didn't have a damn clue what he was agreeing with. As Rupert pulled away, Leon cleared his throat again. If Rupert liked playing dress-up with him that much then…

"What else should I wear?"

Rupert paused. "You're giving me a completely free choice?"

Leon nodded.

"In an ideal world I wouldn't give you anything else to wear," Rupert informed him. "I'd add a matching collar and leash, and that would be it."

Unable to find the words to form an immediate reply, Leon closed his eyes.

"What are you thinking?"

Leon didn't have enough blood left above his waist to lie. "I'm imagining myself naked in the arctic." Finally convincing his eyes to open, he offered the older man an embarrassed little smile. "There's no give at all in these trousers."

Rupert grinned.

The collar idea was hot, and it would be the perfect way to show his lover that he could play any game he liked, and it might be just the thing that would convince Rupert he'd never need to date anyone else, and… And in reality, Leon knew he'd just spend the whole night horribly embarrassed and blushing like a little girl. Hell, his face was probably already bright red just thinking about it!

Rupert stroked his knuckles down Leon's cheek. "I said in an *ideal* world."

And Leon wanted to be ideal. He wanted it so badly he could taste it, but—

"In the *real* world I'd end up spending the whole evening glaring at all the guys who failed to realise your collar was more than a fashion accessory and tried to hit on you anyway," Rupert said, cutting easily through every thought in Leon's head.

Leon scraped up a smile for his teasing.

"Don't believe me, sweetheart?"

"I don't think you'd be the guy getting jealous," Leon whispered.

Rupert laughed. "Even fully clothed, you'd spend the whole evening fighting off half the club if you went there alone." Pulling him closer, Rupert's slid one hand down Leon's back and settled it on his arse as he dipped his head and brought his lips to Leon's ear. "So, it's lucky you're not going there alone, isn't it?"

The warmth of the older man's body called to Leon. He leaned easily into his embrace and let his eyes drop closed. Their bodies rubbed together, coaxing him to rock his hips and press his crotch more firmly against Rupert's thigh. It was so perfect, so easy to pretend that everything was fine, and—

Suddenly, Rupert was gone, leaving Leon thrusting against the empty air. Quickly opening his eyes, Leon turned his head, desperately trying to locate his lover.

"If we get distracted now, we'll never get to the club," Rupert said. He was already standing by Leon's wardrobe.

Within seconds, he'd picked out shoes and a black T-shirt to go with the leather trousers. Leon barely had time to pull them on before Rupert was dressed and ready to leave. Within moments, they were in one of Rupert's fancy cars and rapidly approaching the city centre.

Leon glanced at his boyfriend's profile as the street lights sped past them. Squirming slightly in his seat, he cleared his throat.

"Leon?" Rupert prompted, glancing briefly in his direction before turning his attention back to the road.

"This club," Leon said.

"Yes?"

"Is there, um…" He picked at the seam on his new leather trousers as he tried to find the right words. "Is there anything I should know about it before we get there?"

Rupert's frown was just visible in the gloom. "Such as?"

Leon took a deep breath. "Such as, is it the kind of place where guys really do wear collars and leads and stuff?" The words almost collided with each other as he rushed them past his lips.

For several seconds, Rupert was silent. The purr of the engine faded away, as if the car were holding its breath waiting for the answer too.

"I don't mind if it is," Leon blurted out. "I just…"

"No," Rupert said. "It's not that kind of club. You probably won't be the only man wearing leather trousers, but that's as close to fetish gear as you'll see there."

Leon remembered how to breathe. Closing his eyes, he leaned his head back against the headrest. He was so relieved, his head was damn near spinning, but there was another little voice in the back of his mind that whispered about a far less expected emotion—it felt suspiciously like a touch of disappointment.

"It's just somewhere guys go to drink, dance and let their hair down," Rupert said as he pulled into a car park behind a big, low-slung building.

Leon nodded. "Sounds good," he said, as casually as possible, as if he was in the habit of going to gay bars all the time.

There was a long queue at the front door. Rupert walked straight past it. A handshake with the doorman, in which more money than Leon spent in a week probably changed hands, and they were inside before Leon even had time to look apologetically at the guys they'd jumped in front of.

Rupert slipped his arm around Leon's shoulder as they left the real world on the pavement outside and entered a parallel universe full of dark shadows and pounding music.

Leon looked up at Rupert in surprise at such a gesture taking place anywhere but inside his house, but Rupert's attention was all on the men around them. Even with the confusion of faces swirling through the club, half the guys there recognised Rupert. Men called out to him, but he kept going with no more than a nod or a wave, leading Leon through a mindboggling succession of different dance floors and bars.

As the crowds became denser, Leon leaned into Rupert's body, glad of the way his arm stayed around his shoulders. Somehow, when the press of bodies thinned out, Leon forgot to pull back. He remained tucked tightly to Rupert's side until they finally found a bar Rupert seemed to like the look of.

Leon glanced around them. It was a quieter space than most of these they'd passed through, tucked away in a less shadowy area towards the back of the club. Still, they'd barely ordered their drinks before Leon sensed another man join them at the bar.

"It's been a long time."

Leon looked over his shoulder and barely held back a sigh as he recognised Mr Lewis, one of Rupert's business associates. Suddenly remembering he was as out of place there as he had been at any of the formal dinners Rupert had invited him to, Leon tried to make himself fade into the background as inconspicuously as possible and simply enjoy the way Rupert's arm was still looped casually around his waist.

As Mr Lewis babbled on about some mutual acquaintance, Rupert's grip around Leon's body tightened for a moment. Leon looked up. Rupert raised an eyebrow, as if asking if he was okay. Leon blinked as he realised Rupert had no more interest in what the other man was saying than he did. Smiling slightly, Leon nodded. He was okay and Rupert was merely being polite to a man with whom he did business.

Leon leaned more cosily into Rupert's side, relishing the closeness that being in a gay club apparently allowed. By the time Mr Lewis insisted on introducing Rupert to someone else, Leon was even feeling comfortable enough with his surroundings to assume he was invited too.

Rupert shook his head very slightly.

Leon's confidence evaporated.

Dipping his head, Rupert whispered softly in Leon's ear, "I can't get away from him on the excuse of getting back to my date if you're already with me."

The bored expression in Rupert's eyes told Leon everything he needed to know. He happily nodded his acceptance of what seemed to him to be a very good plan.

"I won't be long," Rupert promised. His smile turned slightly wicked. Bowing his head once more, he offered Leon a brief kiss.

It was amazing what Rupert could do with the very briefest of moments when he wanted to. Leon leaned instinctively against Rupert, sliding his hands up his neck to tangle his fingers in the back of Rupert's hair.

Parting his lips at Rupert's demand, Leon was panting for breath by the time Rupert broke the kiss. The older man smiled down at him for a moment as he calmly went off to be introduced to a guy Leon could no longer remember the name of.

"Thirsty, darling?"

Leon turned to look over his shoulder and found himself damn near nose to nose with a guy he'd never even set eyes on before. Jerking back, he quickly put some space between himself and the stranger. Clearing his throat, he pointed to his glass on the bar. "I've already got a drink, thanks."

The man raked his eyes up and down Leon's body, making him curse Rupert for having picked that moment to play the tease. He wasn't used to talking to strange men while sporting an erection he had no chance of hiding.

"Nice to see you're enjoying yourself."

Leon looked the other guy straight in the eye, cheerfully willing to be damned before he backed down from a man who was so obviously glorying in his discomfort.

The other guy just laughed all the more, and handed him a card. "When Rupert gets bored with you, give me a call. Someone with an arse as good as yours will find me very generous." His palm connected sharply with Leon's backside as he stepped past him and strode away.

He was well out of earshot before Leon could think of a single bloody thing to say.

If the rest of the stream of other guys who joined him at bar didn't actually mention payment for services rendered, they were all very complimentary in a way that made Leon's skin crawl. He would have given almost anything for a coat that could have covered up the skin tight outfit.

Finally left alone for two blessed seconds in a row, Leon glared down at the card the first man had shoved into his hand. Anyone would think he had a flashing neon light above his head marking him as someone who would only ever make it into such an exclusive bar because he was trading his arse with the man who took him there.

When yet another man's hand reached past him and plucked the card from his fingers Leon spun around, not in the least inclined to have it replaced with another card or a higher bid.

"Easy, darling. You're not my type." The guy looked briefly at the card. Wrinkling his nose, he tossed it onto the bar next to the drinks. "Neither is he. I'm Tommy Grant, by the way. I saw you with Rupert earlier. He and I are old friends."

The man held out a hand. Leon, slowly settling back into his usual manners, shook it. "I'm—"

"Leon Powell," the man cut in, with a grin. "I know. Rupert's mentioned you."

"He has?"

Tommy nodded. "Let me see. You're twenty-three years old. You're studying for a master's degree in art history and you met Rupert at an art exhibition a few months ago. I'm sure he could have told me more interesting things, but Rupert never has been one to kiss and tell. How did I do?"

Leon blinked. He took a sip of his drink, playing for time while he wondered just how many people Rupert might have mentioned him to. "You and Rupert are good friends?" he asked.

"Went to school together." Tommy turned away from him to place his order with the bartender.

Leon nipped at his bottom lip as he stared at the back of Tommy's head, wondering if there was a subtle way for him to ask if Rupert had mentioned anyone called Gerald.

"Rupert also said that you were stunning, but I thought that was just him being smug—apparently not..." Tommy laughed again, an easy, friendly sound that invited anyone within hearing to join in with the joke.

Leon just about managed an embarrassed smile.

"He didn't mention just how close to the closet door you are though."

"What?" His smile disappeared.

"You're barely out."

The breath caught in Leon's throat. Was it really that obvious?

As Rupert strode back across the club, he mentally cursed every man he had ever done business with and especially long-winded pillocks who couldn't take the hint, not even when he told them straight out that he needed to get back to his boyfriend.

There was a man standing next to Leon at the bar. Rupert's sped up his pace.

By the time he'd moved close enough to recognise Tommy and realise that Leon wasn't actually in any immediate danger, Rupert was just able catch the tail end of what Tommy was saying...

"Any man who looks like you and isn't used to accepting a compliment from another guy has obviously never set foot on the gay scene before."

"And this ancient wisdom is coming from a man who spent his first night in a gay bar telling everyone he was only there as part of a dare," Rupert cut in, as he reached Leon's side and slid his arm proprietarily around his shoulders.

Tommy grinned at Rupert's rather blatant attempt to mark out his territory.

Rupert smiled back. "Hi, Tommy. What's your excuse for being here tonight?"

Good-natured laugher filled the air. "Hey, not everyone hits the ground running! Has he told you about his first night out of the closet yet?" he asked Leon.

Leon shook his head.

Just out of the shorter man's field of vision, Rupert echoed the gesture.

Tommy caught his eye and hastily changed the subject, but he wasn't quick enough. Rupert could practically feel the curiosity radiating off Leon when he glanced up at him.

By the time Tommy spotted someone else he knew in the crowd and left them alone, Rupert had already said several silent prayers that Leon would have forgotten all about it.

Searching for distractions, Rupert turned to reach for his drink. There was a business card in the spilt coke next to it. Rupert frowned as he picked it up and realised that Tommy's blabbering might not be the thing he should have be worrying about. "New friend of yours, sweetheart?"

Leon took a swig of his drink and shrugged as if it was no big deal. He was still a bloody awful liar.

Rupert said nothing as he slipped the card into his pocket. He wasn't going to spoil their date by getting angry now. No, it was far better to lock away the cold fury that raced through his veins and keep it nice and fresh until such time as he could unleash it more effectively.

Leon caught hold of his sleeve just as the white rectangle started to disappear behind the leather. "What do you want with that?"

"Just a little reminder that I owe him," Rupert said, pushing the card completely out of view.

Leon frowned. "Owe him?"

Rupert stared down at him for a moment. The boy really didn't have a clue. "For whatever it was he said to you."

Deeper furrows appeared between Leon's neat blond brows. He reached into Rupert's pocket. Rupert watched with amusement as Leon fumbled and wriggled his fingers at an awkward angle until he managed to snag a corner of the card and drag it out.

Leon crumpled it in his hand and threw it over the bar, into a bin that was already half full of empty beer bottles. Rupert made no objection. He'd already memorised the name anyway.

"I don't need my boyfriend to stand up for me," Leon snapped.

In any other submissive, Rupert was sure he'd have considered that statement in that particular tone of voice to be evidence of an attitude problem that required immediate correction. But in Leon...

Rupert smiled down at the boy. He just sounded like an enthusiastic pup who wanted to prove to all the big dogs that he really was old enough and tough enough to play with them.

Stroking the back of his fingers down Leon's cheek, Rupert dipped his head and brushed their lips together.

For the first time in almost as long as they had been together, he felt Leon hesitate to respond. Rupert found a few extra mental curses to throw at the name on the card, but he didn't pull away from the kiss. Keeping it all slow and easy, Rupert let their lips linger together until he felt the tension drain from Leon's muscles.

Finally, the boy leaned into his body as he seemed to remember how much he liked being held close by a more dominant man. His hand came to rest on Rupert's chest as he rose onto his toes so Rupert wouldn't have to crane his neck so low.

Drawing the kiss out, Rupert slid his tongue against Leon's and encouraged it out to play. Without making any sort of fuss, he quietly saw to it that Leon had a few moments where he could forget about the club, the men around them and the whole world.

Even when it became obvious the kiss couldn't go on forever, Rupert pulled away from Leon so slowly and with so many returns to brush their lips together just one more time, even he couldn't have stated with any sort of certainty when it actually ended.

Eventually, he pressed a final chaste little kiss to Leon's cheek, just as he had at the end of their first date. Leon smiled slightly, as if he was remembering that night too.

Rupert stroked Leon's hair back from his face and relished the sight of him so happy. "You do know you're not the only gay man on the planet to find his first visit to a gay club a bit intimidating?" he asked.

Leon closed his eyes in a move too long to be called another blink, but just short of complete denial. "Am I an idiot?" he asked, apparently ready more than ready to laugh at himself.

"No," Rupert said, letting no return humour creep into his voice. "You're human. There's nothing wrong with a bit of nerves."

Leon sighed as he dipped his head forward to rest his temple on Rupert's shoulder. "It sounds so bloody simple when you say it."

"But?" Rupert prompted.

"But this was supposed to be a fun night out!" Leon blurted out. "I didn't envisage substantial amounts of gay angst."

"What did you envisage?" Rupert asked.

Leon pulled back far enough to glance up at him. "Um… Drinking? Dancing?" Whatever he was going to say next, he bit it back.

Rupert clenched his hand into a fist at his side as he swallowed down a demand that he tell him what he had been about to say. Leon was his boyfriend, not his submissive, he reminded himself for what felt like the millionth time. Different rules applied. The moment he was sure the right words would leave his lips when he spoke, Rupert nodded. "Then we should dance."

He slid his hand into Leon's, twining their fingers together. Leon followed him willingly enough as Rupert led him through the club. He only hesitated when they reached the edge of Rupert's chosen dance floor.

Still, a little tug was all it took to convince Leon to join him with the other men crowded onto the floor. The beat from the speakers thumped through the room until it felt like every particle of air hummed with it.

Rupert slipped his arms around the smaller man. Before Leon had a chance to worry about how two men should dance together, Rupert saw to it that they were pressed close and already dancing. Or at least they were rocking their hips and grinding their bodies together in time to the beat, which was as close to dancing as anyone got there. Rupert smiled as he felt Leon gradually relax within his embrace.

As Leon pressed against him more firmly, Rupert's erection throbbed behind his fly. He could only imagine how tight Leon was finding his own trousers.

Settling his hands on Leon's arse, Rupert slowly but surely took control of his lover's movements. The boy easily followed his every hint, quick to submit to his control even if he didn't understand that was what he was doing.

A moment passed, and Leon somehow found the confidence to make a move for himself. He turned his face up, tentatively offering his lips to be kissed. Rupert hastily obliged, eager to encourage his lover to relax and feel at home in the club.

Just a moment later, Leon suddenly stepped back. Rupert frowned, unable to work out what had spooked the other man, but when Leon reached back and grabbed his hand, he allowed Leon to tug him off the dance floor.

He seemed to be looking for somewhere. Rupert smiled when he realised exactly what kind of place he was searching for. Apparently Leon really had grown in confidence over the last day or two.

Just the previous weekend, the idea of the shy little novice trying to find some out-of-the-way spot for them to get laid in a gay bar would have been crazy.

Leon glanced at a door marked *Staff Only* only to discount it. He obviously hadn't lost his desire to do the right thing and follow all the rules. Rupert stopped and jerked the door open, not about to obey any rules he hadn't set himself.

It looked like some kind of coat closet. Through a slightly parted curtain on the other side of the room, Rupert saw a sliver of light and the edge of the counter where guys could check their coats on the way in to the club.

Leon peeked past him into the small space between the rows of coats. He hesitated for a second, and Rupert was sure he'd object to it not being private enough and ask if they could go home instead, but Leon stepped in and closed the door behind them with an air of determination. The smell of all the leather coats huddled together on the racks dominated the room, making it feel far more like the kind of club Rupert usually visited.

Grabbing Rupert's hand, Leon led him resolutely between the coats. If he was ready to experiment, then it was possible he wanted to play at being a dom. Rupert bit back a chuckle as Leon nudged him politely towards the wall at the far end of the rows of coats. He knew the boy far too well to think he'd really take to dominance but, God help him, it actually occurred to him that it was sweet Leon wanted to try it. Rupert let his head drop back against the wall. Damn, but he really did have it bad for him.

Leon dropped to his knees in the small dark space. Rupert lifted his head away from the paintwork just in time to see him reach for his fly. In the shadows, he saw the way Leon's hands shook with excitement and nerves. He fumbled with the zip for several long seconds until he finally managed to free Rupert's shaft from the folds of fabric.

Leaning in, he quickly encased the tip of Rupert's cock between his lips, his fingers curling around the hard length as he steadied the shaft.

Rupert took a deep breath. There was no technique in the younger man right then, no attempt to tease. Hands and mouth working together, Leon stroked and sucked as fast as he could, as if the only thing in the world he wanted right then was to taste Rupert's cum on his tongue.

Leon glanced up. Their eyes met through the shadows. No matter who was leading who through the club, Leon's expression was still all submission and a desperate need to please. His eyes begged Rupert to come.

While Leon looked at him like that, there didn't seem to be any reason for him to try to hold back and make it last. Making his submissive work for his reward could wait for another day.

Rupert's hips jerked forward just a fraction of an inch as he came. Leon's eyes dropped closed as if he was savouring his taste as it spilled into his mouth. For just a few moments, there was no sign of nerves or confusion. Leon was all peace and flawlessness.

Even as pleasure raced through his body, Rupert kept all his attention focussed on Leon, drinking in the sight before him just as eagerly as Leon swallowed down his lover's cum.

Several long seconds passed before Leon slowly pulled back and Rupert's cock fell from between his lips. Keeping his gaze down, Leon dutifully turned his attention to tucking Rupert away and zipping him up. That done, he tentatively bent forward and leaned his head against Rupert's hip, resting there as he seemed to fight for some self-control.

Settling his fingers in his hair, Rupert welcomed him close, quite willing to let the younger man lean against him for as long as he needed. No doubt if somebody did need their coat, a generous tip would ensure the coat-check guy forgot he'd ever seen them there.

Eventually, Leon pulled himself to his feet. Rupert frowned when he saw Leon shake his head, wondering if the boy was already regretting his moment of daring. Catching hold of Leon's arm, Rupert tugged his lover around to face him, suddenly wondering if he should have stopped them doing something he could have easily guessed was way out of the boy's comfort zone.

In the dim light, Leon smiled up at him. "I was just thinking that sooner or later we'll both have to get out of this closet."

Rupert chuckled as relief rushed through him, but he didn't let Leon head for the door straight away. "Don't you think we should do something about this first?" he asked as he cupped Leon through his trousers.

Even as he thrust forward and rubbed himself against Rupert's palm, Leon shook his head again.

"You don't want to get off?" Rupert asked, playfully massaging him through the thin leather.

"Not here," Leon managed to say, in the midst of a pleasure-filled moan.

Rupert stilled his hand, waiting for more information before he decided his next move.

"Maybe everyone will know what we've been up to when we walk out of here, but they don't need to hear how much I enjoyed it too," Leon whispered, his voice hoarse with desire.

"Afraid you might be a bit too vocal?" Rupert teased gently.

"Have you ever known me to be quiet?" Leon gasped out. "Damn, I wish I had your control."

"It's not about control, sweetheart," Rupert said, as he allowed his fingers to resume their play once more. "Some people scream, some don't. You trying to make me scream would be like me trying to make you hold your breath."

Leon looked up at him, guilt flooding into his eyes.

"Yes, I noticed," Rupert whispered in his ear. But that was enough talking for now. "Do you trust me?"

Leon nodded without the slightest hesitation.

"I'm going to make you come." Rupert whispered the words very quietly, barely breathing them against his ear. "Right here, right now, and no one will hear you. Understand?"

He nodded again.

Rupert quickly turned the younger man around, so Leon's back was to his chest and the smaller man's whole body rested against him.

Reaching around him, Rupert carefully unfastened Leon's fly and freed his erection. The boy gasped his relief as his cock sprung free from the tight confines. He sagged back to lean even more comfortably against his chest.

Rupert quickly dug into his own back pocket and pulled out a condom. Leon nibbled at his bottom lip as he noticed it.

"I think a lot of people will be far happier if you don't come all over their coats, sweetheart," Rupert pointed out. More importantly, he was sure Leon would be embarrassed if he did make a mess over a stranger's clothes.

"Oh." Other words seemed to be beyond Leon as Rupert deftly rolled the thin latex over his cock.

The moment the condom was in place, Rupert took hold of Leon's hands and guided them back past both their bodies. A little bit of gentle coaxing had Leon's hands nestled snugly in the back pockets of Rupert's trousers.

"Beautiful," Rupert whispered in his ear as he looked down Leon's body. It was also as close as he had come to seeing him restrained. Hard, aching and sheathed in clear latex, the boy was stunning. And he was all his.

Rupert encouraged Leon to rest his head back against his shoulder as he whispered to him again. "Trust me."

A second later, he covered Leon's mouth with his hand, sealing out the air.

Leon mumbled something against his fingers as he squirmed under his hold. Rupert made a soft soothing noise in the back of his throat, hushing him as he wrapped his other hand tightly around Leon's erection.

Bucking helplessly in his grip, Leon immediately let out what would probably have been a loud moan if the sound hadn't been quickly captured by Rupert's palm. Apparently catching on to the idea, Leon nodded his understanding.

"Can you still hear the beat, sweetheart?" Rupert whispered.

Leon nodded again, and Rupert started to move behind him, rocking his hips to the music as he began to jack off Leon in perfect counterpoint.

Leon whimpered into his hand.

"Dance with me, sweetheart," Rupert ordered.

Leon tried to shake his head but neither that movement, nor any sound that might have accompanied it, got past Rupert's hand as the younger man pushed himself forward into Rupert's palm, then back against his fly.

Even with Rupert's hand over his mouth, Leon seemed to be struggling to stay silent.

"Don't hold back, Leon," Rupert ordered. "Scream for me. Let me hear you."

Leon parted his lips under Rupert's palm. He sucked at his skin, as if to gasp for air as much as to obey. Keeping Leon's head pinned back against his shoulder, Rupert maintained the seal tight over his mouth.

"Come for me, sweetheart."

Thrusting into his fist, Leon screamed against his palm as he did exactly as Rupert demanded.

Leon obviously didn't try and hold back a single decibel but, just as Rupert promised, the hand over his mouth made sure that no one except his lover knew how obedient he was. His palm killed every scrap of sound that could ever have made it out of the room.

As Leon collapsed back against him, Rupert carefully removed his hand from his face. The boy didn't rush to move and Rupert found himself quite content to wait while pleasure at his lover's trust made him smile into the shadows.

Eventually, Leon shifted in his embrace, apparently recovered enough to move.

Leaving Leon to wrestle his softened cock back into his trousers, Rupert dispensed with the used condom in a bin in the corner of the closet. By the time he turned back, Leon had almost returned to his normal self—a little bit unsure, more than a tiny bit nervous about the world he was just starting to explore, and undoubtedly as submissive as hell.

On the way home in the car, Leon remained completely silent. As Rupert pulled up at a set of lights, he glanced across at him. Leon's fingers were stroking back and forth across his neck.

Rupert tapped his fingers against the steering wheel in a pleasant little rhythm, wondering exactly what the boy was planning for them now.

Chapter Three

Wednesday

"This is a nice surprise."

Leon hesitated several yards away from Rupert's house as he looked up and saw him standing on the doorstep, briefcase resting at his feet and his front door keys in hand. It was almost unheard of for them to actually arrive there at the same time. On any other day, Leon was sure it would have been a lovely surprise.

As it was, he smiled, and hoped like hell the expression didn't look as forced as it felt. His backpack was suddenly heavier than ever, weighed down by all the items he'd hoped he might be able to smuggle into the house unnoticed.

"Hi," he managed, wiping his hands on his jeans as his palms turned sweaty.

Rupert smiled. It wasn't his usual *'I'm glad to see you, did you have a nice day?'* smile. Leon abruptly quit obsessing about the contents of his backpack in order to make more room for another flavour of panic inside his head. He rapidly rattled through his memories as Rupert looked expectantly down at him from the top step.

Birthday? No, that was next month. Anniversary? Leon tried to put every milestone they'd shared into the right place in his mental calendar but he was damned if he could think of anything that matched that particular day's date.

As Rupert asked about his lectures and his research, Leon answered entirely on automatic pilot, biding his time and hoping like hell that he could work out what was going on before it became obvious that he was more clueless than ever.

Finally, after a shared meal that had seen Leon damn near jump off his chair every time a piece of cutlery rattled against his plate, he knew he had to admit defeat.

"I give up," he announced, as he and Rupert stepped into his bedroom that night.

"Give up on what?"

"On trying to work out why you look as if you're waiting for something extraordinary to happen," Leon admitted.

Rupert's lips twisted into a slightly rueful smile. "I take it the mood has passed, then?"

"Mood?" Leon echoed, blankly.

"You've been in a rather interesting frame of mind the last few days."

Leon opened his mouth, then closed it and mentally rolled his eyes at himself. He hadn't been born subtle and twenty-three years on the planet hadn't improved that.

"Which has made me wonder if you had anything special planned for us tonight?" Rupert continued as he crossed the room to stand directly in front of Leon.

A knuckle under his chin made Leon look up. He rapidly searched Rupert's expression wondering just how much of an idiot his lover thought he was.

No. As their eyes met, Leon was sure Rupert's expression wasn't that of a man who was making fun of anyone. Rupert looked...intrigued? Perhaps he looked a little amused too, but not exactly amused at Leon's expense.

Leaning down, Rupert brought their lips together in a slow, tender kiss that seemed to seek to reassure more than anything else.

By the time Rupert pulled away, all the reasons why Leon was determined to do everything he could to keep the other man interested in him were back in the forefront of his mind, along with the contents of the carrier bag hidden in his backpack.

"Tie me up?" Leon blurted out.

Rupert nodded. His expression didn't betray the slightest bit of shock at the request. "With anything in particular?"

That was his cue. Drawing a deep breath, Leon forced himself to take it. Pulling away from their embrace he retrieved the thick black plastic carrier bag from its hiding place.

Rupert took it and peered inside. A quick glance at Leon, and he tipped its contents onto the bedspread. It landed in a jumble of leather and silver metal, creating a stark, kinky contrast with the crisp white sheets.

Damn! Leon had been so sure he'd removed all the price tags. Lurching forward, he quickly tugged one he'd missed off a buckle before Rupert could see how much of his overdraft Leon had thrown into his latest oh-so-brilliant plan.

Rupert made no comment on anything at all as he calmly sorted through the purchases.

Nipping at a fingernail, desperately trying not to let his uncertainty show any more than was absolutely necessary, Leon watched the other man place some of the items neatly on the bedside table.

Most of the other toys were moved to the top of the chest of drawers on the other side of the room, but one length of leather remained in Rupert's hand. Soon back at Leon's side, he trailed a fingertip very gently over Leon's throat, much the same way Leon remembered doing when he first came up with the idea of showing his lover he could be just as kinky as any of his other boyfriends if he needed to be.

"Have you ever worn a collar before?"

Leon shook his head. "I'm pretty sure I get the theory, though." He held his neck still so Rupert could slip it around his throat and do up the buckle. It was something Leon was certain that no one, not even a broke student, could screw up.

Rupert's lips curved into a smile but his eyes stayed very serious. "I'm going to collar you now."

Leon took a deep breath as he nodded his understanding, but he was pretty sure there wasn't a great deal of blood making its way to any part of his body above his waist. Understanding wasn't easy to come by when his brain was running on fumes. Rupert's tone of voice sent messages to his cock that Leon didn't even have words for.

"Are you going to do exactly as I say until I take it off?" Rupert asked.

It sounded far more like a statement of what Rupert expected, rather than a polite little enquiry, but as

Leon looked up and met his eyes, he realised there really was a question in there. *Is this just bondage or are you offering to submit to me too?* There was a difference, Leon's internet research had taught him that much at least.

"Yes," Leon said, far more softly than he'd intended. Yes — to everything.

Rupert didn't say another word as he deftly fastened the length of soft black leather around Leon's throat. The older man ran his fingertips underneath the collar as if checking the fit in exactly the same way as he would have if he'd placed it on a puppy.

Silence descended and stretched out until Leon had to break it or go crazy. "You said yesterday — about a collar. I just thought…" *I thought maybe if you knew you could be kinky with me, you wouldn't want to be kinky with anyone else.* Leon kept those words back somehow.

Rupert met his gaze, admiration clear in his eyes. "I was right," he said. "It looks perfect on you."

Leon swallowed. The collar shifted around his throat. That sensation rushed to his cock just as quickly as Rupert's words had, giving Leon the horrible suspicion he might actually come before the other man even had a chance to tie him up.

Rupert's attention moved to the top button on his shirt. Leon automatically reached up to help undress them both as quickly as possible, but Rupert's hands wrapped around his fingers before they were even halfway to their destination.

"I didn't tell you to move." Rupert guided Leon's hands back down to his sides. The look in his eyes couldn't have made his expectations clearer. Leon would do to as he was told and keep his hands where they had been placed until such time as he was given permission to do otherwise.

Leon curled his fingers into fists as he instinctively strived to do as Rupert wanted. No authorisation to move was forthcoming. He had little choice but to remain perfectly still as, one by one, each item of his clothing was taken away.

Feather-light caresses brushed against Leon's skin as Rupert exposed more and more of his body for inspection. Leon's eyes dropped closed. Rupert allowed his eyelids that much freedom, but almost any other alteration in his posture was corrected with a kind of stubborn patience that Leon hadn't really seen his lover display before that day. The only other movement Rupert didn't try to rewind was the way Leon's cock hardened and rose to curve back towards his abs.

As he stood in the middle of the room, Leon gradually felt the world condensed down to a very simple place. Rupert's commands were the only things he had to worry about now. Answering machine messages, other men, even the possibility of Rupert being kinkier than he could handle or screwing the whole world as soon as he stepped out of his boyfriend's sight, none of it was scary in that moment.

Leon's eyes sprung open as something brushed against his wrist. Bowing his head, he watched as the cuffs were deftly fastened around his limbs. Rupert's fingers danced over the buckles as if he'd been handling bondage his entire life. First Leon's left, then his right wrist, were quickly cocooned within the restraints.

Leon made no comment. Rupert hadn't told him to talk. There was no reason for him to say a single word as Rupert led him to sit on the edge of the bed so he could crouch down and bind his ankles in the same way.

Rupert evidently knew what he was doing. He didn't hesitate once as he guided Leon to lay back on the bed. He didn't even seem to need to think for a moment about how to go about fastening the restraints to the frame.

Obviously, Leon wasn't the first person to lay spread eagle there. The realisation made the breath catch in his throat. Against all logic, the idea of Rupert tying someone else up was almost as hard to accept as the mental picture of Rupert screwing someone else.

This was important. He sensed it in his lover's mood, in his every movement. This meant as much to Rupert as sex ever would, maybe even more.

Suddenly, Rupert straightened up and stepped away from the bed. For several long seconds, he just stared down at the picture he'd created. Then, very slowly, he smiled.

Leon remembered how to breathe. He'd pleased Rupert—perhaps he'd only done that by staying still and doing as he was told, but success still rushed through his veins as he looked up at the other man, chasing away any embarrassment he might have felt.

Seconds passed and the images Leon had seen on the internet slowly crept into the edges of his mind. Heavy whips, welts on guys' backs, bright red stripes across their buttocks where they'd been caned.

The chains attached to Leon's cuffs rattled as he squirmed. If it was that important to Rupert, then...

Leon swallowed rapidly. He'd take it. He'd take whatever Rupert needed to throw at him without complaint, and maybe he'd learn to love it. But even as Leon told himself that, a shiver of apprehension danced down his spine.

Rupert took another step back. Leon's attention quickly focussed on the present as Rupert stepped out of his clothes. Fabric fell to the floor around him. The older man made no effort to put on a show, but he wasn't the kind of guy who needed to twirl around a pole to be gorgeous. Rupert's actions were all very crisp and practical, but Leon still watched his every movement, as mesmerised by his lover as he had ever been.

Leon's hands itched to reach out and touch him. His muscles tensed as his body begged for permission to sit up and offer his lips to be kissed, or to crawl across the bed so he could dip his head and take the tip of Rupert's cock into his mouth.

The metal links on his cuffs rattled against the bed frame again. Permission wasn't Leon's to grant. The bondage was making all the choices for him. His *lover* was making all the choices for him.

Rupert's smile turned wicked as he sat down, naked, on the edge of the bed. He left far too much distance between them. Leon couldn't even feel the heat of his body and, right then, that alone would have been something he'd have been willing to cherish.

Leon opened his mouth. A fingertip pressed against his lips and silenced him before he had a chance to say a word.

"Do you want to tell me to stop?"

Leon shook his head. Rupert's finger followed the movement.

"Then I'll tell you when you have permission to speak."

Unable to lay there without making any sort of contribution at all, Leon kissed his lover's fingertip to show his acceptance.

A shot of anxiety rushed through him as he wondered if Rupert would be angry with him for that, but the dominant merely stroked his cheek, as if in praise, before taking his hand back.

"I wonder what I shall do with you now?" Rupert mused, apparently to himself.

Leon had to bite the inside of his cheek to keep his own suggestions back. Part of him wanted to beg for a whipping, just to get it over with. Another part was up for anything except that.

As he considered his options, Rupert stroked his fingertips over centre line of Leon's rib cage. His touch was almost absentminded. For all the expression on his face, he could have been tapping his fingers on the edge of his desk.

Leon's hands curled into fists above the cuffs. There was nothing casual about the waves of sensations Rupert's touch sent dancing through his body. Squirming against the mattress, Leon thrust his hips forwards. His cock found nothing but empty air.

Rupert said nothing as he slid his hand down Leon's body to stroke up and down the inside of his thigh. Then, just as Leon was about to lose his mind, Rupert spoke. "Have you thought about this before?"

His conversational tone of voice almost pushed Leon over the edge, but he managed not to say anything sarcastic by simply not saying anything at all.

"Answer me, Leon."

"You told me not to speak."

"No," Rupert corrected, patiently. "I told you that I'd give you permission when you were allowed to speak. That's different."

Leon stared up at him.

"Have you thought about this before?" Rupert repeated, his voice deeper and more gorgeous than ever.

Leon closed his eyes as the dominant's teasing touch disappeared from his leg, only for his knuckles to rub back and forth against the underside of his cock. "My day dreams are usually less frustrating," he bit out.

"Really?" Rupert asked, all polite curiosity. "Tell me about them."

"What?"

"Tell me about your fantasies. I want to know what you think about when you touch yourself like this," Rupert said, tracing a fingertip around and around the tip of Leon's cock.

"That's nothing like the way I touch myself!" Leon protested. He thrust his hips forward, desperately trying to push his erection into the other man's hand but Rupert easily rode out the movements, allowing nothing more than he wished to grant him.

"Do you want to come?"

Leon blinked at the other man. Talk about asking the blatantly bloody obvious!

"Then you'll have to earn that right," Rupert informed him. "Tell me your fantasy and I'll give you my hand. I'll touch you just as you'd want to touch yourself if you were free to do so—but only while as you keep talking. If you stop, so will I."

Leon licked at lips that were suddenly dry with nerves.

"Your favourite fantasy, Leon," Rupert specified. "The one you go back to time and time again because you know it will always bring you off."

Closing his eyes, Leon tried to make his brain work. It wasn't half as difficult as he expected it to be. As easily as the darkness behind his lids enveloped him, the fantasy was there, just waiting to unfold.

A second later, Rupert wrapped his hand around the length of his shaft, ready to give him exactly what he wanted. Leon took a deep breath. All he had to do was tell him what he liked to think about while he jacked off. He could do that. Hell, it wouldn't even hurt!

"Locker room," he whispered.

Rupert slowly stroked from the base of Leon's cock all the way up to the tip and closed over the glans, smearing pre-cum across his palm. Leon fell silent, savouring that first stroke of the dominant's hand as it retraced its path down his shaft.

Rupert stopped.

Whimpering at the loss of friction, Leon searched for more words, anything to get his lover's hand moving again. "I go into the locker room at a gym. There are loads of fit guys in there. Most of them are naked."

Rupert began to move his hand again, slow and steady.

"Some of them are coming out of the shower, water dripping off them. Other guys have just got there and all the energy they've saved up for their work-outs is still bubbling away inside them. Some of them know each other, but none of them know me."

Rupert's grip on him tightened slightly, making Leon whimper at the sheer excellence in the other man's touch, before he quickly scrambled for the next words he needed.

"They're all laughing, telling dirty jokes, talking about whoever they screwed on the weekend. Some of them are gay, some of them are talking about women, but everyone's thinking about sex."

Leon paused for a moment to lick at his lips as he turned his head on the pillow, eyes still closed very tightly.

"I start to get undressed as if I'm just getting changed to do a work-out. But...but I'm not. I'm there on a bet or something. The details don't matter, I just know that someone told me I have to go in there and offer myself to the first man who speaks to me. I have to promise to do whatever that man wants right there in the changing room."

Rupert's hand sped up, encouraging Leon's words to tumble out faster and faster.

"I'm so nervous. I'm shaking," Leon whispered, as he watched the mental image of himself fumble at a zip. "I can barely get my clothes off. I keep my eyes on the floor because I know that as soon as I undo my fly, everyone's going to see how turned on I am. I'm still waiting for someone to say something to me. I close my eyes, because I can't bear not knowing who it will be."

Leon closed his eyes even tighter. The chains on his cuffs rattled as he squirmed.

"Someone turns to speak to me. I don't really hear the words, but I look up. It's you."

In spite of everything, Leon felt the heat race to his cheeks at the admission.

"It's you," he whispered again. "But I don't know you—I've never met you before. There are guys all around us, but I manage to stutter the words out. I offer to do whatever you want. The whole room goes quiet and everyone's staring at us but you don't even seem shocked. Someone behind me puts his hand on my shoulder, but you grab his wrist and make him let go. You won't let him touch me. You could—if you tell me to do what he wants, I'd have to. I'm so scared you'll hand me over to them, but you tell him that you don't share. But you'll let them watch though. You..."

Leon bit his lip, whimpering and trying desperately to keep talking as the pictures flashed through his mind more and more rapidly. Images of himself on his knees, worshipping Rupert's cock while other men commented on how good he was. Rupert bending him over the bench in the middle of the room and burying his cock deep into his arse while the other guys cheered him on.

Rupert's hand stopped. Leon desperately sought for words as he writhed and jerked against his cuffs.

"You tell me you're going to screw me, but you want my mouth first." The words were barely coherent, but somehow, they kept Rupert's fist moving. "You tell me to suck your cock and get it all nice and wet for you. You're soft at the start. I have to work you from scratch."

A gasping breath and Leon pushed on.

"You hold back and I know you're making me work for it. I lift my hand to cup your balls, but you shake your head, so I put my hands down by my side. Everyone's talking about us. Someone puts his hand on the back of my head and pushes me forwards on your cock, but you swat them away. You push my hair back from my face, in that way you do when you're relaxed and sleepy and want me to take it really slow. You only ever do it then," Leon babbled. He tossed his head as he instinctively looked for the older man's hand with his scalp.

"Just…just as I start to get the taste of you on my tongue, you pull away. You bend me over the benches in the middle of the room and push your fingers into my arse, until I'm begging for your cock. Finally, you give it to me. You hold onto my sides so hard I know there'll be bruises. I want to touch myself but I can't move my hands or I'll fall off the bench, so I just cling on. You push my head down, so my forehead rests on the pine and you screw me so hard."

Leon gasped as he fought to get a purchase on the blankets with his feet and find some leverage. It was impossible. Rupert kept the same rhythm, the same grip, the same everything no matter what he did.

"I forget about the guys around us, I forget about everything but you. You come inside me, I can feel it," he went on. "God, you feel so good inside me. And when you've finished you pull away, and I feel so empty. I'm still desperate to come. I try to touch myself. But you tell me to put my hands back on the bench.

"You say that you're going to have a swim. You'll come back for another round later. I have to stay right there until you come back. And you just leave me kneeling, arse up, on the bench. I can hear all the other guys walking around me, chatting to each other — gossiping about me. But I know they won't touch me because you promised me they won't, and you'd never break a promise like that. And I...I..."

Rupert tightened his grip, just the tiniest fraction, and suddenly words were no longer necessary.

"Come for me, sweetheart."

It was more a case of well thought out timing of an order than true obedience, but as Leon rushed towards his orgasm, Rupert couldn't resist the temptation to slip the idea of being able to come on command into his mind.

Leon tossed back his head and screamed as his cum spilled against his stomach in long white ropes. At the same moment, Rupert moved his other hand more quickly over his own erection, allowed himself the pleasure of coming into his palm just a moment after the submissive came.

As Leon's triumphant yell faded slowly from the air, he blinked his eyes open. His gaze fell on Rupert. There was so much shock in his expression — it would have been funny, if it hadn't been so bloody wonderful.

Dropping his head back onto the pillow, Leon turned his attention to the ceiling, apparently not ready to meet his lover's eyes. Giving him a moment or two to pull himself together, Rupert deftly cleaned them both up before moving on to undoing Leon's cuffs.

"You have permission to make yourself comfortable. You don't have permission to leave the bed."

Leon nodded as he wriggled into a more relaxed position. Rupert studied the boy's movements carefully. The bondage hadn't been taught, and he hadn't been in it long. He didn't appear to be the least bit sore after his first foray into leather. Everything was going exactly to plan.

Rupert couldn't help but think the world was a bloody brilliant place as he stretched out on the bed next to Leon. "Thoughts?" he prompted, as he turned onto his side and supported his head on his hand.

"How the hell did it take me twenty-three years to be sure I was gay?" Leon asked. Apparently more than a little light-headed with afterglow, he giggled as he rolled his eyes at himself.

Rupert smiled as he stroked Leon's hair back from his face. It wasn't a gesture he'd really thought about when he'd done it before, it certainly wasn't something he'd ever have guessed Leon liked enough to mention in the middle of his fantasy. "It takes many men a lot longer than that."

"How old were you?" Leon asked, as he turned towards him.

"I was nineteen," Rupert admitted. "I had my suspicions before, but that was when I actually came out of the closet and stopped dating women."

"The women at those dinner parties you go to are enough to put a guy off women for life."

Rupert smiled. "My taste improved a hell of a lot when I moved on to guys."

Leon looked away as he blushed. "You know, you're way past the point where you need to flirt with me. I'm pretty much a sure thing with you, if you hadn't noticed."

"Is it unfashionable to tell your lover that you think he's beautiful these days?" Rupert asked.

Leon's blush deepened.

Rupert stroked the heated skin with his fingertips. "You are. If you won't believe me, you must have realised it was true when we went to the club. Damn near every man in the place was panting after you."

"Rupert!"

He chuckled. "Any boy who can dream up that fantasy shouldn't be able to blush at a simple little compliment."

The observation made the blush darken even further, just as Rupert knew it would.

"If I'd met you when I was fifteen, everything would have been so much simpler," Leon complained.

"If we'd met when you were fifteen, you'd have been both illegal and far too young for my tastes. Anyway, I've always thought it's good for a gay man to fool around with girls for a few years before he comes out. Otherwise women would always be in the back of his mind, and he'd be wondering if the grass was greener on the straight side of the fence."

And this way, I never have to worry about you getting curious and wanting to try out a woman, Rupert mentally added.

Leon nodded. He seemed to get lost in his own thoughts then. Quite content to merely admire the view, Rupert lay quietly next to him and waited him out.

"What did Tommy mean about your first night at that club?" Leon finally asked.

Rupert held back a sigh. It had obviously been too much to hope that Leon would have forgotten all about that. "It wasn't that club," he corrected, as he rolled onto his back to stare up at the ceiling. "The one he was talking about was just outside Oxford. I doubt it's even open now. The building should have been condemned long before I stumbled into it and that was long enough ago to be depressing."

"You make yourself sound ancient. You're not that much older than me," Leon protested, as he moved closer and propped himself up on his elbows so he could stare down at him in a neat little reversal of their earlier positions.

Rupert smiled at the submissive's earnest expression, wishing that was true. There was enough age difference in real years. In terms of experience, he wasn't sure he had *ever* been as young or as innocent as Leon.

Silence fell over the room.

"You still haven't told me what you did in that club," Leon reminded him as he dropped his gaze to stare at his hands.

Rupert stroked along the other man's neck, tracing the line of the collar. Leon already seemed to have forgotten he was wearing the strip of leather — he was that comfortable in it.

The sight of him marked out that way only made Rupert all the more determined not to screw things up. "You're supposed to be doing what I say, not the other way around," he pointed out, but there was no bite to his words.

Leon looked down at the blanket between them. When he looked up, Rupert could tell he thought his reluctance was some kind of slight. Tugging at the collar, Rupert quickly encouraged Leon closer, to curl into his side and rest his head on his shoulder.

"It wasn't my greatest moment," he said.

"Tommy seemed to think it was."

"When I was nineteen I probably thought the same. Looking back..." Rupert shrugged. He trailed his fingers up and down Leon's back, following the line of his spine. "Looking back I was a complete slut."

Leon pulled away and blinked down at him.

Rupert couldn't help but smile at the boy's expression. He'd been right in his initial assessment— he'd *never* been that innocent.

"So, it, um...didn't take you long to get into the whole gay scene?" Leon asked.

Rupert shook his head.

"The first night you were out?"

"Yes."

"You...?"

"Let's just say, by the end of that night there weren't many firsts left in me," Rupert said. "Vanilla or kinky."

"Oh..."

Rupert mentally cursed his nineteen year old self.

"You must think I'm an idiot..." Leon whispered.

"You think I'd want you to act the way I did when I was your age? You deserve better memories than a hurried fumble in the corner of a club." And Rupert had made damn sure Leon's memories were a lot better than that too—it was one of the few things in his sex life that he really was proud of.

Leon's eyes opened very wide, suddenly all concern.

Rupert shook his head. "Don't take it into your mind that I wasn't a very willing participant. I'm sure I enjoyed it a great deal at the time—for one thing, I didn't know anything could be better than that."

"And most guys do the same, don't they?" Leon asked, once more dropping his gaze to examine his bitten-short fingernails. "As soon as they come out they're happy to screw anything that moves, to try anything and everything."

Rupert frowned. "Like I said, it's not something I'm proud of."

Leon was silent for a few seconds. "You know if there was something you wanted us to do, you don't have to wait for me to catch up or anything. You only have to say. We could—"

Rupert cut him off with a glare. "Have I ever told you I'm not completely satisfied with what we're doing now?"

Leon shook his head. Then, he smiled slightly, as if that little bit of reassurance was all he'd needed.

They lay in silence for a few moments. Rupert continued to trace lines across Leon's skin. The whole world was so relaxed right then, and they'd managed to discuss their different approaches to life just after they'd come out, without the world imploding. And—

"I told you my fantasy."

Rupert nodded. "Yes, you did," he agreed. And one hell of a fantasy it had been…

"Tit for tat?" Leon suggested. As he looked up, he bit his lip at his daring.

It couldn't be easy for a man with such a natural flare for submission to make that request. Rupert smiled as he stroked Leon's collar again, pleased his lover trusted him enough to make it.

"So many fantasies to choose from…" he murmured, as he tried to pick the most suitable one to share. "I've imagined us doing so many different things." And he was reasonably sure that Leon wasn't ready to hear most of them.

Sorting through each erotic little moment very carefully, Rupert finally selected one that he hoped might push Leon's envelope slightly, without risking ripping the content of it to shreds. "Do you know, I pictured you in a collar just like this one the first time I saw you?"

Leon shook his head.

Rupert chuckled. "I remember walking up to you in that gallery. You turned around and looked up at me. I forgot what I was going to say." Rupert stroked a line along Leon's jaw, remembering the moment as if it were just that morning.

"You asked me if I was exhibiting a collection there," Leon reminded him.

"I couldn't think of anything else to say," Rupert admitted. "It felt like I stood there for ages. Then I snapped back into it. Something finally registered in my brain—art gallery—art—talk about that!"

Leon dipped his head as if he didn't believe him, but Rupert pushed forward, determined to let him know he was just as invested in this as Leon could ever be.

"You looked so shocked when I stared flirting with you, I thought you must be straight. But you kept looking up at me through your lashes and you blushed as if at least part of you liked it. You looked stunning."

Leon shook his head again.

"You looked stunning," Rupert repeated. "I was supposed to meet some guy there. I called up and cancelled as soon as I set eyes on you."

"You didn't tell me you had a boyfriend!" Leon protested, horror dropping off every syllable.

"Because I didn't. It was just a date—hardly the same thing."

"Oh…"

Rupert made the younger man tilt his face back to look at him. "Leon?"

"He didn't mind you cancelling at the last minute?"

"I'm sure he found someone else to enjoy himself with quickly enough. It was a casual thing."

Leon nodded as if he understood the difference, but there was still something off about his expression.

"What's going on in that mind of yours?" Rupert stroked his fingers through Leon's hair again, as if that would somehow help him work out what was happening inside his head.

"You're supposed to be telling me about the first day we met, and your fantasy," Leon reminded him.

"You had a white T-shirt on. It had a black neckline, and I pictured you like this, wearing a collar I put on you. That was my first fantasy about you." And he'd been desperate to see him in his collar ever since. Rupert smiled slightly at himself. It probably served him right for scoffing at all those idiots who believed in love at first sight.

"I told you a lot more than that!" Leon protested.

Rupert hesitated. It was one thing for Leon to fantasise about dangerous things in the safety of his own mind, quite another to hear his lover say them, to realise his boyfriend had every intention of making at least some of those fantasies come true.

"I imagined you wearing nothing but that collar, kneeling in the middle of the gallery after everyone else had gone home. I pictured you looking up at me through your lashes. I knew from the start that you weren't a slut. I guessed that you probably weren't even properly out and that I'd be the first man you ever dated. You were so perfect. I couldn't wait to get your clothes off, but I think you would have had a seizure if I told you what I wanted then." Rupert smiled at the memory. "You weren't even sure about letting me drive you home. I thought you were going to run for the hills when I kissed your cheek."

"I wanted you to kiss me properly," Leon whispered.

Rupert leaned in and brushed their mouths together. He teased Leon's lips apart with his tongue. The boy's eyes dropped closed as he leant forward, instinctively looking for more contact, more everything with his future master. When Rupert broke the kiss, Leon stayed perfectly still for several long seconds. Then, his tongue sneaked out to caress his lips.

A frown crept onto Leon's forehead, as if he was struggling to remember something. "You were telling me about your fantasy..." he said again.

"Was I?"

Leon nodded, determinedly. "If you'd thought I'd...dated other men. Would you have told me about it the first night we'd met?"

"Maybe," Rupert allowed.

"Tell me now?" There was a hint of begging in his voice.

Eager to teach him that if he chose to offer him his submission, his master would see to it that he had anything and everything he ever wanted, Rupert went on. "In the fantasy, I told you I wanted to stay behind after the exhibition for a private viewing."

Leon just stared up at him, his eyes pleading with him to continue.

"After everyone else had left, I walked back into the main gallery and found you waiting for me in the middle of all the art work. You were kneeling naked on a low plinth and you were the most beautiful thing there—especially with the light pouring through that huge stained glass window turning your skin all different colours."

Leon swallowed, but he didn't interrupt.

"I made you wait like that while I looked around all the other pieces on display, as if I hadn't seen it all before, as if I really gave a damn about any of them."

Rupert stopped to stroke his fingers across Leon's chest, brushing a knuckle against one tightly-pebbled nipple and making him jump.

"I could hear your breaths in the silence. I could hear you trying to control them, too. Neither of us said anything. Finally, I came back and walked around you as if you were just another exhibition. I touched your cheek. You looked up at me, just the way you did earlier that day when I started flirting with you. A little bit scared but so determined not to show it, even though you couldn't hide your blush."

That was all it took to have the colour racing back to Leon's cheeks.

"You know how much I love looking at you," Rupert said, softly. "Sometimes I think about locking you up in my own private gallery, right here in this house, just so I can go in and look at you for as long as I want. I'd put you behind glass so no one else could ever touch you, and I'd make sure you couldn't touch yourself either. You'd just have to wait right there for me. You wouldn't be able to get yourself off, you'd have to earn that right."

Leon whimpered.

"Just like right now." Rupert caught Leon's hand as it wondered sleepily towards his cock. "While you wear that collar, you aren't allowed to come without my permission."

"But…" Leon trailed off.

"Do you want me to take the collar off?"

Leon covered the buckle with his other hand and shook his head quickly, a touch of real panic rushing into his eyes at the idea of it being taken away.

Rupert stroked his hair very tenderly. "Keeping it on means doing what I say," he said, as gently as he knew how.

"I will," Leon promised.

Rupert stroked his cheek. He looked him over again and teased Leon's cock with the back of his knuckles. "I like to pretend you are all mine," he admitted.

Leon hesitated for a moment, as if searching for the right words. "Maybe, when I wear it, I am all yours?"

Pure delight rushed through Rupert's veins at the words.

Leon smiled shyly at him, apparently very pleased that he'd pleased his lover.

Rupert brushed their lips together. "Do you like that idea, sweetheart, belonging to me that way?"

Leon nodded.

Rupert kissed him again as he stroked the collar, but all too soon reality nudged at the back of his mind. "You should get some sleep—we both have an early start tomorrow."

"I haven't. My lecture got cancelled."

Rupert looked down at him, his thoughts quickly picking up that idea and running with it. "You'll be home all morning?"

"Yes."

"I've got a few hours free around lunch."

"You could come back here," Leon suggested, enthusiastically.

Rupert chuckled. "Sounds like a date."

"I'd like that."

Another gentle brush of lips and Rupert reached for the collar.

Leon pulled away. "What are you doing?"

"You don't want to sleep in this."

"Yes, I do!"

Rupert stroked his fingers over the leather. "I put it on you. That means it stays on until *I* take it off," he pointed out. "I doubt you want to be woken up early so I can do that, do you?"

"Leave it on?" Leon asked. "Let me be all yours for a little while longer?"

Rupert couldn't help but relent. "But you remember what I said. It stays on until I come home to take it off."

Leon nodded.

"It's important, sweetheart," Rupert said, making no attempt to make the issue sound less serious than it really was.

"I'll keep it on." Leon swore. "Promise."

Rupert nodded his permission. And in spite of all the promises he'd made to himself over the last few months, he couldn't keep his next words back. "Good boy."

Chapter Four

Thursday

A shiver ran down Leon's spine as he peered around Rupert's hallway. Looking up from a kneeling position, everything looked very big, very daunting.

But this was still a good idea. He kept repeating those words over and over inside his mind. It was a good idea. He wasn't making a fool of himself. And even if he was, he was pretty sure Rupert would be very polite about that fact.

Rupert wasn't stupid. He was bound to realise what Leon was trying to do—what he was trying to offer to him. Turning his attention to his skin, Leon watched the blue, red and green pattern sparkle across his body. He checked the way the pattern extended onto the tiles to either side of him.

The sun had moved slightly further along its arc across the sky since he first arranged himself there. Leon shuffled a few inches to his left, so he knelt precisely in the middle of the pattern created by the stained glass window set over the front door.

A sudden metallic scrape heralded a key sliding into the lock. The colours fled from Leon's skin as he jumped halfway to his feet and cast a longing glance towards the stairs.

He could run up there before the door swung open. Rupert would never be any the wiser. It would only take him moments to slip into his usual jeans and T-shirt. Or he could just jump into the bed, snuggle under the blankets and pretend he hadn't surfaced all morning. Maybe Rupert would actually prefer finding him ready and waiting in his bed?

No, he was going to do this. Leon's hand went to the collar at his neck. *This* was what Rupert wanted. Leon lowered himself back to his knees.

The door swung inward. Leon bowed his head and placed his hands neatly behind his back, just like the guy in the photo he'd found on the net earlier that day.

A cool breeze swirled around the hall as Rupert stepped inside. Two footsteps echoed around the room as they fell on the tiles. The door clicked closed.

Silence.

Leon forced himself to stay perfectly still and keep his gaze on the delicate mosaic pattern. He didn't have an art gallery with a huge stain glass window in it. All he could do was pray this was close enough to Rupert's fantasy to at least earn him points for trying.

Leon closed his eyes once more, fighting against a rush of panic as he heard Rupert come closer.

"Open your eyes." The words emanated from right in front of him.

Leon opened his eyes. His gaze fell on Rupert's shiny lace ups.

He could do this. If all those guys on the internet could do it, so could he. Leon leant forward and pressed a chaste little kiss against the highly polished toes of Rupert's shoes, left first then right.

As he sat back on his heels, Leon was aware of Rupert crouching down in front of him, but he didn't lift his gaze to look the older man in the eye.

Rupert stroked his cheek with his knuckles. Leon could feel his attention caressing every other inch of his naked body as Rupert silently studied him. His cock thrived under the dominant's contemplation, even as Leon felt the breath catch in his throat and fear threaten to overtake him.

Suddenly, Rupert was gone—on his feet and two yards away.

"Stand."

Leon did as he was told, doing his best to keep his movements as neat as possible. But he couldn't resist the temptation to glance towards the leather lead he'd left in a prominent position on the hall table.

Rupert followed his gaze. He stepped up to the table and picked up the lead. Wrapping the leather around his fist several times, he tugged at it, as if testing the quality. Staring down at his hand, Rupert considered it for a little while, before setting the lead back on the mahogany table and turning to Leon. "I think I can trust you to walk at heel, can't I, sweetheart?"

Leon nodded, but he wasn't entirely sure if Rupert's words were supposed to be a threat or a promised treat. When Rupert stepped forward, tucked a knuckle under his chin and made him look up, Leon realised that they could easily be both. If he wanted the lead, all he had to do was leave Rupert's side. If he didn't want the lead, all he had to do was be good and stay at his heel.

Either way, he'd remain exactly where Rupert wanted him and Leon got the distinct impression that was all that mattered to Rupert right then.

"Your safe word is concrete. Understand?"

Leon nodded again. Safe word. His time looking stuff up on the internet had been well spent. At least he knew what that was now.

"Tell me what a safe word is."

"It means stop—especially when people are playing games where saying stop can mean 'yes please'," Leon recited.

Rupert smiled slightly. Amusement danced in his eyes, but Leon didn't have time to worry about that, because Rupert had already turned away and was walking through to the living room.

Leon felt the heat race to his cheeks as he rushed after him, staying as close to his heel as any obedient little puppy ever could.

Sitting in the centre of the huge sofa, Rupert picked up one of the cushions and dropped it on the floor between his feet.

Leon didn't wait for a command. It was kind of obvious what Rupert wanted him to do. He was kneeling on the cushion before Rupert even opened his mouth. His fingers were halfway to his lover's fly when Rupert wrapped his hand around his wrist and stopped him short.

"When I got home, your hands were behind your back."

Leon stared up at him, helpless to do anything but return Rupert's gaze.

"Put them back there. I'll tell you when you have my permission to move them again."

Leon slowly did as he was told. It felt like he was moving through thick treacle. With every one of his senses far more heightened than he'd even guessed was possible, each movement felt very important, every decision had the power to make or break his whole world. Except... Leon frowned slightly.

"Speak up."

Leon blinked at Rupert.

"Tell me what you're thinking."

"All I have to do is obey your orders?"

Rupert thought about the question for far longer than Leon expected. "That's part of it," he finally allowed. "But it's not all of it. There's a lot more to submission than that."

Leon nodded as if he understood, and hoped like hell Rupert couldn't tell he was faking it.

"If it's something you want to try, I can teach you everything you need to know about it," Rupert offered. "There aren't many kinks I haven't dipped a toe into over the years."

Leon felt his brow crease as his frown deepened.

Rupert traced the line across his forehead with one fingertip. "I'm not a mind-reader, Leon. If something's wrong, you need to tell me what it is."

Leon shook his head. "It's nothing."

"A big part of submission is telling the truth and not holding anything back. If you do that, it will impress me far more than any kind of obedience could."

The words slipped straight past any kind of higher thought process and caught the part of Leon that wanted to please Rupert by the throat. "This was supposed to be your fantasy," he blurted out. "It wasn't supposed to be about you having to play the teacher with me."

Rupert chuckled.

Leon completely failed to see what was so damn funny.

"Don't you think that's a role any man who's interested in dominance would enjoy?" Rupert asked, as he slid his fingers into Leon's hair and pushed the strands back from his face. "Don't you think I'd love introducing you to new things, guiding you through them, watching you do something you've never done before?"

Leon cleared his throat. "So you don't get bored waiting around for me to buy a clue then?" he whispered.

Rupert shook his head. "You're one of the few men I know who shocks the hell out of me on a regular basis. I never quite know what you're going to do next."

Leon nibbled at his bottom lip. After the last few days, Rupert must either think he was insane or on something illegal.

Leaning back in his chair, Rupert tapped his lap. "Come up here. Kneeling at your lover's feet might be very pretty and very submissive, but too much of it will give both of us a crick in the neck."

Leon pulled himself to feet. With his hands still behind his back, he had no idea how to maintain his balance as he tried to straddle another man. With one knee on one side of Rupert's legs, he tried to move the other leg to the opposite side of him. One moment he was just about managing to keep his poise, the next, he was face first into the sofa cushion behind the other man's shoulder, his body pressed tightly against Rupert's torso.

Strong hands settled on his shoulders and straightened him up. When Leon regained his equilibrium, Rupert's didn't rush to pull his hands away. He slid them down his arms, caressing his bare skin all the way to where Leon's right hand was wrapped around his left wrist behind his back.

Rupert smiled as he slid his fingers back up Leon's arms before moving on to his torso. From there, he slid his palms across Leon's chest until one strong confident hand settled over Leon's heart. There was no way for him to hide how fast his pulse was racing then.

"I..." Heat rushed to his cheeks once more. There was nothing else for Leon to say, no excuse for freaking out all the time like a little kid who had no chance of ever being man enough to have Rupert all to himself.

"Tell me what's scaring you," Rupert suddenly ordered. "The first thing in your head. No holding back."

"You've never said you were into any of this before." And that scared Leon far more than anything he'd read on any website, more even than the whips and crops. The fact that they could be together for so long, that he could be so far in love with Rupert and not really know what he was actually into wasn't so much scary as completely terrifying.

"I don't think I've ever hidden the fact that I like to be in control from you, have I?" Rupert asked.

Forgetting all about keeping his hands behind his back, Leon reached up to touch his collar. "But you never actually —"

"There's no rush to bring out the toys. And if it turns out you're not into this" — his hand joined Leon's on his collar and squeezed his fingers before guiding his arm back behind him — "that's not an insurmountable problem either."

Leon looked away. He wasn't an idiot. He knew that Rupert would find it really easy to get a fix of whatever Leon couldn't provide elsewhere — there had to be enough kinky guys around that would fall over themselves to have Rupert tying them up and making them scream.

Rupert took great care to keep his voice very calming, very gentle when he spoke up again. "There's nothing to be scared of."

If anything, Leon's heartbeat sped up another notch under his palm.

"We're not going to do anything you don't want to do."

That didn't do anything to reassure the Leon either. Rupert frowned as the other man closed his eyes. His own heart was racing just as fast as Leon's, even if there was no way the boy could know it.

He couldn't screw this up. With any other man it would have been easy to launch in and damn the consequences. With Leon... Yes, with Leon, the problem had everything to do with what was going on in Rupert's heart.

"I understand that you want to do this for me," Rupert said, carefully. "And I love the thought behind the gesture, but it's only going to happen if we *both* enjoy it. I'm not going to use you like some sort of sex toy."

"But you would if I was someone else?" Leon asked.

Rupert leant back against the sofa cushions as he ran his hands over the younger man's torso. No lies — rules like that went both ways. "Someone who had enough experience to know what they were getting themselves into — yes," he admitted. "I've used people like that in the past, just as they've used me, and we've both enjoyed ourselves a great deal in our own ways."

"Then why not me?"

"Because you're not them. You're *you*," Rupert said, unable to keep a little snap out of his voice. Anyone who couldn't see the difference had no business calling himself a dominant.

Leon turned his head aside. "Sometimes I wonder why you bother with me for anything at all—"

Rupert caught hold of Leon's chin and jerked his head back to face him. "No! You don't ever doubt the way I feel about you."

Leon's eyes opened very wide. "I'm sorry, I…"

He should have spoken to him more gently, Rupert knew that, but the idea that Leon could really believe he didn't give a damn about him tore right through Rupert's mind, leaving a gaping hole in its wake.

Leon tried to look away again, but Rupert held him still, determined to see some sort of understanding dawn in his eyes, on that point if nothing else.

"You could have anyone," Leon finally whispered. "Why waste your time with me?"

Rupert stared at him in shocked silence, horrified that Leon really did seem to doubt how much he cared for him. After all the time he'd spent trying to show him how safe he was with him. Rupert swallowed down the bitter taste in the back of his mouth. Obviously he'd been right to be concerned that a lifetime of leather bars and experienced submissives hadn't in any way prepared him for a man like Leon.

"You could have gone into that bar on Tuesday and half the men there would have begged you to screw them or whip them, or do anything else you wanted to them, right?"

Rupert didn't bother to deny it

"So why waste your time with me?" Leon repeated.

"I can get sex any time I want and submission damn near anywhere, too," Rupert agreed. "Any man with enough money in his wallet can. But, I can't get *you* anywhere."

Leon looked down. "What's so special about me? That you like to look at me? In case you hadn't noticed there were plenty of other twinks in that club wearing tight leather trousers."

Rupert smiled slightly. What was special about him? He wasn't sure he knew where to start. "You know that we're much more than a casual fling, right?" he finally said. "This is more than just sex or even kinky games to me?"

Leon held his breath, as if waiting for him to add something else. Rupert had to bite back his tongue to stop the L word escaping in response. It was far too soon for that. Even if it were true that he was in love with the boy, there was no need to admit it out loud right then. Not when it would be more likely to scare Leon off than anything else.

Silence filled the room as Rupert trailed his fingertips down Leon's body until they reached the pale little happy trail of hairs leading to his cock.

Leon gasped as Rupert gently brushed his fingers along his shaft.

"I meant it when I said that we can do whatever you want—" Leon began.

Rupert covered his mouth with his other hand, only to hesitate and hold back his automatic response. "Whatever I want?" he checked.

Leon nodded.

"Good." Rupert took his hand away. "Then we're going to talk."

Leon looked at their respective positions.

"And you're going to look me in the eye while we do that," Rupert added.

Leon slowly lifted his gaze. "Okay…"

"Putting you on the other side of a table when you're naked and collared would be a waste. So you're going to sit right here on my lap while I ask you whatever I want, close enough that I can touch you however I want, aren't you?"

Leon nodded again.

"But first, you're going to walk over to the shelves next to the window and get the lube and condoms out of the box on the left for me."

The boy was so eager to obey, he almost landed flat on his face as he launched himself off Rupert's lap with far more enthusiasm than co-ordination. He was all the way on the other side of the room before he remembered that his hands were still locked behind his back by his lover's orders.

Leon looked over his shoulder for help. Rupert raised an eyebrow and stayed exactly where he was, withholding permission to break posture, just to see what Leon would do. Biting his lip as he frowned with concentration, Leon turned his back on the shelf and squinted over his shoulder as he fumbled with the box.

His own fingers working far more deftly, Rupert undid his belt and his fly in anticipation. By the time Leon had turned back to him, lube in hand and success shining in his eyes, Rupert's fist was wrapped snugly around his cock, jacking himself off as he admired the sight of his lover, naked and squirming his way through an unnecessarily difficult task in an effort to please him.

Leon stalled halfway across the room as his eyes dropped to where Rupert was stroking his cock and stayed there, seeming to feast on the view of his lover playing with himself as if he'd never seen anything so magnificent.

"Come here." It was an order rather than a request. For once, Rupert didn't make any attempt to disguise that fact.

Leon stepped forward, but he didn't look up. His head remained bowed to stare at Rupert's open fly. He almost tripped over the cushion still on the floor at Rupert's feet. Shocked into looking up, Leon met Rupert's gaze.

"Turn around."

With a reluctance he was apparently completely incapable of hiding, Leon did as he was told. Rupert took the condoms from his hand and dropped them on the sofa next to him. Taking the lube from him too, Rupert placed his other hand on the small of Leon's back and guided him to bend at the waist.

A tap from Rupert's shoe against the inside of Leon's ankles encouraged him to spread his legs wider, offering himself more overtly to his lover. Rupert quickly spread lube on his fingers, and dropped the tube. He moved his left hand to his shaft as he smeared the lube across Leon's hole with his more dominant hand.

He could feel the tension thrumming through Leon's body. He wasn't used to being put on display in that sort of position, not used to his lover leaving him feeling exposed and vulnerable. It had to feel very different to relaxing on the bed and being able to reach out and touch his lover in return as Rupert carefully prepared him. Perhaps it felt just a little more like that fantasy Leon had told him about.

"You can move your hands," Rupert allowed. "Put them on your knees to balance yourself."

Leon followed the order without question.

"Good boy."

As Rupert felt Leon relax, he carefully worked his fingers inside him, slowly coaxing the tight ring of muscle to loosen around the digits.

"You've never thought about dominance and submissive much until recently, have you?" Rupert asked, forcing his voice to remain perfectly level, perfectly controlled.

Leon shook his head.

"Verbal answers until I give you permission to answer in another form," he ordered.

"O—Okay," Leon managed to stutter out.

"Good boy," Rupert murmured again.

"I hadn't really thought about it at all," Leon admitted, his voice already shaking with need. "Not before I met you."

"But I'll bet you've been doing some research today, haven't you?"

Leon whimpered. He nodded. A moment later he seemed to remember his previous order. "Yes."

"And I'll guess the history's deleted on my internet now?"

Leon nodded again. "I'm sorry—"

"You have nothing to apologise for," Rupert cut in.

"You said you liked the teacher thing," Leon whispered.

"Yes, I did. But that doesn't mean..."

Part of Rupert already had the whole speech lined up in the front of his mind. *Don't trust a dominant who insists on being your only source of information. Don't walk into anything without checking.* The first words were already rushing to his lips when he realised any such lecture would be supremely pointless.

Rupert bit back a smile. Leon didn't need to be warned about other doms. He was only going to have one, and Rupert couldn't help but love the fact that his own opinions were the only ones that needed to be explained to the submissive. There weren't going to be any leather-clad monsters hiding behind rocks waiting to jump out and carry the novice submissive away.

Leon moaned his approval as Rupert found his prostate. His hips rocked, trying to push himself back and lodge himself more firmly around the offered penetration. Rupert stilled his fingers and watched with pleasure as Leon rode the digits. A glance in the mirror above the fireplace confirmed that Leon's eyes were closed. He was lost in his own world, thinking about nothing but his personal gratification.

Leon let out a mewing little sound of displeasure as Rupert finally stopped the show by taking his fingers away. He left Leon bent over in front of him as he opened the condom and deftly rolled the latex down his shaft.

"Hands behind you. Turn around."

It took Leon a very long time to obey the order, as if he was no longer in complete control of his body, but finally he faced his future master.

Placing a hand on either hip, Rupert led Leon to straddle him once more. Leon's movements were clumsier than ever, but Rupert didn't let him stumble this time. With his guidance, Leon was soon lowering himself over Rupert's erection.

Leon tilted his head back and looked up to the ceiling as he settled down around him, as if simple animal instinct made him desperate to bare his neck and show his submission to a more dominant male.

Rupert growled his approval as he wrapped his fingers around Leon's cock. He stroked once or twice, then just left his hand there wrapping loosely around Leon's erection offering nothing but static warmth.

Leon's head dropped forward as his muscles tensed and he struggled not to thrust into his grip without permission.

"Do whatever research you want," Rupert offered.

Leon blinked open his eyes and frowned his confusion as if he'd completely forgotten what they were talking about.

"As long as you don't start treating every daft website you stumble across as a check list of things you *have* to do, I've no problem with you looking things up for yourself. If you read something and think—wow, I really want to do that! Great. Let me know what it is and we'll try it. Other things might not rock your boat." Rupert shrugged. "No one is into everything."

Leon squirmed on his lap. It was impossible to tell if he was trying to move his cock within Rupert's grasp or ride his lover's erection, but for once, Rupert didn't give him more of whatever he might want the moment he asked for it.

Leon's frown deepened. He stilled as he seemed to realise he'd only increase his frustrations by trying to move. "What are you into?" he asked, very softly.

Rupert shook his head. "I'm into being the one asking the questions today."

Leon immediately dropped his gaze and turned his face away.

"And if you look away from me while you answer them, I'll think you're hiding something. I'll think you're lying to me," Rupert said.

"Maybe I'm trying to hide how much I like this?" Leon hazarded. It honestly sounded like he didn't know. He looked so lost, so out of his depth.

Rupert turned Leon back to face him and pressed a tender kiss to his temple. "Tell me what you like and

I'll tell you something I like in exchange," he offered, gently taking him by the hand and leading him back towards the shallow end of the D/s pool for a little while.

Leon nibbled at his bottom lip.

"All you have to do is tell me something you've heard of or read about on the net that you liked," Rupert explained. "Then I'll tell you something I like in return. Does that sound fair?"

Rupert studied Leon's eyes very carefully. Fair was important. If Leon understood that they were starting out as equals, he'd have a much better chance of explaining that he still thought of him as worthy of equality when some of the things they did in the future might make him think otherwise.

Leon shifted uncertainly on Rupert's lap. His erection pressed against Rupert's hand more firmly. Leon whimpered and pushed his hips forward, rubbing himself blatantly against his palm as his arousal got the better of his self-control.

"Tell me what's turning you on, sweetheart."

"You."

Rupert smiled and brushed their lips together in a brief approval, but there was no reason to go *that* easy on him. "I want far more from you than that."

"I liked it when you said I was yours," Leon whispered, obviously relishing the way the word tasted on his lips. Their gazes met through Leon's lashes.

"I like the way you do that," Rupert offered in return. "I like the way you bow your head and look up at me through your lashes. I love that you're terrible at hiding things when you look me in the eye too."

"That's cheating." Leon tried to pull away, but there wasn't anywhere for him to go.

Rupert's grip tightened over his erection, not so much holding Leon in place as reminding him why he didn't want to go anywhere. "How exactly is it cheating?"

"I told you something that turns me on," Leon complained. "You're supposed to do the same."

Rupert chuckled. He ran the fingertips of his other hand over Leon's eyes. "You don't think you can turn me on with a look? You're underestimating yourself."

Leon shook his head, apparently not the least bit convinced.

Maybe he did deserve a little more at that. "It's also as submissive as hell. Keeping your eyes lowered and looking up at me though your lashes like that. It gets to me every time."

Leon glanced up at him. Barely a second had passed before he seemed to realise he was doing exactly as Rupert had just described. Leon blushed and quickly looked away, over his shoulder and down to where his hands were clasped behind him.

"How does having to keep your hands behind your back make you feel?"

"Like last night, when you tied me up," Leon offered.

Rupert stayed silent, letting Leon know the answer wasn't enough to satisfy him.

It didn't take him too long to work out that more was required. "It almost feels like you're holding me there. I can't move my hands until you tell me to and—" Leon frowned as if struggling to get his thoughts in line inside his head. Barely a fraction of a second later, his hips rocked—apparently, his body had already given up trying and was more than happy to return to more pleasant tasks. "It feels like everything depends on you—like you can do whatever you want with me and there's nothing I can do about it." His voice faltered on the last few words.

"And what do you think I'd want to do with you?"

Leon nibbled at his bottom lip. "I don't know. I think part of me likes that too. It likes not having to make decisions," he whispered, as if he wasn't sure if that made him strange.

Rupert brushed their lips together in praise, eager to wipe away any such idea. "Perfect," he whispered into the kiss. It made him perfect.

As he leant back, Rupert rocked his hips a little. His own body screamed its frustration at not being able to move, even while Leon's body was wrapped tightly around his cock and the boy's muscles contracted around him every time he squirmed.

Forcing himself to concentrate on more important things, Rupert stroked his fingertips over his lover's body, enjoying showing Leon exactly what it felt like to be touched but not be allowed to touch in return— to have no choice but to concentrate on his future master's touch because he had nothing beneath his own fingertips to distract him.

Leon's shoulders tensed and Rupert knew he'd tightened the grip on one of his hands around the opposite wrist. The boy's eyes fell closed. His hips thrust forward as he tried to arch into Rupert's touch and get the stimulation he wanted. Rupert smiled to himself as he altered his movements to make sure he received the exact opposite.

Leon stilled for a moment, apparently deep in thought. When he moved again, something akin to reverse psychology was obviously taking place.

Rupert immediately switched to complying with everything Leon signalled his desire for.

Leon whimpered his disappointment. He opened his eyes, looked up and met Rupert's gaze.

"I love your faith in how easily I can be manipulated," Rupert teased.

Leon bit his lip. "That's cheating, too."

"Then I'll tell you I find it incredibly erotic that you would try submitting to me for no other reason than you thought it would please me. I love the way you trust me. And yes, I get turned on just from the fact you're sitting on my cock accepting whatever I give you, that you didn't even hesitate to give up the right to demand anything else."

Leon whimpered. More and more pre-cum slicked Rupert's hand as Leon's desperation increased as he continued to toy with the boy's erection regardless.

"You know I love going down on you, but I love this too—jacking you off so slowly that you can't help but writhe around me." Rupert began to stroke him more quickly as he said it. His grip tightened, his fingers closed over the head when he reached the top of each stroke, covering the glans and teasing Leon's foreskin.

"I...I like it too."

"It's a control thing," Rupert said, almost managing to make his voice sound casual and conversational. "I love being completely in control of you. And it doesn't make any difference to me if that involves twelve foot of rope or your word you'll do as I say. I love possessing you."

Leon whimpered.

"Do you like that idea, too, pet?"

"Yes." His eyes dropped closed.

"Open your eyes. Watch what your master's doing to you," Rupert ordered.

Leon obeyed.

One hand wrapped around Leon's erection while the other moved to the boy's hip to steady him, Rupert gradually sped up his strokes even further, encouraging Leon to move with him. Each time he lifted himself and thrust into Rupert's hand, Leon's hole milked Rupert's cock that little bit harder, taking each of them closer and closer to the edge by the moment.

As Leon's gaze remained on his cock, Rupert focussed on his lover's eyes, watching both the pleasure and the submission blossoming in them. He held Leon on the edge for as long as he could until they both came together. Leon's semen spilled over Rupert's hand to land across both his partially bared torso and his shirt in milky white lines.

Pure bliss raced through Rupert's body. All thoughts and plans were pushed aside as, for just a few brief moments, physical ecstasy was allowed to reign supreme. There were no questions that needed to be asked as lightening shot through every muscle and nerve ending, no doubts that Leon belonged to him in every way a man ever could.

Leon half collapsed forward as his pleasure drained away. His forehead came to rest against Rupert's shoulder. He gasped for breath, his whole body trembling with the effort. Moving one hand to rest on the back of Leon's head, Rupert let him relax there as several minutes silently past them by.

As Leon straightened up, he moved his hands from behind his back, automatically reaching for a wipe from the end table to clean up Rupert's chest. No doubt he wasn't intending to disobey, but still…

"Leon." There was only the tiniest note of correction in Rupert's voice.

The boy couldn't have tensed up more quickly if someone had screamed their anger with his failure at the top of their voice. His expression faltered as he realise he'd made a mistake. Very slowly Leon put his hands back behind him. Uncertainty flooded his eyes as he looked up.

Rupert smiled his forgiveness, pleased with how quickly Leon realised his little mistake and that his first instinct had been to correct it, even after he'd come. Dropping his own gaze for a second, Rupert slid his finger through where Leon's semen decorated his chest and offered it up to Leon's lips.

The younger man hesitated as he looked down at the sticky fingertip. "That's your next thing?" Leon checked. "That's something that turns you on?"

"Yes."

Leaning forward, Leon took the fingertip in his mouth with obvious caution and carefully sucked it clean.

"That's right, sweetheart," Rupert whispered. He took another finger full of cum from his skin.

This time, Leon didn't hesitate. He held even Rupert's eyes as he suckled on the digit, so damn eager to please.

When he didn't rush offer him more, Leon carefully lifted himself off Rupert's softening cock and backed away to kneel on the cushion between Rupert's legs. Bowing his head, he leant forward to lap his cum directly from Rupert's skin.

He looked up through his lashes. A moment later, Rupert stroked the submissive's hair back from his face in just the way Leon had said he liked.

Leon lapped his way across Rupert's chest with apparent enjoyment. He didn't pause until he'd cleaned every trace of cum away, even licking the worst of the stains from his shirt along the way.

He didn't seem to know what to do with himself when he was finished, but that was easily fixed. Adopting a tighter hold on Leon's hair, Rupert pulled him back up onto the sofa and brought their lips together.

Demanding access, he licked the taste of Leon's cum from his mouth, more than willing to share in it.

"That's right," Rupert whispered in his ear as lack of oxygen forced him to break the kiss. "Good boy." He let Leon rest until they both caught their breath, but the moment their breathing settled into an easy rhythm, he knew he couldn't put off the inevitable any longer or he might lose the strength to do what needed to be done at all.

"I'm going to take your collar off now." Rupert shook his head when Leon tried to object. "It's time, sweetheart. You've got a lecture this afternoon and I have to get back to work soon. I won't be here to take it off just before you go."

"I could keep it on," Leon suggested.

Rupert shook his head once more. "No. This is just between us." Leon was his, and he'd be damned if anyone else would get the chance to see him in a collar before everything was final between them.

Leon nodded, but his reluctance was obvious. "Okay."

"When I take it off, you can move your arms."

"Okay."

Rupert took the collar off and laid the length of leather neatly on the sofa next to them.

"Do you have to go right away?" Leon asked.

If he was trying to make the question sound casual, he failed completely. Leon sounded far more like exactly what he was — a natural submissive who'd just taken his first shaky steps into exploring that side of himself and now needed a little bit of a fuss made of him, a little bit of gentle after-care to reassure him he was on the right track.

"I've got a little while."

Leon hesitated as he looked at their positions and appeared to decide he shouldn't remain on his lover's lap forever. Rupert let him pull away, but only allowed him to go as far as his side before he tugged him back to rest his bare skin against his lover's almost entirely clothed body.

Afternoon business meetings could wait.

Chapter Five

Leon tapped his fingers against the bedside table. There was no more time to waste on the idea he could get away with only playing those particular games that appealed to him. There was no way in hell he could risk everything on the assumption that Gerald hadn't called back, or left another message for Rupert—one that he'd actually received.

Leon reminded himself of all those things several times. This had to happen, and it had to happen tonight—even if the skin on his back winced at the very idea.

Taking a deep breath, Leon stared down at where the collar rested just next to his fidgeting fingers. As he pushed his hair back out of his eyes, he couldn't help but pray that he'd be able to convince Rupert to put the collar on him from the start.

In a way Leon didn't really understand, he was sure that a whipping would be far easier to take if he had the little strip of leather wrapped around his throat. There was strength in that collar, maybe even a little bit of magic in it. Somehow, it was almost impossible to believe he could ever fail to do whatever Rupert wanted while he was wearing it. It had also been strangely difficult not to call him sir, like the submissives did on the internet.

Leon tensed as the bedroom door clicked closed and Rupert's footsteps crossed the room. Rupert obviously knew he had something planned for that evening. The fact that his boyfriend had to work really late hadn't changed that.

Leon could damn near feel the expectation rolling around the room. Rupert seemed to sense his nerves too. Stroking his hands down Leon's shoulders, he gently turned Leon around in his embrace. As much as he tried to hide it, Leon knew Rupert felt the little shiver that ran through him as he took a deep breath.

Tucking a knuckle under his chin, the taller man tilted Leon's head back and kissed him in that tender reassuring way he had. It was as if every touch of his lips promised that all Leon had to do was follow his lover's lead and everything would be fine.

Leon went with that idea, tipping his head back further and lifting himself onto his toes as he parted his lips. Rupert was a great kisser. The whole world became a very simple, very wonderful, place as Rupert's tongue teased his bottom lip.

A few moments passed. Rupert rocked his hips slightly, pressing their bodies closer together, leaving Leon in no doubt that he was already hard and ready for anything.

There was no answering tent in Leon's jeans. Mentally cursing his cock for picking that night, of all nights, to get bashful, Leon pulled back a few inches and looked up at his lover, wondering if Rupert had noticed that and how pissed off about it.

The taller man smiled down at him, amusement dancing in his eyes.

That...that really wasn't the reaction Leon had expected.

"So far this week we've had welcome-home sex, semi-public venues, bondage and submission. I have to admit I'm curious about what tonight's topic of exploration might be."

"I thought maybe we could do something else," Leon said, keeping the words as calm and level as he could.

"Such as?" Rupert asked as he stroked Leon's hair back from his face.

Leon leaned into the touch. He wasn't sure what he loved more, the calming caress or knowing Rupert did it even more often ever since he had mentioned he liked it. "Whip me?" he blurted out.

"I don't think you have a unanimous vote on that idea," Rupert said, twitching his leg and leaving Leon in no doubt that he had indeed noticed every little detail. Stepping back Rupert moved to sit on the end of the bed.

"I really don't need to be turned on to be whipped," Leon pointed out, as he allowed Rupert to guide him forward.

"Actually, the most essential thing is for *both* of the guys involved to want to get the whip out in the first place," Rupert corrected as he led Leon to sit on the bed next to him.

"I do want to," Leon said with every scrap of confidence he could muster. "I'm just...um...a bit nervous?"

"So we'll wait a little longer before we try that—until you're less nervous," Rupert said, as if it really didn't matter to him at all.

Leon frowned down at the carpet between his feet, wondering why the hell it would matter, when it was obvious just how easily Rupert could find someone else to play those games with in the meantime.

A minute passed. Rupert stroked his fingers down Leon's cheek as he turned him to face him. "Not that I haven't enjoyed the side effects, but what has been going on with you this week?"

Leon leant back until he lay halfway across the bed. He stared up at the ceiling as if the entire universe was laid out there, all neat and easy to understand. "It doesn't matter," he muttered. It had been a bloody stupid plan from the start. He'd made an idiot out of himself for nothing and now Gerald would be in town and...

Thoughts faded from Leon's mind as Rupert half turned and peered down at him. He raised an eyebrow. Leon knew that particular look. It meant that Rupert would happily wait all day for an answer, so long as he got his answer eventually.

Leon shook his head. "It was nothing. I mean, I just thought..." It was bloody hard not to tell Rupert whatever he wanted when he looked at him like that. Leon shook his head again, but it did no good. "I wanted to ask you something..." he admitted.

"So, ask me," Rupert said, in something that was dangerously close to the tone of voice that was able to make Leon obey him, no matter how scared he was.

Leon somehow managed to hold strong and shake his head once more. "Not now. Afterwards."

"You wanted to ask me something after I whipped you?"

Leon nodded, his gaze flickering from Rupert to the ceiling and back again.

Rupert's face lost any trace of expression. "Ask me something or ask me *for* something?"

Leon had never heard Rupert sound that way before, so cold, so completely unemotional. "Sort of, both?" he said, looking quickly back to the ceiling.

Rupert caught hold of his chin and turned Leon to face him. There was no caress in his touch. "There are names for people who ask for things in exchange for sex or submission, Leon. They aren't nice names."

The blood drained out of Leon's face. Pulling sharply away from Rupert, he scrambled towards the edge of the bed only to stop there, with his back to Rupert, as every joint in his body froze up.

Was that really what he was doing? Was he really asking for exclusivity in exchange for his submission, in exchange for letting Rupert hurt him?

Suddenly Leon was pretty sure he knew the answer, and he didn't like it at all. "I…" He trailed off as he realised making excuses wasn't going to help.

Behind him, Rupert sighed. The mattress moved as he shifted his weight. Via the shadow Rupert cast on the carpet, Leon saw him push his hand through his hair. He hardly ever did that unless a big deal was falling apart.

An extra shot of horror ran through Leon. He couldn't have started this conversation on a day when Rupert had lost something that was really important to him. Even he couldn't be that stupid.

Rupert took a breath so deep it almost sounded like another sigh. "Leon, you know if there's something you need — or even something that you want this badly, I'll make sure you get it. But you're far too important to me for me to let our relationship become about this sort of manipulation."

Leon closed his eyes, unable to even look at Rupert's shadow.

"I won't have you exchanging your submission for whatever it is that you want. I've had that off too many people in the past. You're better than them — you're better than this, and I won't be the man who changes that."

"I wasn't trying to manipulate you," Leon whispered, clenching his fists tightly around the edge of the bed.

"But you thought I might react differently to your request after I whipped you — after you gave me what you thought I wanted from you?" Rupert asked.

"It wasn't like that," Leon said, but he was less and less sure of his position by the moment.

The sadness in Rupert's voice was far worse than his anger could ever have been. Leon pulled his feet up onto the edge of the bed in front of him and hooked his arms over his knees. Disappointing Rupert was somehow so much worse than merely pissing him off could ever have been.

Rupert took another deep breath, as if he was struggling to stay calm too. Another movement rocked the mattress. Rupert's slid his arm around Leon's shoulders. "Forget about everything else for the moment. Tell me what you wanted to ask me for?"

Instinctively leaning into an embrace that implied he might have screwed up, but not past the point of forgiveness, Leon tried to make his brain work through his fears.

Somehow Rupert seemed to have pulled himself together. When Leon risked a glance up, he realised that, in spite of everything, Rupert had somehow even managed to pin an encouraging smile to his lips.

"I just thought we could talk about us, maybe, being exclusive," Leon whispered.

Rupert tensed. The arm around Leon's shoulder retreated. "Who?"

Leon blinked at him. "I don't underst—?"

"We've been together for almost six months. If you're dating someone else I think I have a right to know who it is." The words sounded strained, as if Rupert were suddenly struggling to hold on to every scrap of the composure he'd regained.

"Me?" Leon protested. "I'm not the one who's—" He cut himself short as he looked away.

So, they were going to have this talk regardless of his complete inability to prove he could play all the games Rupert enjoyed so much? Great. That was just bloody great...

"So this has all been because you think I'm cheating on you?" Rupert demanded, as he jerked himself to his feet and took several steps away from the bed.

"I'm not an idiot," Leon said, as he looked up at him. "You never said you wanted us to be exclusive. I should never have assumed that you intended us to be. Loads of men like you have lots of boyfriends, lots of submissives. I get that now. I just thought it was something we could discuss."

"After I whipped you," Rupert put in.

"Yes. I mean, no!" Leon shook his head. "I just thought that if everything went well you might be more inclined to agree not to see other people. I mean, I couldn't ask you to stop playing around with other guys until you knew things could be good between us, that I could play those games too." Leon wasn't even sure if his words made sense or not. His head was swarming with too many emotions for clear thoughts to stand a chance.

"So you thought I might agree we should be exclusive, providing I proved to you that I'd really enjoy whipping a man who obviously has no interest in pain?" Rupert bit out. He turned away then, and began to pace back and forth across the bedside rug.

"Maybe not straight away… I mean, maybe once I got the hang of it all?" Leon analysed his own words and found them severely wanting. They sounded so much like payment for services rendered it almost turned him sick.

"And you've assumed I've been running around behind your back since the start?" Rupert demanded as he retraced his path once more.

Leon watched his feet go back and forth, unable to risk lifting his gaze and meeting Rupert's eyes. "We're not exactly from the same world, are we? I don't expect you to think about things the way I do."

"And when did you experience this revelation that you and I don't think about things the same way?" Rupert demanded. "When you realised I like leather?"

Leon shook his head. "Gerald phoned."

Rupert stilled. "Oh?"

"He left a message on your answer phone when I was in your study, waiting for you to come home. He's in town this weekend. I deleted the message, but I can remember the number if you want it." The damn thing was pretty much etched into his brain.

"Yes, I will need the number, Leon," Rupert said, suddenly very calm again.

Leon nodded dejectedly. Of course Rupert wanted Gerald's number. Hell, he'd probably gladly take the number of any guy who acted sane right then…

"I should at least call him back and tell him that I'm not available," Rupert continued. He put every scrap of composure he could muster into the sentence. To his relief it came out damn near level.

Leon glanced up, a jerky little gesture that screamed his discomfort with the situation. He looked so damn ready to bolt.

Go slow. Be patient. Let him get used to gay vanilla before you get too kinky. Show him you care. Look after him. Protect him.

Everything Rupert had been telling himself since he first looked into those big blue eyes circled around and around inside his head. His hand clenched into a fist at his side. Making the boy feel worthless because he hadn't jumped into a leather harness on the first date hadn't been part of his plan.

"Not available?" Leon echoed, as if he wasn't familiar with the concept.

"It's what I've been telling everyone since we met," Rupert admitted with that same forcibly calm voice. "If I intended dating anyone else, or playing with anyone else, while we were together, I'd have told you that from the start."

"You would?"

"Have I given you any reason to believe I'd lie to you?" Rupert asked as he forced his fist to unclench. The calm tone was much easier to maintain now. It almost felt like he'd gone all the way through panic and into the numb, peaceful place on the other side.

Leon shook his head.

Rupert took a deep breath. He supposed that was something. The boy might think he was a cheating bastard, but he didn't think he was a *lying*, cheating bastard. "Even if I was used to open relationships, I knew you weren't. I wouldn't have let you assume we'd be exclusive if I had any plans to the contrary."

Leon dropped his gaze. Rupert could almost see the relief rushing through him, and he cursed himself for not having realised something was wrong earlier.

"Rupert…" From just that one word, Rupert knew Leon's relief was gone, already replaced with new worries.

"Yes, sweetheart?"

Leon hesitated. Crouching down in front of him, Rupert stroked his hair back again from his face in the way he knew Leon loved so much.

"I'm sorry."

"Isn't that my line?" Rupert asked. The teasing fell flat. Leon didn't even force a smile in response.

"I didn't think about… I wasn't trying to manipulate you. It's just… If you were playing all these kinky games with other people, it seemed logical to wait until *we* were playing them before asking you not to go to other guys. But…"

Rupert continued to stroke Leon's hair as he forced himself to stay silent and let the boy get all his words out.

"But I didn't want to wait until you suggested it, because you didn't seem to be in any rush, so…" Leon closed his eyes. "God, you're right. I was acting like a whore."

Rupert mentally cursed his temper. "I shouldn't have said that."

Leon shook his head. "No! You were right—"

Rupert pressed a fingertip to Leon's lips, silencing and stilling his head at the same time. "You acted like a guy who's scared he might lose someone who means a lot to him. I can understand that." Hell, he felt like he'd been living in that state ever since he set eyes on him! "I'm not mad at you—and I certainly don't think you're a whore."

Leon nodded, but only when he seemed to realise the silence would continue until he did so.

"But, I did mean what I said about not manipulating me," Rupert continued, as he held his lover's gaze. "I've had that off other people for too long. I don't want us to be about that. You're different—and I want you to stay different. Okay?"

Leon nodded again.

Rupert found himself nodding too, but their sudden ability to reach an agreement about something so basic didn't change the way thoughts kept racing faster and faster around his head. He glanced at the bed, then at Leon. He wasn't really in any condition to sleep, or to do anything else with either item, right then.

"Is there anything else you want us to talk about right now?" he checked.

Leon shook his head.

"You understand that you don't have to worry about any of this anymore? That I'm not going to do anything with anyone else?"

"Yes."

Rupert didn't let out a relieved sigh, but it took a lot of effort to keep it back. "It's getting late, why don't you get into bed?"

Leon obediently began to turn down the blankets.

"I won't be long," Rupert promised, as he moved towards the door.

"You're going?"

Rupert turned back to him. "Only as far as the kitchen—I'll just get a hot drink before I turn in. Do you want one?"

Leon silently shook his head.

Downstairs in the kitchen, Rupert leaned against one of the old-fashioned oak cabinets that lined two of the walls, and ran a hand down his face. How the hell any man could manage to inspire so little trust in a submissive was beyond him.

If one phone call from a man Leon had never even heard of could shake his confidence in his would-be master that much, there had to be an underlying problem that went far deeper and —

"The kettle will boil a lot quicker if you switch it on."

Rupert's attention snapped towards the door leading in from the hallway. Leon stood on the threshold, still in his jeans and long-sleeved T-shirt.

Leon walked quietly across the flagstone floor and picked up the kettle. He carried it across to the sink and calmly filled it with water before setting it to boil. Only then did he turn back to Rupert. "If you prefer not to be in the same room as me, I'd rather you just tell me to leave your house."

It was obviously a statement he'd been practicing on his way down from the bedroom.

"If I wanted you to leave, I'd have told you that." The words sounded very loud in the otherwise silent room. "I want you to stay."

Leon nodded. His shoulders relaxed as if his worst fear had already been relieved. He pushed his hands into his pockets as he leaned against the counter adjacent to Rupert.

There was a very determined expression in his eyes. Now that Rupert stopped to think about it, he realised he'd seen it increasingly often over the last few days. A submissive who was determined to do what he believed was right, however hard he found it…

Just the sight of him like that rushed straight to Rupert's cock—which was pretty much why he'd been so sure it would have been far better for him to think the whole mess through on his own.

"I can understand why the way I acted would put you off," Leon suddenly blurted out.

For a few seconds, Rupert was completely speechless.

"I know you have a thing about guys being after your money and—"

"And you never have been, so you can stop worrying about it," Rupert cut in.

"I can tell when you're disappointed in me," Leon whispered.

"In this particular case, you're wrong." When Leon would have spoken, Rupert cut him off with a shake of the head. "You're not the man I'm disappointed in."

Leon blinked at him as if he suddenly didn't have a clue what they were talking about.

"I should have made everything perfectly clear from the start," Rupert admitted. "You shouldn't have had to worry about this."

Leon straightened up. "It's not your fault."

"If I was the kind of man you could have spoken to more easily—" Rupert cut himself short before he ended up either angry at his own stupidity or feeling sorry for himself. Maybe if he'd dated a few guys like Leon in the past rather than club sluts and experienced submissives, then—

"It's not your fault," Leon repeated, with even more conviction. He stepped forward until he stood directly in front of Rupert.

So like a sweet little sub, to take the blame, even when it was obvious his would-be master was the one at fault. "It's not the end of the world, sweetheart,"

Rupert said briskly, turning to take two mugs out of the cupboard. "It's just something we'll have to work on."

"What is?"

"On my being more approachable," Rupert specified. "On you not having to worry before talking to me about things like this, and—"

"No."

Rupert set the cups on the counter top and turned around. "Leon," he begun.

"No," Leon repeated, folding his arm across his chest. "I'm not working on that."

Rupert raised an eyebrow at him, wondering if Leon was actually going to stamp his foot too.

"The only way I would have spoken to any guy about this without worrying about it, would be if I didn't give a damn what his answer would be. I'll obey any other orders you want to give me, but I won't work on you being less important to me!"

Rupert smiled slightly.

"You're important," Leon whispered, his hands burrowing back into his pockets as he tried to hide his nerves and failed. "I don't want to screw up what we have."

Rupert nodded. "Okay."

"But you still don't like it," Leon observed.

"If all I was interested in was a one-night stand or a quick scene, I wouldn't care too much about your opinion of me or of dominance and submission, but I want more with you than that." Despite everything, there was no way Rupert could keep the words back right then.

"More, as in…?" Leon asked.

And in that moment, the whole truth was impossible to avoid. There was only one thing Rupert could say. "I want you to belong to me."

Leon stared back at him in silence for several long moments. "I'm not an idiot. I do know what all those individual words mean—I'm just not sure what they mean when you put them all together," he finally admitted.

"It means…" Rupert took a deep breath. "It means lots of different things." He frowned as he tried to find the right words, ones that Leon might be able to understand. "You don't hear it used so much anymore, but when I was first starting to explore this kind of lifestyle, a common phrase was that a dominant took a submissive under his protection."

Leon made no comment.

"That's what I want," Rupert said. "I want to take you under my protection."

Even as he nodded his understanding, Leon frowned slightly.

Rupert half chuckled. "That doesn't help at all, does it?" He pushed his hand through his hair as he looked up at the ceiling for inspiration.

"It means doing as you say—obeying your orders?" Leon hazarded.

"It means trusting that I will always give you the right orders. It means giving control of certain parts of your life over to me—maybe because you aren't interested in controlling them yourself, or you think I'll do a better job of it, or maybe just because you think it could be hot to do that."

"And if I disobey you?" Leon asked.

"It would depend on the exact circumstance," Rupert said slowly. "But it's very likely you'd be punished for it."

Leon nodded slowly. "On the internet…" He trailed off, as if not sure he should be starting a sentence that way.

"Go on," Rupert encouraged, leaning forward but somehow managing not to step away from the counter.

Leon folded his arms across his chest once more. "The submissives were kept in cages on some of the sites," he rushed out. "They slept on the floor at the bottom of their master's bed. They weren't allowed to have jobs — they just did the housework and stuff."

Rupert waited to see if there would be more forthcoming, but that seemed to be the entire list of worries in the forefront of Leon's mind right then.

"If I ever put you in a cage, it would be as part of a scene, what you might call a game we were playing, and it would be used in the hope it would let both of us enjoy the game more. You'd sleep in my bed with me every night." Rupert paused for a moment, wanting to make sure he was giving Leon the whole truth. "I suppose it's possible that would only change for a limited time as part of some sort of punishment, but it's unlikely. I like having you in my bed far too much to throw you out of it on a whim."

Leon managed a small smile as he nodded his understanding.

"As for the rest — you'll be expected to put your degree to good use. I expect to get a job you enjoy and work hard at it. I don't care if you get paid or not, but you will have a worthwhile occupation outside this house, and whatever rules I made for you would take that into account."

He waited for a few moments for that to sink into Leon's mind.

"I'm not asking for a sex toy who just sits around to be at my beck and call every time I get a hard on. I want to own the whole man. And, providing you pick up after yourself, everything else can be left to the housekeepers," he added, as he remembered the last point on the list.

"I think…I think I'd like that," Leon whispered.

"If this is going to work, you'll need to belong to a dominant you can talk to. Someone you're not afraid of," Rupert forced himself to say, even when every instinct he possessed screamed at him to simply wrap his arms around Leon and pretend everything had been solved with those few simple words.

"We talk," Leon protested as he stepped forward, bringing their bodies together.

His attempt to make Rupert feel better might have been sweet, if it hadn't been so damn embarrassing. Reassurance was all well and good, but Rupert was pretty sure it should be flowing from the man with all the experience and towards the novice, not the other way around.

"We talked lots yesterday, when I was riding you, remember?" Leon pushed.

Rupert couldn't help but chuckle as he looked down at him. As if he could have forgotten their lunch date.

"I told you things I'd never have told anyone else," Leon told him, still completely serious.

Rupert stroked his fingers through Leon's hair. "Then tell me what you want right now, the truth."

Leon looked down for a moment. "Be pleased with me?"

Rupert frowned slightly.

"That's what I want more than anything," Leon said. "I want you to be pleased with me."

"I am," Rupert said, entirely honestly.

Leon thought for a long time before he made another attempt at an answer. "And let me belong to you?"

"In all the most important ways, I think you already do, sweetheart," Rupert said softly. "I certainly think of you as mine. And tomorrow, I'll prove that to you."

"You don't have to prove anything to—"

"Tomorrow, I'll prove it," Rupert repeated.

It was time that one of them remembered that he wasn't a scared little novice. Rupert was an experienced dominant, and he knew what to do with a submissive—and it was about time he proved to them both that he even knew what to do with a submissive he was in love with.

Chapter Six

Saturday

Leon considered his options very carefully as he walked up the steps leading to Rupert's front door. During a morning spent cheering on his younger brother from the football side-lines and reassuring his parents for the thousandth time that his new boyfriend really was a nice guy, he'd had plenty of time to get his thoughts in order.

He shuffled his feet as he slid his key into the lock. On the one hand, yes, he trusted Rupert at least one hundred and twenty-six percent. The other man wasn't going to cheat on him, and that was great. But it didn't actually change the fact that this Gerald guy was still in town. It probably couldn't do any harm to remind Rupert exactly why he planned to tell all the other guys on the planet he was unavailable.

As he stepped into the house, Leon's jeans rubbed against his rapidly hardening cock. If Rupert couldn't be brought to believe that he was ready for a whipping then maybe a... Leon wasn't precisely sure. A paddling? What was one step below a whipping? It still had to be something pretty hardcore if it was going to do his cause any good and —

Leon's breath caught in his throat as he saw Rupert lounging in the doorway leading into his study. He looked as if he might have been waiting there for him for quite some time.

Closing the front door, Leon took advantage of the brief moment when his back was to Rupert to pull himself together. "Later on, would you like to —?"

"No."

Leon frowned at the old woodwork. A few quick footsteps were his only warning before he found himself pushed forward. He raised his hands and braced himself against the door just in time.

"What the —?"

Rupert's erection pressed hard against the seat of his jeans. The older man dipped his head. Teeth scraped against the skin on Leon's neck. He quickly tilted his head to the side, inviting more. As easily as that, he completely forgot what he'd been intending to ask.

Rupert's lips worked their way up to whisper in his ear. "You can stop playing the dominant now, sweetheart."

"I wasn't —"

"Leon?"

"Yes?" It was harder than ever for him to bite back the word 'sir'. He'd just read it too many times on the internet, that was all. He didn't really need to say it, he told himself.

"When I want to know your opinion, I'll ask you for it," Rupert informed him. "Until then, just relax and do as I say."

There was no way in hell Leon could give a one-word answer then. "Yes, sir."

Rupert smiled against the sensitive patch of skin by his ear. "You'd best be careful of that habit. If you're going to start calling me sir every time you feel submissive towards me you'll raise a lot of eyebrows when we visit vanilla venues."

Leon tried to get a view of Rupert over his shoulder. They were too close together. All he could see was a blur. "I thought we might stay in tonight, and—"

"We're going out."

Leon hesitated. He really wasn't in the mood for sharing Rupert with anyone—even if it was just people who happened to be eating at the same restaurant as them.

"Upstairs and change." Rupert stepped back and gave him a sharp tap on the arse to send him on his way.

"Hey!" Leon tried to look offended. It was a hard look to achieve when he realised he wouldn't really mind feeling him do the same thing again...

Rupert grinned. "Go on—or we'll be late."

"You're sure you want to go out?" Leon asked.

"I'm always sure—about everything," Rupert said, without missing a single beat.

"I don't suppose we have time to—"

"Go!"

Leon dodged another swat aimed towards his buttocks, and instantly regretted making the successful swerve. That first tap had sent a surprisingly pleasant wave of warmth through his backside.

Rupert laughed. "Next time, stay still and you might get what you want."

Blushing, confused by why the hell that should feel even vaguely good, Leon moved quickly up the stairs and across Rupert's bedroom towards the en-suite, shrugging off his clothes as he went. He was just about to step into the bathroom when he heard Rupert speak again.

"Leon?"

He paused in the doorway, entirely naked, without even one piece of clothing lingering in his hands to hide his flourishing erection. "Yes?"

"You don't have permission to jack off while you're in there," Rupert warned, as he appeared in the bedroom doorway.

"I wasn't going to—"

Rupert merely raised an eyebrow at him. "Shall I come in and supervise or can you be trusted?"

Leon gawped across the room at him. Rupert was perfectly serious. That had never been more obvious in all the time they had spent together.

"You can trust me," Leon whispered, "…sir."

"Good boy."

Leon found himself smiling at the praise as he finally slipped into the bathroom and closed the door behind him, conveniently forgetting to lock it, just in case Rupert wanted to check on him at some point. Maybe it was only praise for not coming without permission, but still, it was praise and it sent a mini-orgasm's worth of pleasure rushing through his veins.

When Leon stepped out of the bathroom a few minutes later, his hair damp from the shower and his cock still hard and curving back towards his stomach, his eyes immediately went to the clothes laid out on the bed.

He stepped closer.

They were his clothes. More specifically, they were clothes that had obviously been bought to fit him rather than Rupert. They weren't actually the kind of things he owned, or that he'd have ever been tempted to buy for himself.

Leon turned and looked across the room. Rupert was already dressed, all in black—from the top of the high polo neck, all the way down to his highly polished boots. He stared back at Leon with obvious admiration, but he made no move to approach him. "Get dressed."

"Yes, sir." The words fell from Leon's lips almost without him having to think about them.

Turning back to the clothes, he picked up a familiar pair of leather trousers. It was even harder to get into them than it had been last time. They brought back far too many memories of the coat closet in Blacks. Leon could damn near feel Rupert's hand covering his mouth as he squirmed and tried to tuck away his erection. His tongue flicked out to taste his lover's skin only to be disappointed when it found nothing but empty air within its reach.

Leon parted his lips to ask a question instead, then thought better of it. The evening might not be going as he expected, but it did seem to be going quite well. Or at least in a direction that had nothing to do with Rupert wanting to meet up with Gerald. There was no need to rock the boat any more than was absolutely necessary.

"You're allowed to speak."

Damn! Rupert had the vision of a bloody hawk.

"I just wondered if I was allowed to ask where we're going tonight?" Leon said.

"Why wouldn't you be?"

Leon shrugged. "Do submissives ask questions like that?" He bent down and gave his boots his full attention as he pulled them on and attacked the laces with gusto.

Rupert crouched down in front of him and waited until Leon gave in and looked up.

Leon hesitated when he saw Rupert's smile. His fingers forgot what they were supposed to be doing. "You like that I trust you enough to tell you I don't know what I'm doing?" he hazarded.

"Yes, sweetheart, I do."

"Yeah, well." Leon managed a rather embarrassed return smile as he turned his attention back to his laces. "I'm really pleased for you, but I'd far rather actually know what I'm doing."

Rupert stood up. "You are allowed to ask, and we're going to the Falcon."

Leon nodded. They hadn't been there together, but the other man had let enough slip over the months for Leon to know it was Rupert's favourite club—Rupert's favourite *leather* club. "Are we celebrating, sir? I didn't think you'd know about the new deal until next week."

"Can't I just want to take you out and show you off?"

Leon froze, still hunkered down the side of the bed, with his second lace half-tied. "Um…how exactly are you intending to do that, sir?"

Rupert had retreated to the other side of the room to lounge against the wall next to the door. He raised an eyebrow in query when Leon looked up at him and their eyes met, but it morphed into a frown when he saw Leon's expression.

Leon took a deep breath as he straightened up. Smoothing out his already perfectly crease-free trousers, he played for time.

"I don't think I'm as into that sort of thing as you are, sir," he finally blurted out. He forced himself to hold Rupert's gaze properly as spoke, no looking through his lashes, no flirting, just the kind of honesty Rupert had said he wanted from him. "The idea of bringing anyone else into these games with us kind of freaks me out."

Rupert tilted his head slightly to one side, as if literally considering him from a new angle. His lips twitched into a smile. He beckoned Leon across the room.

Leon moved to stand in front of him, pretty sure he was the butt of the joke, but not at all sure what the punch line might turn out to be.

Rupert brushed their lips together.

"What?" Leon asked, when he couldn't stand it any longer.

"I must be more subtle than I thought," Rupert mused, apparently more to himself than anyone else.

Leon took a deep breath to push down both badly-timed sarcasm and nerves.

"Didn't you notice that I barely took my hands off you, even in a vanilla club? The only reason I let Frank Lewis talk me away from your side for two minutes was my complete conviction that you had to think I was far too possessive of you and that you'd appreciate some room to breathe."

"Possessive?"

Rupert stroked his jaw line, trailing his hand down Leon's neck to rest against his throat. "Yes, I'm as possessive as hell, and it's entirely your fault."

Leon blinked at him.

"I never had trouble sharing before," Rupert informed him. "You bring out a jealous side I didn't even know I had."

"Rupert…" Leon protested, more certain than ever his lover was lying to make him feel better.

"I wasn't talking about showing off your skills as a submissive in that way," Rupert said. "I'd be quite happy if I was the only man on the planet who ever saw how perfect you are when you offer yourself to me."

"We could stay in?" Leon offered hopefully.

"No." There was no room for argument in the word. "We're going out. Everyone is going to see us together, and know that we are together. And they're going to know that we aren't interested in anyone but each other."

Leon nodded. That idea was far more palatable. Then, he frowned. "How exactly are they going to know the last bit, sir?"

"Leave that to me."

Leon nodded again and turned his attention back to the clothes laid out on the bed. There was only one thing left there. It was impossible to put off the set of leather straps that represented the top half of his outfit any longer.

Rupert's hand settled on the small of his back. He turned Leon to face him as he picked up the leather. In his hands, it quickly morphed from a confusing jumble of connected strips into a harness, just like some of those he'd seen men wearing on the websites he'd visited over the last week.

"Yesterday, you asked if submission was just about obedience. If it was, then the only reason you'd wear this is because I told you to."

"I don't mind—"

"That's not what I want," Rupert cut in. "I want you to wear it because you trust that I wouldn't tell you to wear something that wasn't suitable for where we were going—because you realise I have more experience in this field than you do and I'll use it to lead you in the right direction. I don't want you to obey me, Leon. I'd much rather you put yourself in my hands instead, step under my protection. Submit to me," he invited.

"Yes, sir."

The last buckle snapped into place and Rupert stepped back as if to get a better look at him. Leon stared down his body. The black stood out in stark contrast to his skin. Before he had time to worry if his lover liked the way it looked or not, Rupert stepped forward with another length of leather in his hand.

One click, a flash of silver, and the lead Leon had offered Rupert a few days before was connected to the silver ring that joined all the leather straps in the centre of Leon's chest. It joined him to Rupert too.

"Ready?"

Leon was pretty sure he wasn't the least bit ready, but he nodded anyway. He hadn't been ready for anything that week and it hadn't turned out too badly so far.

* * * *

Members only. No guests permitted.
Failure to abide by club rules will result in instant expulsion from the club.

Leon tried to look away from the succinct list of rules posted just inside the club door, but his attention kept straying back to it as if magnetically attracted to the rusty old thing. It was almost more distracting than the fact he was only wearing a few strips of leather beneath the jacket Rupert had loaned him, although perhaps not quite so disturbing as the fact that, at some point, he was going to have to take that jacket off.

"Those rules are meant for other people," Rupert said, as he led Leon towards the coat check desk.

Leon looked up at him in confusion, pretty sure that rules were supposed to apply to everyone.

"The owner is an old friend of mine."

"Is that why this place is your favourite, sir?"

Rupert's lips twitched as if he was holding back a sudden grin.

"Sir?" The word still felt good in Leon's mouth every time he said it. It tasted even better when he realised that it didn't really matter if anyone overheard him say it right then.

Leon's eyes travelled slowly over the slew of leather-clad men who surrounded them. As Rupert checked both their jackets, Leon couldn't help but take some mild form of reassurance from the fact that he wasn't the only man wearing a harness, or showing quite a lot of skin between his bits of leather. He doubted the men there would be shocked by *anything* anyone could say or do. An honorific wasn't even going to make anyone blink.

A tug on his lead and Rupert guided Leon deeper into the club. The lights grew lower. Shadows crept out from every surface, threatening to take over the whole world at any moment. A shiver ran down Leon's spine, making him desperate to look over his shoulder just in case someone or something leather-clad might launch itself out of the gloom and attack them without any warning.

Rupert pulled him forwards a little. His hand came to rest on his back, as if reassuring him there was nothing behind him that he needed to be the least bit nervous about. Rupert was in control and he wouldn't let anything hurt him. Within moments of them entering a crowded room, he'd found them a place at the rough wooden bar.

Even after they stopped moving, Rupert's hand stayed on Leon's back, just resting there, warming his skin below the leather straps.

"You were going to tell me if that was why this is your favourite club," Leon reminded him.

Rupert's lips twitched as if he were fighting back a smile. "No, the fact we won't be thrown out for ignoring a few rules has nothing to do with it. You're forgetting that I could buy and sell practically any place I wanted to play in twenty times over and count it as small change."

Leon blinked. Rupert never talked about money with him. It simply didn't happen.

"My point is," Rupert went on. "Any businessman who wants to stay in business would think twice about throwing us out of their establishment for anything less serious than a multiple homicide."

Leon's eyes opened very wide. "Rupert!"

The other man's lips twitched again.

"You can't do things like that," Leon whispered to him, looking around, hoping no one else had overheard either of them.

"Why not?" Rupert asked, still as calm as ever.

"Because…because you can't do things like that!" Leon hesitated, then shook his head at himself for being so bloody gullible. "You wouldn't really put someone out of business just because they threw you out of their club," he realised.

"No, probably not," Rupert said. "But I certainly would if they threw *you* out." He turned and ordered their drinks from the bartender as a skin-head in a leather waist-coat approached.

When he turned back to Leon, Rupert smiled at his expression.

"Bankrupting people is not romantic," Leon hissed, dropping his voice as a huge bear of a man walked past them leading a much smaller guy who was crawling on all fours at the end of his lead.

"But it is very effective," Rupert pointed out. "Word like that gets around quickly."

"Sir!" Leon protested again.

Rupert tugged him closer with the lead and pressed a kiss to his temple. "Okay, sweetheart, no bankrupting anyone while we're on a date. I promise."

When the drinks arrived Leon took refuge from his confusion by reaching for his wallet, except there was no wallet. He didn't have any pockets to put one in — even if he had thought about bringing one with him. Rupert made no comment as he paid for the drinks.

"Sorry," Leon muttered. "I — "

"Some dominants don't like their subs to carry money when they come to clubs like this — I'm one of them," Rupert said easily, as if it were no big deal — as if he wouldn't think any differently if Leon was a millionaire.

Leon frowned as he twirled his coke bottle around on the bar.

Rupert took a swig of his drink, his lips caressing the edge of the bottle as if he was about to give it the most amazing blowjob in the world. "Did you have a good day?"

Leon took a sip from his own in an effort to cool his throat and stop his next words from coming out in soprano. "It was okay. Ben scored two goals and his team won." He took a deep breath as he set his drink down. "On a side note, do you think I'll ever manage an entire date without substantial amounts of angst about us?"

Rupert settled his arm around Leon's waist and coaxed him to stand closer, until his bare skin rubbed against the larger man's shirt. "As I recall, the angst is never actually about us—it's about the rest of the world. You're fine with us. Being out about everything—that's more complicated. Angst is to be expected the first time a man puts on his leather."

Rupert seemed to consider his own statement very carefully then. "Unless, you do what I did and screw, drink and bluff your way through it until it all feels natural. I wouldn't advise it. The hangovers are murder once you sober up."

Rupert stroked Leon's hair back from his face in the way that made Leon very glad he still hadn't found time to get it cut. Leon smiled up at him in return as he started to relax a little. Peeking over Rupert's shoulder, he was even able to look around without worrying that anyone would see too much of him in return.

"Rupert!"

Leon froze. His smile congealed. He knew that voice, even when it wasn't being mangled by an answering machine.

"Gerald," Rupert said, as he turned away from Leon. "It's good to see you."

Beyond Rupert's shoulder Leon saw a man approach. Tall, tanned and reeking of old money, he fitted into the club perfectly. He was just the kind of man Leon could easily imagine Rupert going to university with, who he could easily imagine Rupert screwing. He'd bet Gerald had never hesitated before getting the toys out. Broad-shouldered and muscle-bound, he could probably take a whipping without even blinking. Right then, Leon was more than willing to hate him for that, let alone for anything else.

Rupert and Gerald shook hands. Gerald clapped Rupert on the shoulder, standing closer to him than anybody needed to be simply to greet an old friend. Hell, he might as well have jumped him right there next to the bar!

Leon's hand curled into a fist at his side. Another, less real fist, clamped down around his stomach. It was more luck than judgement that it didn't make Leon throw up right then. Tilting his chin back, he did his damnedest not to let either of the other men see his queasiness.

"You must be Leon." Gerald smiled at him, all perfect white teeth and dark designer stubble. He held out his hand.

Leon managed to unclench his fist and shake the guy's hand. He even forced a smile.

A few moments later, Gerald turned away to check his coat. Leon somehow resisted the temptation to rub his palm against his trouser leg and wipe Gerald's touch from his skin until he was out of sight.

Rupert raised an eyebrow at him as he noticed the gesture. "You have about three minutes before he gets back in which to get it out of your system."

"You invited your ex-boyfriend to meet us here?" Leon said. Against all his expectations, the words came out perfectly calmly.

"Actually, I invited an old friend with whom I used to go to clubs, to drop by and share a drink with us while we're here, but broadly speaking, yes."

"Why would you do that, sir?" Leon asked, very carefully.

"Because he's not important."

Leon opened his mouth. He closed his mouth.

"You seemed to think he was somehow significant to me. The easiest way to prove to you that he isn't any threat to us is for you to meet him and see that for yourself."

"You're insane," Leon whispered. "Completely insane."

Rupert smiled, his hand still stroking Leon's back.

Leon leaned into the touch regardless of Rupert's mental state. "I know you're not screwing around, sir," he whispered. "You told me you weren't. That was all I wanted. A show and tell demonstration isn't necessary."

Rupert stroked along Leon's jaw, encouraging him to tilt his head back so he could brush their lips together, which was all very nice. Leon would still have preferred him to say, 'okay, let's go home' instead.

"I never thought I'd see the day when you settled down," Gerald's voice interrupted. "Not that I can't see the attraction—I've never seen a cuter arse in my life."

Leon felt the blush rise to his cheeks as Gerald returned to stand next to them at the bar.

Rupert's hand tightened around his waist. Leon glanced up at the taller man. If looks could kill…

Gerald grinned. "Since when are you the jealous type?"

"Since now."

Gerald shrugged. "Fair enough. Tommy said you were serious about him. So, I suppose a threesome is out of the question?" He held up his hands in mock surrender as Rupert's gaze narrowed, but his eyes still danced with humour. "Okay. But don't be a hypocrite, Rupert. I'll bet you make him blush on purpose all the time."

Rupert bowed his head once as if in acknowledgement of that fact, but his grip on Leon's waist didn't relax in the slightest. Leon was pretty sure that there would be a bruise on his side the next day—a perfect impression of his lover's fingertips. He could hardly wait to admire it when it arrived.

Gerald turned his attention back to Leon.

Leon forced himself to meet his gaze without faltering.

"So, um…art history, right?" Gerald hazarded.

Leon nodded. "I'm halfway through my master's degree. What do you do?"

"Nothing at all," Gerald said happily. "Some people have the sense to lay back and enjoy life if they can afford to. Is Bertie here still a workaholic?"

Leon looked up at Rupert. Sure, he worked hard, but a workaholic? "Not really," Leon offered.

Rupert smiled down at him. The hand at his waist relaxed a little.

Gerald looked from him to Rupert and back again. "Completely smitten." He shook his head. "Do you know how many people have tried to seduce him into not thinking about boring business meetings twenty-four-seven?"

Leon blinked.

Gerald just laughed as he looked over Leon's head and apparently met Rupert's eyes above him. "My, how the slutty have fallen!"

* * * *

"So you've finally lost interest in your bit of rough trade?"

Rupert looked up as a shadow fell across the table where he and Gerald were sitting.

James Campbell.

Rupert pointedly turned his attention away from James. "He's called Leon."

"Oh, that is sweet, you'd even learned his name." James sat down on the third chair around the table uninvited. "But then, as I remember, you always have had an aversion to soppy endearments, haven't you?" James continued.

"With most people," Rupert agreed. It had certainly surprised him just how easy they were to apply to Leon once he made the effort to start. James also brought various adjectives to his head, none of them the least bit polite.

"Well, I hope you got your key back—that's all I can say. You can't be too careful with people like that," James sneered. "Are you done slumming now, or will we be subjected to a whole string of second-rate boy-toys traipsing through our midst before you're finally ready to turn your attention to the kind of submissive who you wouldn't be ashamed to take out…in…public…?"

The words ground to an uncertain halt as James realised that no one was listening to him. Rupert barely even noticed the silence take over. His attention was all on Leon as the boy made his way back to the table, carefully balancing his tray of drinks.

He mentally nodded his approval as he noticed that Leon was far less bothered by the admiring glances that tracked his progress now. A few yards from their table, Leon looked up. He obviously saw James, but his footsteps didn't seem to hesitate for a moment.

Out of the corner of his eye, Rupert noticed James turn his head and follow his line of sight. James' lips pursed. His eyes narrowed. A few moments before, an objective eye might have considered him classically handsome, but Rupert saw any hint of that die as James' expression turned sour.

Leon smiled brightly as he lowered himself to the cushion placed on the floor on the other side of Rupert.

James snorted. "I should have guessed you wouldn't mind having to share, so long as Rupert keeps picking up the tag—"

"I don't share," Leon said, very calmly, as he set his tray on the table and handed out the drinks. "But I don't give up without a fight either." Looking up, he turned all his attention to James. "That's the thing about people who weren't born with everything handed to them on a silver spoon—they don't run away at the first sign they might actually have to *work* to keep something they want." His tone was cooler than Rupert had ever heard it, holding more anger than Rupert had ever believed was possible.

Suddenly everything clicked into place inside Rupert's head.

James dropped by before you came home.

I heard a guy named Gerald leave a message on your answering machine.

Rupert ground his teeth together. Every muscle in his body tensed. Even his toes curled up in his boots.

"You really think you can keep him?" James demanded.

"No," Leon said, with obvious honesty. "I don't think anyone could *keep* a man like Rupert. But I have every hope that he will decide to keep me under his protection for a very long time."

James looked from Leon to Rupert.

"What? Did you forget he was here?" James snapped.

"Leon doesn't need his master to stick up for him." Rupert didn't even bother to look in James' direction. He took a sip of his beer as he held Leon's gaze.

The boy blushed slightly as he heard his own words quoted back at him. Rupert had to admit that Gerald had been right about that one thing, at least. It was very hard to resist the temptation to send the colour rushing to Leon's cheeks for the sheer joy of seeing it there.

Rupert tore his gaze away just in time to see James look Leon up and down. "Rupert usually has better taste than to play around with the sluts and strays," he bit out.

It took everything Rupert had in him not to speak up. He glanced back towards the younger man, sure he'd see hurt in his eyes, but Leon was giving what looked like a surprisingly calculated 'I'm clueless and innocent' expression.

"But that can't be right," he said, with a sweet little frown. "He's screwed you, hasn't he?"

Rupert's lips twitched.

Gerald burst out laughing on the other side of the table. "Careful, Jamie, he might prove to be quite a bit smarter than you."

James scowled at him. "And you're obviously over the moon. Are you going to take it in turns with him?"

"I've got more sense than to mess with Rupert's…" Gerald paused. "Significant Other?"

"Submissive," Leon corrected, glancing up to Rupert as if to check that was okay.

Rupert considered the term for a second and nodded his approval.

"And I don't give a damn what Rupert says about Leon standing up for himself," Gerald went on. "He'll send anyone who upsets Leon straight to hell and enjoy every minute of it—and if you weren't so bloody desperate to find a rich dom stupid enough to pay your way out of debt, then you'd have more sense than to play such a dangerous game, Jamie."

James pushed back his chair. Wooden legs screeched on bare floorboards. "You'll get bored with the novelty soon enough," he predicted.

Leon watched the silly little fool walk away, but Rupert's eyes never left his submissive. Against all expectations, the boy was on the verge of laughter.

Rupert shook his head at him as a chuckle escaped from Leon. "Your sense of humour leaves a lot to be desired."

Leon nodded, covering his mouth in a half-hearted effort to keep the rest of his laughter back. "You're probably right, sir."

"Enough about that," Gerald cut in, leaning forward and resting his forearms on the table. "I want to know what you're plotting?"

Rupert raised an eyebrow. "Whatever makes you think I'm plotting anything?"

"I've known him for a lot longer than you, so I'll give you some advice," Gerald said, turning towards Leon. "If Rupert's pissed off and not doing anything about it, it'll only be because he's got a plan to do something really evil in the not so distant future."

"Evil?" Leon echoed.

"Rupert does an excellent range in revenge served hot or cold. You'd best be careful who you wind up," Gerald said.

"I'll be sure to remember to mind my manners," Leon murmured, politely.

"Oh, not you! You could start World War Three and Rupert would probably still be besotted with you," Gerald said, with a careless wave of his arm. "I'm talking about being careful who you allow to get to you. You can be damn sure that this 'Leon doesn't need his boyfriend to stick up for him' bull stops as soon as you're out of earshot. You're his, and Rupert protects what's his."

Leon looked down at the coffee table, but unless Rupert was very much mistaken, that was only to hide his pleasure at being called 'his'. Rupert smiled himself, very pleased with the label. Reaching out, he casually settled his fingers in Leon's hair.

"Gerald?" Rupert said.

The other man glanced at him over the top of his glass, his expression suddenly wary. "What?"

"When was the last time you and I had sex?"

Gerald leant back in his chair. He looked from him to Leon and back again. "If you've really started believing that a quick fumble in an alleyway constitutes sex, Leon has my sympathy…"

"And the last time we did a scene together?" Rupert asked.

"What would be the bloody point in that?" Gerald asked with a frown. "Two doms aren't going to have a good time together, are they? You're not going demented on us, are you?"

Rupert didn't bother to answer, Leon was staring up at him and it was obvious that he knew why Rupert was asking, even if Gerald didn't, and that was all that really mattered.

"Hold that thought," Gerald muttered, with a quick, perplexed look at Rupert. Apparently spotting someone he knew across the room, he rushed over to say hello.

A moment later, something in that same part of the room caught Leon's attention. Rupert followed his gaze until he spotted Gerald put his arm around a young red-haired man and head for the door.

Gerald raised a hand in farewell as he left. Rupert absentmindedly raised a hand back.

"Do you mind him leaving, sir?" Leon asked.

"Of course not." He'd served his purpose very well.

Leon nodded his understanding, but said nothing.

Rupert tucked a knuckle under his chin and tilted his head back, trying to work out what was going on in his head.

"He was right, wasn't he?" Leon asked. "About the whole protective thing."

Rupert nodded. "Yes. Does it bother you?"

Leon shook his head. "I'm just not used to you like this. You're different when it's just you and me at home, sir."

"Yes, sweetheart, I am."

Leon hesitated. "Are you pretending to be someone else when you're with me, sir?" he asked, barely managing more than a whisper.

"No."

"Because you really don't need to," Leon pushed on. "I—"

Rupert stroked his fingers through the boy's hair once more, in that way which was quickly becoming a very pleasant habit in which to indulge. "I'm more myself with you than I am with anyone I've ever met."

Leon glanced up, but there were still doubts lingering in his eyes.

"You don't believe me."

"I think the real you would have ordered me to call you sir a long time ago."

Rupert leant back in his chair a little. "Did I" — he searched for the best word — "temper my inclination for dominance for a while? Yes." There was no point in denying it.

A little of the tension drained out of Leon with the announcement.

"Do you want the complete truth?" Rupert asked.

Leon nodded rapidly. "Yes, please, sir."

"It would have been very easy for me to ride roughshod over you the same night we met. Within a few hours, I could probably have had you agreeing to let me screw you, tie you up, whip you and a dozen other different things." Rupert made no attempt to soften his words. "You were a gay natural submissive who'd never even dated another man. Any dominant who knew what he was doing could have taken advantage of that."

"But you didn't, sir."

"No. I wanted you to make your own decisions, move at your own pace," Rupert said with a slight shrug. "Not at my pace. And not at James' either."

Leon glanced up at him when Rupert's tone of voice changed slightly.

"Is there any particular reason why you didn't mention to me that James was there when you heard Gerald's message?"

Leon stared down at the black leather cushion beneath his knees. "He made it sound like I should have known you'd keep seeing other guys until you told me you wanted to be exclusive," he admitted.

"He always did enjoy screwing with people's minds far more than he actually enjoyed screwing," Rupert muttered. "Rumour has it the recession hasn't been kind to him. So, he's decided it's time for him to find a suitable sugar daddy dominant and I'm to be the lucky man."

"He's a submissive?" Leon asked.

"More a pain slut, really, but yes, he's been known to call himself a submissive when it suits him. Although, in his mind, being the heir to a title makes him far superior to any other submissive." He thought about that for a moment. "And to most dominants, come to that."

Leon shook his head as if he really didn't understand any of it.

Rupert smiled slightly, but the expression quickly faded away. "How much of what we've done together this week would you have suggested if he hadn't filled your head with rubbish?"

Leon looked up. "I don't regret any of it, sir."

That was something. Rupert quietly cherished his sincerity. "Good, but that doesn't answer my question."

"I think I just needed a nudge, sir."

Rupert let his silence speak for itself.

Leon frowned slightly as he seemed to search his brain for another answer. "I wouldn't have had the balls to do any of it," he admitted. "But I'd have wished I had."

Rupert reached out and stroked his thumb across Leon's cheek.

"If I'd known it would have convinced you to be yourself with me, I'd have made myself do it all, and more, weeks ago."

The boy had known his lover had been holding something back from him. As Rupert looked into the submissive's eyes, that much was suddenly obvious.

Leon had known that Rupert wasn't being himself —
that was what had held him back too.

"I wouldn't trade the orders you've given me
tonight for all the patience in the world," Leon
whispered.

"Then it seems that it's time for you to make a
decision, Leon. Is this what you want?" He waved a
hand, indicating the way Leon knelt at his feet, the
club, the leather they were wearing and everything
else. "Do you want me to be your boyfriend or your
master?"

Leon opened his mouth. Rupert already knew what
he was going to say, but he covered Leon's lips with
his fingertips before he could get a word out.

"If I become your master then it's very unlikely we
can go back to the way we were before. It's not a bell
that can be easily unrung, so don't rush your answer."
Rupert dropped his fingertips away from Leon's lips.

"I want this, sir. I want you to be my master," Leon
said, without even waiting for a single beat.

Rupert had never heard any sweeter words spoken
in his life. Reaching into his pocket, he took out a
length of silver chain.

Leon frowned at it, apparently not the least
impressed with his master's choice of mark.

"A little bit more subtle than a leather one. You'll be
allowed to wear this one all the time."

The frown faded away. "Yes, sir."

Rupert had it fixed around his neck in just a few deft
movements. "Most people will think it's just a bit of
silver jewellery, but we'll know different."

Leon nodded.

"Every time you feel it move around your neck,
every time you take a breath, it's going to remind you
who you belong to now. Understand?"

"Yes, sir." The words were barely a whisper. Leon lifted his hand to the collar and traced his fingers delicately along the links.

Just a moment later, Rupert's hand was wrapped around Leon's wrist as he led him out of the club, unable to share him with the rest of the world for another moment.

Leon made no comment on that. He didn't say a single word as Rupert drove them back to his place, or as Rupert nudged him upstairs towards the bedroom.

It was hard for Rupert not to smile at the still silent figure as he came out of the bathroom and saw his new submissive studying the chain's reflection in the mirror on the dressing table.

"Sir," Leon began, as their eyes met in the reflection.

"Tomorrow," Rupert cut in.

Leon turned to face him, uncertainty flashing in his eyes.

"Whatever it is you're going to suggest we do," Rupert said, "it can wait until tomorrow."

Stepping forward Rupert hooked his fingers into the younger man's collar, the same way Leon had during his entire ride home. "Today is about this. Whatever you think it is that you need to do to prove to me that you really want to belong to me, it can wait until tomorrow. No arguing."

Chapter Seven

Sunday

By eight o'clock the following morning, Leon had already stared up at the ceiling above Rupert's bed for so long, his eyes were starting to ache. The urge to wriggle and 'accidentally' wake up his lover…and accidently wake up his *master,* was almost over powering.

Today, of all days, Rupert was apparently choosing to sleep late.

Taking a deep breath, and only just convincing himself not to let it out as a sigh, Leon turned his head to the side to admire the sleeping form for what already had to be the hundredth time.

At the sunlight creeping around the edges of the curtains might allow him to make out the details of his morning stubble this time, and —

Rupert peered back at him, eyes wide open and no trace of sleepiness in his expression.

Leon jolted at the unexpected sight.

Rupert's lips twitched.

Leon cleared his throat and tried not to make any more of an idiot of himself than was absolutely necessary. "How long have you been awake, sir?"

"Quite a while," Rupert said.

Leon nodded, not sure what else to do. "Do submissives make breakfast?" he asked, cautiously. It sounded a lot more polite than asking if Rupert had meant they could do whatever he wanted *first thing* tomorrow.

Rupert's smile widened. "Just coffee for me, and I think I'll have it in bed. I'm not in any rush to get up today."

Leon saw the humour dancing in his eyes and knew that Rupert was well aware of his impatience to get on with things. Sliding out from between the blankets, Leon reached for his jeans.

"Go down as you are."

Leon frowned slightly as he looked over his shoulder. "Naked?"

"Yes."

Leon nodded his understanding—his head moving without any permission being given by his brain. If Rupert wanted him walking around the house naked, Leon was sure he could do that. Even if it was surprisingly chilly now that he'd lost the warm cocoon of the blankets.

"Just until you get back to bed," Rupert promised. "If you're very good, I'll even help you warm up when you get back."

Leon smiled as he slipped from the room and hurried down the stairs. There was no one else in the house, Leon knew that, but he still found himself peeping around corners, checking that the coast was clear before scurrying forward to the next piece of furniture he could hide behind.

There was something about running naked around the house that made him feel silly. Lightheaded and giggly, he was grinning widely at his own foolish pleasure when he carefully operated the door handle with his elbow and backed into Rupert's bedroom.

The older man hadn't moved a muscle. He remained stretched out on the bed, the blankets almost completely covering him. In the half light, he was still gorgeous. The bedding didn't soften anything about him. It only made Leon all the more eager to burrow underneath and find the muscles hidden away there.

Crossing the room, Leon reached out to put the coffee on the bedside table. Halfway through the motion, he thought better of it. Lowering himself carefully to his knees by the side of the bed, he proffered both mugs up to his lover like a sacrificial offering.

Even in that moment, Leon had no doubt that he'd be creeping out of bed the following morning to make his master his morning coffee. It was far too enjoyable a ritual to simply abandon after one outing.

Still very much wide awake, Rupert gazed down at him with what looked suspiciously like approval. Sitting up, he took both cups of coffee and set them on the bedside table before offering his hand to Leon. A firm tug guided him back under the blankets with his master.

Rupert's body was deliciously hot. It was impossible for Leon to resist the temptation to snuggle and warm his skin against him. Rupert looped his arm around his shoulders, welcoming him close, as if he wasn't the least bit worried about an ice cube invading his bed and spreading its chill around.

For a few minutes, neither of them said anything. It was as if the moment were too important to spoil with words. Rupert was welcoming him into his world and it was far cosier and more comfortable than anyone could ever believe if all they saw of the other man was the stony-faced business tycoon who attended those fancy parties or even the serious dominant who visited those clubs.

Finally, Rupert moved. Dipping his head, he pressed a kiss to Leon's temple as if to declare the moment sufficiently well marked. "Okay, go ahead. You have permission to tell me what it was you wanted us to do last night."

With his head resting on Rupert's chest, his lover's heartbeat counting out the seconds beneath his ear, Leon didn't have to meet his eyes. Somehow, that made it easier. "Spank me, sir?" he asked.

"Why?"

Leon frowned, not sure what the other man expected him to say in response.

"There must be a reason," Rupert said. "Because you think that's what *I'm* into? Because you think *you* might like it? Because you don't think a man can be a real submissive unless he allows his master to hurt him whenever the mood strikes him?"

Leon's frown deepened as he traced fingertip trails over Rupert's chest. He had the distinct feeling that failing to come up with the right answer would mean Rupert deciding not to lay a hand on him for a very long time to come.

"Because," he said slowly. "Because I want to see what it's like?"

"Do you think you'll like the way it feels?"

Leon rubbed his knuckles against the dark triangle of hairs in the middle of Rupert's chest. "I think I'll like how it'll look," he whispered, well aware that his words didn't make the least bit of sense, but unable to exchange the inconvenient truth for a more believable lie.

"You like the idea of me leaving a mark underneath your skin as well as around your neck?"

"Yes!" Leon leaned up on his elbow and looked down at Rupert. That was it! "That's what I want!"

Rupert smiled up at him. "Okay."

Leon grinned. That expression lasted for all of two seconds before his mind turned to practicalities.

Rupert's expression didn't change at all as he sat up and positioned a pillow against the middle of the headboard so he could lean against it in comfort. The central heating's timer must have kicked in to operation. As the blankets fell back, the chill Leon expected to feel was almost entirely absent. Leon backed away a little, to give his lover room to do whatever it was he was doing, but Rupert shook his head.

"Come here."

Crawling over the blankets, Leon made his way obediently back to Rupert's side.

"Over my lap."

Leon looked at Rupert's lap as if he'd never seen it before. "Right now?"

"Yes. Right now."

A moment earlier, Leon had wanted nothing more than to get on with it before his nerves could get any worse, but now...

Looking up, he met his master's eyes. There was no impatience in them, just acceptance.

"You like the idea too, sir?" he checked.

Rupert nodded. "Yes, I do."

Leon moved clumsily forward. His limbs all seemed to have developed lives of their own. His co-ordination was more erratic than ever as he lay across Rupert's thighs and wriggled himself into what he hoped was an appropriate position.

The blankets had fallen back far enough that the only thing he felt beneath him was bare skin. Rupert was already hard. His erection pressed against Leon's stomach. Right then, Leon's own cock was still a little less certain about the idea.

"Do you want to do something else first?" Leon asked, as he felt his lover's pre-cum smear against his skin. "I could — "

"Hush." Rupert's hand settled on his arse and stroked gently over the skin.

Nibbling at his bottom lip, Leon fell silent.

The whole world was equally eager to obey Rupert. As hard as he strained his hearing, Leon couldn't hear a single sound coming from anywhere. Squirming slightly, he tried to push down his nerves and his rapidly increasing arousal.

The light caresses to his arse were going straight to his cock, making his shaft harden and press against Rupert's bare leg. Bowing his head closer to the sheet beneath him, Leon took a deep breath.

Without any warning, all the air he'd managed to cramp into his lungs rushed out in a surprised yelp. Unexpectedly fierce pain flared through his left buttock.

Leon's whole body jerked forward as he half turned over on his lover's lap and looked up at him. Rupert reached out and stroked his hand over the abused skin just as gently as it had before.

He made no move to pull Leon back into position. He didn't even issue an order. Leon was free to jump off his lap and out of his bed if he wanted to, but as the heat from the smack radiated through his body it morphed into something unexpectedly moreish, just like it had when Rupert tapped him on the backside in the hallway. And, just like then, Leon found that he really didn't want to go anywhere.

Very slowly, he rolled himself back to an easily spankable position on Rupert's lap. The other man's left arm settled over the small of his back, securing him in place and Leon had no doubt that he'd just passed some sort of test.

He'd chosen to be there, even when he knew what it felt like. Closing his eyes, Leon waited for the next fall of his lover's hand. He didn't have to wait long. Rupert's hand connected sharply with his right buttock, sending a wave of heat spreading through that muscle too.

Leon murmured as he rocked his hips slightly. He wasn't sure if he was encouraging his lover on, or trying to hump Rupert's leg as his cock rapidly hardened, but it didn't matter.

Another loud smack filled the air, then another. They quickly took on a solid rhythm as Rupert got into his stride. Leon's heart raced faster in response, adding another layer to the percussion-filled arrangement playing inside him.

Again and again, Rupert's hand fell, building the heat inside Leon's arse until he felt as if the skin stretched across his buttocks might burst into flames at any second. He was almost sure he could hear the sound of the burning logs crash down into the smouldering undergrowth, smell the smoke in the air around them.

He clutched at the edge of the mattress as he tried to keep some sort of hold on reality. His head swam with too many sensations it had no time to process. Murmurs and groans of pleasure filled the air, mingling with the other sounds of the spanking and Leon had no doubt that his backside was already red and bearing his master's hand prints.

Part of the other man was inside him, part of Rupert's dominance was now part of Leon's body. The bed creaked as Rupert's movements grew larger. Then, just as the orchestra was on the verge of a crescendo that might send the whole world spinning out of control—nothing. Silence flooded back into the room. Nothing but cool air caressed Leon's arse.

With his face pressed into the mattress, Leon could barely raise the energy to look over his shoulder. He sensed Rupert move slightly beneath him and prayed that the older man was only taking a moment's rest before the second symphony, but when Rupert's hand returned to him, his touch had nothing to do with corporal punishment.

Fingers made hot by the spanking slid between Leon's buttocks and spread lube across his hole. Quickly realising that was exactly what he needed, Leon spread his legs. Lying over his lover's lap, he prayed that Rupert wouldn't take as long to prepare him as he often did, that there would be no teasing this time. He needed more of his master inside him—now.

"Please, sir?" The words were whispered into the blankets. Leon wasn't even sure if his master heard them, but someone, somewhere did. His prayer was answered.

Within seconds, he was off Rupert's lap and positioned head down and spanked arse held high in the air as his lover moved behind him. The sound of a condom wrapper being torn open was his only warning before Rupert was buried inside him to the hilt with one deep thrust.

Leon gasped as other man's hips pressed against his tenderised backside, sending another wave of bliss and endorphins rushing through him. A brief moment to let him adjust, and Rupert pulled back.

Leon held his breath until Rupert rocked forward and filled him once more. A whimper of pleasure left his mouth as Leon swayed back to meet the thrust. He was so close to the edge already, and Rupert was riding him just a little more roughly, a little more *perfectly* than he usually did.

His master wasn't holding anything back from him. That knowledge rushed through Leon's body, colliding head-on with a wave of ecstasy from his prostate and there was no way his control was capable of surviving the combined onslaught.

Leon came, hard and fast, bucking against the mattress as fireworks exploded within him and his mind went blank—unable to contain anything but bliss. Rupert's rhythm faltered just a moment later. Leon was aware of harsher, deeper thrusts pounding into him as his lover came and somehow managed to coax another wave of ecstasy from him.

Several minutes later, as Leon finally found himself able to think and concentrate on the world outside his head, he realised they had both collapsed forward onto the bed. He was trapped beneath the larger man, protected from the whole world by Rupert's body.

He smiled into the mattress. His expression didn't change as Rupert lethargically separated their bodies, disposed of the used condom and pulled the blankets over them once more.

Warm and content, with his master's body spooned tightly against his, Leon tried to slip back into the sleepy haze, but his brain only worked faster. There was no way to stop his thoughts forming and demanding his attention.

"What's wrong?" Rupert murmured into the back of his hair.

Leon shrugged. "Nothing."

"Don't lie to your master. Tell me the truth."

It sounded so much like an order, Leon automatically found himself obeying it. "I was just thinking."

Rupert tugged at his arm.

Leon reluctantly took the hint and pulled a pillow under his head as he turned to face his lover. He sighed as he tried to work out what to say. "Girls have it easy," he finally blurted out.

Rupert's lips twitched into a half smile. "Sore, sweetheart?"

Leon blushed and shook his head as he realised what Rupert thought he was complaining about. "Well, only a bit, sir. In a good way."

Rupert fell silent, apparently waiting for the real explanation.

"It's just, girls can say anything they like after sex and it's not being soppy or effeminate, it's just being female, isn't it? But a guy would always sound like an idiot if he said the same thing," Leon whispered, half his mind still swirling with afterglow while the other half became a tangle of thoughts.

"I'm sure that makes sense inside your head, sweetheart," Rupert said. "But I have no idea what you're trying to tell me."

"I was thinking about Sandra," Leon admitted, turning his head into the pillow a little as if that might help him hide from the memory. "This girl I knew a while back."

"Oh?"

Leon nodded. Then something in the back of his mind registered the tone of voice in that expression. He looked into Rupert's eyes rather than at a random point on his shoulder.

"I wasn't thinking about having sex with her," he said, quickly. "That wasn't really very successful… I mean, she was a nice girl. I'm sure if I wasn't gay I would have had a really great time with her, but we didn't have any sort of chemistry at all and…" Leon trailed off.

"I see."

Leon looked back to Rupert's eyes for a moment. "No! I didn't mean I don't think we have chemistry. We do, I mean, at least from my side we—"

Rupert silenced him with a kiss. "Plenty of chemistry on both sides. What does this have to do with Sandra?" he asked patiently.

"Nothing. Like I said, I wasn't thinking about having sex with her," Leon tried to explain, unable to believe just how much he was managing to screw this up.

"Leon?"

"Yes?"

"Try to focus on what it is you're trying to tell me, sweetheart."

Leon nibbled at his bottom lip. "We only went out together a few times, more as friends than anything, then one night we got back to her place and one thing led to another." Leon frowned. "Still not quite sure how that happened, I never just fell into bed with people, even girls."

"Focus," Rupert repeated.

Leon cleared his throat as his nerves built even further inside him. "Yeah, anyway, afterwards we're lying next to each other and I'm wondering how the hell I ended up there with her when I was really sure I never even had any intention of having sex with her and hoping that things wouldn't be really awkward between us because we really had to finish this group project we were working on about Van Gough."

"Focus," Rupert said again, just a touch of amusement mixed in with growing concern.

"And she turns over and says she's in love with me," Leon rushed out.

Rupert was silent for a few seconds. "I take it you didn't feel the same way?"

"I thought she was insane. But the thing is, women are kind of allowed to do things like that, aren't they? But if a guy were to do the same, anyone would think he was crazy, right?"

"I think it counts as crazy regardless of gender," Rupert said.

Leon nodded. "Yes, sir—you're probably right."

"Not that I don't want to know every single thing about you, but it does seem a strange moment to share all this with me," Rupert mentioned as he stroked his fingers over Leon's bare skin.

Leon shrugged. "You asked me what I was thinking. I was thinking that anyone would think a guy that said something like that right after they did something with someone for the first time was crazy. I'm not a very good liar so I told you the truth."

Rupert tucked a knuckle under his chin and made him look him in the eye. "I love you, too," he whispered.

Leon felt the blush race to his cheeks. "I wasn't thinking it just to get you to say it back, sir."

Rupert smiled as he brushed their lips together. "Technically, I can't say it *back* unless you actually say it at some point."

Leon found that point on Rupert's shoulder again. He shrugged. "I do love you, sir," he whispered.

"And I love you too," Rupert repeated. He kissed him again, a slow tease of lips and tongue.

In that moment, as Rupert rolled him onto his back and the world once more faded from his mind, the last thought that made itself known in Leon's head was that, against all logic and reason, being told that his lover was cheating on him was actually one of the *best* things that had ever happened to him.

WHILE UNDER
THE
INFLUENCE

Chapter One

"Truth or dare?"

Elijah March knocked back another shot of vodka, then squinted as he did his best to focus in on his cousin.

Louisa tossed her drink back with a great deal more co-ordination than Elijah had been able to manage for at least an hour and a half. There was a good reason why he'd sworn off playing drinking games with his cousin. Unfortunately, at that particular moment, Elijah was far too drunk to remember what that reason was.

Blinking uncertainly at the girl who'd been his best friend ever since they'd started school, and who'd been getting him into trouble for just as long, Elijah pulled himself into a more upright position on the sofa and brushed his hair back from his face.

The wavy chestnut strands were too long. They kept falling in his eyes. Maybe that was why Louisa looked blurry! Elijah smiled, pleased he had solved that particular mystery.

"Truth or dare?" Louisa repeated, flicking her own blonde mane over her shoulder as she reached for the vodka bottle again. She must have spilt quite a bit of it at some point, Elijah decided, because there was a lot less in the bottle than there should have been.

Opening his eyes very wide as he tried to resolve Louisa's image into one person rather than two, Elijah considered his options. Louisa had one hell of a strange sense of humour when it came to dares.

From what Elijah remembered of their last night out together, he'd ended up stark naked on a building site. It had been damn cold there too. At least they were tucked away safely in their shared flat this time. There was a greatly reduced chance of getting a chill. But still…

"Truth," Elijah finally said, with all the confidence of a man who had more alcohol than blood flowing through his veins.

Louisa smiled.

Elijah bowed his head and covered his face with his hands. He knew that smile.

He was pretty sure this was how the pretty blonde heroine in the horror films felt when she decided to wander into the dark, scary forest in search of her pet kitten, or whatever. Elijah knew he was going to get slaughtered, but there really wasn't any way to change the role he was destined to play in the scenario.

"Favourite sex fantasy," Louisa purred, obviously relishing each word. "In detail."

Elijah kept his face hidden. "Is it too late to say dare?"

"Drink your shot, Eli. Get some courage in you," she ordered.

Elijah peeked between his fingers just in time to see Louisa toss back yet another shot.

"Snap," he blurted out. "I will if you will."

Louisa laughed, kicked off her shoes and tucked her feet underneath her, making herself completely comfortable on the opposite sofa. "My favourite fantasy…" she mused. "The company football team."

Elijah straightened up, a frown gathering on his brow. If he was going to confess his own worst sins, he'd be damned if he didn't get some good mileage from Louisa in return. "You said we had to give details. Who from the football team?"

The image of the Clarkson Financial Services company football team sprung up inside Elijah's head. He had to admit there were some really fit guys on there and—

"All of them, of course!" Louisa giggled with glee at the idea. "I'd take them all, one after another. Form an orderly queue, boys, there's plenty for everyone!"

Elijah shook his head, not sure he wanted to hear any more, but it made no difference. Louisa was already well into her stride.

"We'd all be in the changing room after they've won a big game. I'd give the man of the match the first turn with me, then just work my way down the line." Louisa walked her fingers daintily along the arm of the sofa as she spoke. "I'd start with my back pressed against the lockers, my legs wrapped around the team captain and his cock buried as deep inside me as he can get it. Once I've come a few times, I'd move over to the wooden bench running down the middle of the room so a couple of different guys could get their hands on me at the same time. We could all finish off in the showers, and I'd be trapped between as many slippery soapy bodies as I can squeeze in under the spray."

Louisa closed her eyes. Her head dropped back to rest on the high back of the sofa. "All those naked fit men, all of them pumped up from their big win. So much adrenaline, so much testosterone, and so many possibilities... Sometimes, I imagine the guys getting so worked up they can't control themselves and start to mess about with each other while they wait their turn for me." She let out a satisfied little sigh as she opened her eyes and turned her attention back to Elijah.

Finally regaining control of his slack jaw, Elijah closed his mouth. "And to think, you used to be such a nice girl..."

Louisa laughed out loud. "No, sweetheart. *You* are a nice boy. I am, and always have been, a complete slut."

Elijah helplessly pictured his Aunt Susan's face. "Your mother would turn in her gave, and she's not even dead yet."

"A slut, Elijah," Louisa announced, in the tone she always used when she was attempting to educate Elijah about the big bad world, "is merely a woman with the morals of a man."

Elijah couldn't help but smile.

"Half the guys at the firm are screwing their way around the temping pool. Why should the testosterone cadets get all the fun?" She tilted her head to one side and considered Elijah through narrowed eyes. "You take life too seriously. You need to go out more, have more fun, have more sex."

Elijah downed another shot and held out his glass to be filled again. At least three glasses weaved about in his grasp, but that was okay. Louisa, clever girl that she was, managed to hold exactly the same number of bottles and re-fill all his glasses at the same time.

"You're cute, single, twenty-one and living in the big city," Louisa chided. "You're supposed to be having the time of your life!" Rolling onto her back, Louisa threw her legs over the arm of the sofa. "Now, ante-up, sweetheart. What's your fantasy? Or shall I guess? Something nice and sweet for a nice, sweet boy, right?"

It was that same patronising attitude that had seen Elijah sneaking out of school and tasting his first beer. Louisa and her truly infuriating way of making him feel as if he was a decade younger than her rather than a whole three days, was going to be the damn death of him.

Suddenly not caring what he said as long as it took the smug look off her face, Elijah blurted out the first thing that popped into his head—unfortunately, that happened to be the truth. "A rent boy in a gay bar."

Shot glass to her lips, Louisa choked on cheap vodka for the first time in living memory. "What!" She sat up, suddenly far more interested in Elijah than he had ever seen her. Her expression alone should have been enough to sober him up in a hurry. "You're gay?"

Elijah blinked rapidly. He hadn't actually said that out loud, had he? "No?" he hazarded.

Louisa lurched forward to the very edge of her seat, grabbed the vodka bottle and poured another shot for herself. When Elijah held out his glass, she handed him the bottle instead. That was good. He needed it.

"You're gay," she repeated.

"No." Elijah wasn't going to have that conversation while he was drunk. Come to that, he wasn't going to have that conversation *ever*. "I am not gay."

"Of course not. You just fantasise about buying a rent boy for the night," Louisa pointed out. "You know, this explains so much!"

"It doesn't explain anything," Elijah corrected. "Because, I'm not—"

"I've been throwing the prettiest girls I know at you for years and there was me thinking the only reason you didn't catch any of them was because you're shy."

"I'm not shy, and I'm not gay. And I do not have fantasies about paying by the hour," Elijah informed her very carefully. Unfortunately, the last statement was the only one that sounded anything like the truth. He hadn't been the one handing over the money— he'd been the one taking it.

Lifting his gaze from the vodka bottle, Elijah glanced across at Louisa. She was peering at him like he was some rare and interesting specimen trapped beneath a microscope.

"Don't look at me like that."

Louisa paid as much attention to that order as she had to any he'd given her over the years.

"I'm not gay."

"Bi?" Louisa suggested.

"No." Elijah had decided he was straight a long time ago. He'd be damned if he'd let a few fantasies about having hot sex with big strong men interfere with his long-held belief that he'd find a woman who appealed to him one day.

"Tell me the fantasy."

It took Elijah a moment to remember the question that had landed him in this mess in the first place. His fantasy…

Elijah shrugged, even though he had no real hope of avoiding fulfilling his end of the deal.

"I told you mine, Eli."

Elijah sighed. He pushed his hand through his hair, tugging at its roots in the process. "Bearing in mind that I spent a whole summer a few years ago believing that I was an alien—" he began.

"It was sixteen years ago, Elijah," Louisa cut in. "You were five. You kept colouring yourself green. Your mother hid all the paints so you stuck grass all over you. What does that have to do with anything?"

"It points out that I often have strange thoughts," Elijah explained, as soberly as he was able. "They don't mean anything. I have phases and I grow out of them."

"Details," Louisa demanded, leaning closer in anticipation.

Elijah closed his eyes. He wanted to water it down so badly it made his head spin. He knew he should turn it into something sweet, something his cousin would easily believe he fantasised about on a regular basis. But, with equal amounts of adrenaline and alcohol racing through his veins, the idea of coming out with anything tamer than the truth almost seemed worse than…well, coming out.

"I'm in a gay bar," he finally said. "In the gent's toilets." He trailed off, allowing the familiar picture to build in his mind.

"Elijah!" Louisa demanded. She was always so bloody impatient.

"Hush," he muttered. "I'm thinking." For once she left him in peace for several consecutive moments.

"It always starts the same," Elijah whispered, as the details fell into place, one by one. The grubby tiled floor. The bare light bulb swinging overhead. The dripping of a leaking tap. It was all there.

Taking a deep breath, Elijah somehow found the will to try and put it into words. "I'm the only one there, but I can hear voices and music floating in from the dance floor. There's this beat that seems to pound within the floor and sneak up through my feet. My whole body's pulsing with it."

He blindly held up a hand, sensing that Louisa was about to interrupt, but not willing to put up with that.

"The door opens behind me. I'm facing one of the sinks and I glance in the mirror above it to see who it will be. I'm there to make money. I'm a rent boy and I can't afford to be choosy, but when I see this guy in the mirror" — Elijah swallowed rapidly as his mouth watered at the sight — "God, he's stunning. Tall and blond, with the most gorgeous green eyes I've ever seen. He's so serious, so strong. He could pick me up and pin me against the wall with one hand — and I'm sure he will if I don't behave myself. And he's hung too. I can't tell that by the reflection in the mirror, but there's no way a man that stunning wouldn't be — nature wouldn't be that cruel."

Elijah closed his eyes even tighter. It was all he could do to keep his breaths even enough to maintain the flow of words.

"This guy could have anyone. He could snap his fingers and everyone would just drop to their knees, their mouths open, begging for a taste of his cock, without him needing to hand over a single penny."

He barely held back an enthusiastic whimper at the prospect of doing just that.

"Our gazes meet in the mirror. I turn around. The guy runs his eyes up and down my body and asks me 'how much?'. He knows what I am just by looking at me."

Elijah bit down on his bottom lip for a moment.

"I tell him my price. Fifty pounds for whatever he wants to do with me. The guy nods and hands over the money as if it's nothing more than loose change to him. And, as easy as that, I belong to him for the rest of the night."

Elijah lifted his hand to his mouth.

"He puts me on my knees right there in the toilets. Anyone could walk in and see us. The floor's hard. My lips are stretched around his cock. It's not nice or romantic. He's not treating me the way a nice man treats a lover, or the way anyone treats a nice guy. His hand's on the back of my head, he's thrusting into my throat, and damn if I don't love every minute of it."

"Does he tell you his name?"

Those words came from somewhere far, far away. They didn't belong in that fantasy. Elijah frowned. "He doesn't need to," he mumbled, desperately trying to cling to the scene playing out in his imagination. "I know who he is."

"So it's always the same guy?"

Elijah shook his head, but the voice still failed to disappear from his make-believe world.

"Yeah, it is," he admitted, if only to stop that voice interrupting him by repeating the question. His eyes remained closed. Any sober part of his mind was busy on its knees enjoying the fantasy. That was the only reason he could have ever have been stupid enough to say it aloud. "Aaron Heath."

Elijah sighed to himself as he slumped back on the sofa. Aaron Heath—Clarkson's Financial Services head of personnel and the one common denominator in every one of Elijah's fantasies ever since he had first set eyes on the man. The solo reason for so many sleepless nights and one-handed work outs, the—

"And you're still trying to deny you're gay?"

"What?" Elijah's eyes snapped open.

Louisa was perched on the very edge of the sofa opposite him, her eyes glittering with fascination. Even with his mind clouded by both alcohol and arousal, Elijah still knew that was a very, very bad thing.

He closed his eyes again and let his head drop back onto the sofa cushions behind him. This time, the darkness that descended around him was just a little bit blacker.

* * * *

If he stayed very still and didn't move at all, Elijah was pretty sure he'd survive his hangover for long enough to spend the whole day wishing he was dead. "I'm never drinking with you again."

"You say that every time."

Elijah flinched and held up a hand. "Don't, Louisa."

"What?" Her tone was all wrong. Even after years spent trying to master it, she still couldn't pull off anything that sounded even remotely like innocence.

"Don't be bright and cheerful and rub it in that you never get hangovers."

Louisa pressed a hot cup of coffee into Elijah's hands. Murmuring an unintelligible thank you, Elijah swallowed a large mouthful of the scalding liquid. It burned as it rushed down his throat, but it still felt good to have something other than alcohol in his stomach.

Sitting carefully on the edge of the sofa, Elijah cradled his coffee cup in both hands and tried to make the room stop spinning. "You're going to hell, you know that, don't you?"

This time, he really meant it when he said he wasn't drinking with her again. The girl had the constitution of a backwoods still.

Louisa swished long blonde strands of perfectly styled hair over her shoulder and balanced herself prettily on the arm of the opposite sofa. "We need to get you a guy."

"You're going to hell," Elijah repeated. "And I'm there already." He risked rubbing at his right temple. Taking his fingers away, he inspected them for bloodstains. It felt like someone had hit him over the head with a sledgehammer at least seventeen times the previous night, but they'd apparently managed to do that without breaking the skin.

"We have to get you a guy and get you laid. It's the only way we'll know for sure if you're gay or not," Louisa declared. Unable to stay still for two sodding seconds in a row, she began to pace around the room.

Elijah closed his eyes as his coffee threatened to leave his body. "That," he managed to say, "has to be the most stupid idea you've ever had — including those that have led to me almost being arrested for indecent exposure."

"You need to try a guy for size."

The pictures those words forced into Elijah's head really weren't compatible with a hangover. Although, in his only bit of good luck since Louisa opened the first bottle the previous night, the blood redirected from his brain towards his cock did slightly ease the headache.

"It's no big deal," she told him. "So you prefer to catch than pitch. It's true what they say, you know — all the good ones are gay anyway." She clapped her hands — Elijah had heard quieter thunder storms.

"We're going to have so much fun once I drag you out of the closet."

Elijah shook his head very carefully, just in case it fell off.

He liked the closet. He had spent so many years in there it was like home. But, now that Louisa was in the closet with him, it was getting far too crowded. One of them was going to have to go soon.

"I've made out with other girls," Louisa announced.

"Good for you."

"Does the thought of me with another woman do anything for you?" Louisa asked.

Elijah put his coffee cup on the low table next to the sofa, careful not to let the china clink too loudly against the wooden surface. "You're my cousin, Lou. The thought of you doing *anything* with *anyone* creeps me out."

"But two women, the idea does nothing for you?"

"No." Elijah pulled himself to his feet and stumbled unsteadily towards the bathroom.

"Definitely another tick in the gay column," Louisa declared, trailing along behind him. "You've never done anything with a guy, right?"

"Have never done and have no intention of ever doing," Elijah corrected, walking across to the sink. Turning on the cold tap, he scooped up large handfuls of icy water and splashed them against his face.

Louisa murmured something that sounded like agreement from the doorway.

Bending over the basin, Elijah cradled his sore head in his wet hands. Whenever Louisa sounded like she agreed with him it was a bad sign. It damn near always meant she was planning to do something that she didn't want him to know about until it was too late.

Elijah took a deep breath. There were only three things he was sure of. He needed more coffee, a new head, and a new cousin—and not necessarily in that order.

Chapter Two

"Truth or dare?"

"Unless you're going to dare me to finish this project tonight, go away." Elijah didn't even look up from his paperwork as Louisa opened the door and walked into his bedroom without even bothering to knock.

If there was a reason why he'd agreed to share a flat with her, he couldn't remember what it was.

Louisa sat on the desk right next to his laptop, casually pushing his things aside to give herself more room. Elijah only just rescued a folder full of notes before it toppled onto the floor. He glared up at his cousin. She merely smiled, obviously not the least bit concerned that she was pissing him off.

"I need to—"

"Give it up, Eli. I was at the same meeting as you. I know you don't need to have it finished until the end of the month."

Elijah sighed, leant back in his chair, folded his arms across his chest and waited. Louisa was dressed to go out, with a skirt barely long enough to cover her knickers and heels high enough to give more sensible people vertigo.

"What if I were to offer you the chance to forever silence your favourite cousin regarding your inclination to take it from a big strapping brute rather than give it to a pretty little princess?" she asked.

Elijah took a deep breath. Part of him really wanted to point out that half the gay men having sex had to be tops rather than bottoms in the arrangement, but that would only lead to more and more detailed questions about his exact preferences. "I've been trying to silence you for years, Lou. I learned my limitations a long time ago."

"Just come to this new club I've found, have a drink with me and I promise you I'll never mention the gay thing again."

"You never keep promises like that." Elijah pushed a hand through his hair and resolutely scrolled back up to the top of the page he'd been trying to type. He had no idea what he'd written as Louisa came in, but he doubted his boss would be impressed with it.

"Scout's honour!" Louisa offered.

Elijah glanced up at her. "You were never a boy scout and that is certainly not the way they're taught to hold their fingers up!" He tried to sound annoyed, but his lips betrayed him. It was impossible for him to hold back a smile.

Louisa grinned.

"You really are a brat, Louisa. You know that, don't you?"

"Yep. I count it as a life skill."

Elijah sighed.

Louisa ignored him.

Rolling his eyes at himself, Elijah gave in and saved what he had done on the project. "Where are we going?"

"Just an adorable little place I've discovered recently."

Adorable inspired a nice, quaint picture in Elijah's head. He wasn't naïve enough to set any store by that. Louisa's idea of adorable tended towards body shots, dancing on tables and waiters in g-strings. He'd learned to ignore the first two. As for the third, Elijah lifted his gaze heavenward…

"You'll need to get changed first."

Elijah sighed once more, but when they left the flat half an hour later without him being bullied into anything more adventurous than a pair of black jeans and a long-sleeved black T-shirt, he was cautiously harbouring the hope that he wasn't about to find himself crammed onto a dance floor with two hundred insane people popping pills and waving fluorescent wands.

"Hurry up!" Louisa's heels clicked on the pavement as she strode ahead.

Elijah obediently walked faster. He caught up with her just as she turned into the doorway of a club. Elijah squared his shoulders and stepped inside after her.

It was… Actually, it seemed surprisingly pleasant. Complete mellowness was obviously too much to hope for—music loud enough to make him wince pumped out from the huge speakers set at either end of a dance floor—but it wasn't as crowded as most of the pubs and clubs in the area.

Elijah made his way a little further inside. A relaxed, comfortable atmosphere gradually surrounded him, promising to soothe his soul and make him forget about his workload for a few hours.

Raising himself onto the high stool next to Louisa's at the bar, Elijah glanced around the room. They were sitting far enough away from the dance floor that the music was bearable. There were no drunks, no obvious drug dealers. There weren't even any crowds of psychotic football fans watching the latest match on a wide-screen TV.

Elijah was tentatively willing to like the place, right up until the moment he noticed one strange, and suddenly very important, anomaly. "Louisa," he said, carefully. "Why are you the only woman in here?"

"Am I?"

Elijah tried to take a deep breath, but giant fists seemed to have wrapped themselves around his lungs. He couldn't get any air. "No, you wouldn't do this to me..." Elijah shook his head. No, she couldn't have. Not even Louisa would put him in this position...

"Come on, I'll buy you a drink," she offered, waving a hand at the whole range of bottles that lined the shelves behind the bar.

Elijah shifted uncomfortably on his stool. They were already getting more than their fair share of strange looks. "And how do you intend to explain you being here?" he hissed, leaning closer to his cousin. "You stand out like..."

"Like a woman in the kind of gay bar that doesn't welcome women?" Louisa shrugged. "If anyone asks I'll tell them I'm a lesbian."

Elijah looked heavenward, but whoever's job it was to answer the prayers of closeted cousins, it must have been their day off. Without any sort of celestial help coming his way, Elijah knew there was no arguing with Louisa.

"One drink, then we're going," he stated.

The barman handed a tray of drinks to someone further down the bar, and headed in their direction. He gave Louisa a slightly strange look, but he smiled widely when he turned his gaze towards Elijah.

Elijah instantly felt the heat rush to his cheeks. Stupid! The man worked in a bar. He probably smiled at everyone. He was probably just angling for a bigger tip. The guy wasn't hitting on him. He really wasn't. There was no need to hyperventilate.

Elijah stared at the water mark the bottom of a wet glass had left on the bar. His heart pounded so loudly in his ears, he didn't even hear Louisa give their order. A lifetime seemed to pass before the drinks were set down in front of them and Elijah felt safe raising his gaze.

"Are you homophobic or something?" Louisa demanded.

"What? No, of course I'm not."

"Because you seem to have a big problem with admitting you're gay."

"I'm not…"

"See," Louisa smirked.

Elijah took a sip of his—"Louisa, what is this?"

"Apple juice."

Elijah frowned at his glass. "You ordered me an apple juice? What am I? Eight?"

"If you get lucky, you'll need to be able to get it up. You're strictly on soft drinks tonight, sweetheart," Louisa calmly informed him. "Now, truth or dare?"

"Louisa…" Elijah ran his hand through his hair, messing up the style she'd forced on him before they left the flat, and only just resisting the temptation to pull out several strands by the roots. "Truth." He wasn't stupid enough to choose a dare in that club.

"What do you have against the possibility of you being gay?"

She just couldn't stop pushing. Elijah shook his head and took a swig of his juice.

"You like the idea of having sex with men," she stated, with the air of someone who was going to get to the bottom of her chosen subject, even if she killed off the object of her fascination in the process.

"I liked the idea of sex with girls too," Elijah muttered into his glass. "Until I tried it." An extra wave of heat rushed to his cheeks as he remembered that horrible night. His brain had been so excited at finally getting into a girl's knickers. His cock had been so…not excited at all.

She was silent for a few seconds. "So you don't want to try out guys only to be disappointed again." It was a realisation, not a question.

Elijah just shrugged.

"Truth or dare?"

"Isn't it my turn?" he asked.

"Like I give a damn about fair play."

Elijah opened his mouth to give his usual safe answer, only to close it again without saying a word. He'd had enough of truth. The truth was screwing up his life.

In that second, he was past the point of caring what happened next. He looked around the club and considered his future without even the smallest drop of alcohol to give him optimism.

What was he going to do? Stay celibate for the rest of his life? Have bad sex with women for the next couple of decades, while frantically imagining he was topping a man every damn time? "Dare."

Louisa put down her glass and smiled. "Do it."

Elijah didn't even bother to look up from his juice. "Do what?"

"Your fantasy. I dare you to do it." She nodded to the sign for the gents' room on the wall behind them.

"What?" Elijah tried to put his glass on the bar and almost missed.

Louisa grabbed hold of the juice before it could spill. "I dare you to go in there and offer yourself to the first guy who walks through the door." She caught Elijah's gaze and held it. "I dare you to do whatever he wants for fifty quid."

"I am not whoring myself out for a dare!" Elijah snapped, leaning forward and dropping his voice. The guy working behind the bar gave him a strange look over Louisa's shoulder.

"Stop whining, Eli. You can give him the money back afterwards if you're going to be all prudish about it. But, for the sake of your sanity, you're going to have to at least see what happens when you get up close and personal with a guy."

"But—"

"There's only one way to know for sure, Elijah," Louisa cut in. "And that's to suck it and see."

Suck it and see? Elijah shook his head and tried like hell to avoid noticing the way his mouth watered at the prospect.

"Look," Louisa said. "There are two ways this evening can go. Either you go in there and find yourself a man. Or I'll find one for you out here. It's your choice."

Elijah could so easily imagine the various ways Louisa might try to throw him and some random guy together. He felt the blood drain from his face. All at once, he knew that trolling in the gents was actually going to be the *least* embarrassing way his evening could go.

He stumbled off his seat without a word. The gents' sign pointed along a corridor. Elijah strode down it as fast as he could without actually breaking into a run.

Pushing the door open, he made the most of his momentum and stepped inside before he could change his mind. There was no one in there. Elijah closed his eyes for a moment and sent up silent thanks.

His hands were shaking, and he was just standing in a deserted room. He could only imagine what he'd have been like if some poor guy had been taking a leak when he'd walked in.

Pacing over to the sink, Elijah ran cold water into his cupped palms and splashed it over his face. By the time he'd dried his cheeks with a paper towel, he had a plan. It was a good plan.

He was going to lie.

He'd lurk around in there until some poor unsuspecting man arrived on the scene. Then he'd escape and tell Louisa that he'd completed the dare, but the man he'd propositioned wasn't interested. Once that was done, he'd go cheerfully back to their flat, back into his room, and back to being in denial.

Elijah examined the plan from every conceivable angle. There were no flaws in it. He'd simply leave the room with both his pride and his closeted status intact, and the next time Louisa turned up at his bedroom door he was going to get into his actual closet and hide there until she went away.

Filling in time, trying not to just stand around and look like he was waiting for an easy hook-up, Elijah washed and dried his hands once more.

His gaze strayed to the mirror above the basin. That was a stupid thing to do. As he caught sight of his reflection, Elijah was catapulted straight into his fantasy. His mind disintegrated into tiny little pieces and scattered across the none-too-clean bathroom floor.

The man who looked back at him from the reflection was someone else — someone who wasn't worried about whether having sex with a man would be good because he already knew it was always fantastic.

The guy who stared back at Elijah was someone who didn't care what the world thought of him — someone who'd come out with pride rather than stumbled out of the closet in a drunken stupor and confessed his guilty little secret to the one person who was bound to drive him insane about it.

Would a guy actually want to screw him anyway? Elijah wondered.

He had no doubt that any sensible person's ideal man was all chiseled jaw and washboard abs. Anyone with any sense would want to screw a man who was all muscle, all attitude, all orders and leather and stern gazes.

They'd want the opposite of him…

Trapped, with no way to expel rapidly increasing levels of nervous energy, Elijah pushed his hand through his hair disordering the chestnut waves even further.

A moment later, he shoved his hands into his pockets. No, he couldn't do that. It would look like he was playing with himself. Elijah snatched his hands away from his crotch and cast a guilty glance around the room.

Even though he knew full well that he wasn't stupid enough to go through with the dare, his palms were already slick with sweat. He wiped them on his jeans. They were his best jeans. They were also too damn tight. His brain knew nothing was going to happen. His cock had spent too long in the fantasy version of a club's gents' room to understand he wasn't in a daydream anymore.

Elijah adjusted himself as subtly as he could and pressed the heel of his hand to his growing erection. The door leading into the bathroom swung open. Elijah turned quickly back to the sink and fiddled clumsily with the tap, hoping like hell it looked like he was in there for perfectly innocent reasons and had just washed his hands.

The mirror above the basin called to him again. Elijah helplessly peeked into the glass.

No…

His eyes met those in another man's reflection.

No…

Elijah couldn't look away. He couldn't breathe, either. The air lodged in his throat and threatened to choke him.

No… This wasn't happening. It couldn't be. The world couldn't be this cruel to him.

* * * *

Two days earlier…

"Hi! It's Aaron, right?"

Aaron Heath glanced up from his lunch and straight into the eyes of a stunningly attractive woman. He only just managed to hold back a sigh when he saw the expression on the girl's face.

He'd learned how to spot when a certain kind of woman was plotting his downfall a long time ago. All he had to do now was wait until she let slip if she'd be hitting on him for her own benefit or if she was trying to set him up with one of her friends.

"I'm Louisa March, from the advertising department. We worked on the Berkshire project together." She sat down on the other side of the table without waiting for an invitation.

"I remember," Aaron admitted, with vague politeness. He adjusted his reading glasses slightly and turned his attention back to the report in the open folder lying next to his plate of spaghetti. He really was going to have to find somewhere other than the restaurant directly opposite his office to have his lunch.

"Rumour has it you're single."

Aaron raised an eyebrow at the girl. She had to be at least a decade younger than him, barely into her twenties. "Nought out of ten for subtlety, but full marks for getting to the point."

"So, you are single?" Louisa pushed.

"Single, yes, but not looking," Aaron corrected.

"Bollocks."

If nothing else, she now had his attention. Aaron stopped even pretending to study his report. He took off his glasses and met the woman's gaze head on. "Miss March, with all due respect, whatever it is you have in mind, I sincerely doubt that—"

"So Elijah's not your type then?" she cut in.

"Elijah?" Aaron repeated blankly.

"Elijah March, he works in accounting. Cute little guy, bit shy—but sweet as hell once you get to know him. He's my cousin."

The description was completely superfluous. Aaron knew full well which guy she was talking about just from the name.

So, Elijah March was gay? The picture Louisa had painted of him was accurate enough, as far as it went, but she'd completely forgotten to mention that the guy damn near screamed his need for a dominant lover with each and every mannerism.

Louisa smiled. "You do swing that way, right?"

I did before – Aaron cleared his throat and cut that line of thought dead in its tracks. "Whatever my sexual preferences are—"

"How do you feel about virgins?"

"What?" Aaron narrowed his eyes. He sat up a little straighter in his chair.

"I know you like guys in general," Louisa said. "Now, I just need to know if you have any objection to being the first man to screw a particular someone."

Aaron stared across the table for several long seconds. His only consolation was that he knew that his expression remained completely blank while his mind raced faster and faster. A virgin would be...

Aaron twirled one arm of his glasses between his fingers. There would certainly be a few very specific advantages to the scenario. It just might be exactly what he needed in order to...

"He's never—?" Aaron cut himself short and shook his head. "I'm not interested in being set up with anyone."

"He's sweet and cute—all he needs is someone to kick him out of the closet. And I'm pretty sure you're the only man who can do that."

A virgin who needed to be rescued...? "Is there some particular reason why you believe that?"

"He's got the world's most massive crush on you."

And he's never done anything with another man. One annoyingly persistent part of Aaron's psyche—that part of him that was wired directly to his cock and only cared about getting laid after such a prolonged dry spell—repeated that fact over and over.

It really had been a long time—too long. And there was no reason to believe the problem that had arisen during his last few attempts at enjoying the company of a submissive, would be repeated with Elijah.

Whatever Louisa saw change in his expression, it made her smile, as if she was suddenly sure she had won. "Here's the deal," she informed him. "He has this fantasy. All you have to do is play your part in it, get him out of the closet and have some fun with him."

Aaron leant back in his chair and folded his arms across his chest. "What's the catch?"

"There isn't one," Louisa promised, echoing his pose exactly. "Oh, apart from the fact I'll have your balls for a new pair of earrings if you hurt him." Her smile didn't waver in the slightest as she said it.

Aaron found himself smiling as he unflinchingly returned her gaze. For just a few moments, Aaron almost felt like the same man he'd been back before his ex had decided to drop the parting bombshell which had destroyed such a large part of Aaron's world.

* * * *

The figure stood perfectly still in the bathroom doorway for so long, Elijah had almost convinced himself that Aaron was just a figment of his imagination. Then Aaron's reflection stepped forward.

Elijah managed to take a breath, but only one, and only because his body took over from his mind and demanded oxygen before he passed out.

"How much?"

Elijah tried to clear his throat and failed. All the images from every permutation of his fantasy closed in around him. It was only pure survival instinct that allowed him to drag another breath into his body. "I…"

Aaron moved closer. Lord, he was stunning. Elijah had rarely been that close to him and he'd never been lucky enough to find himself in a room alone with his fantasy. He desperately wanted to turn around, lower his gaze and take in every detail of Aaron's body, but Aaron's gaze held him, trapped, facing the mirror.

"How much?" Aaron repeated, his voice even lower and richer than Elijah remembered it being at work.

"For what?" Elijah whispered, doing his very best to maintain a fingertip touch on reality as it threatened to slip away from him entirely.

"For whatever I want," Aaron said, as if that should have been obvious.

Reality be damned. Elijah whimpered his complete approval of impossible daydreams.

Aaron stepped forward again, closing the gap between them just a little more. His voice dropped to a whisper. "How much would it cost for me to have you all to myself for the rest of the night? For you to promise to do anything I ask? For you to give me your mouth, your arse, your cock, and any other part of your body I want?"

Elijah could barely even blink.

Aaron was right behind him now. His voice hadn't lost any of its strength or confidence as his tone became hushed. "How much?" he asked again.

Elijah's head was empty, his brain running on autopilot. The fantasy rose up in his mind and the words were on his lips long before he could make his consciousness understand it wasn't a good idea to say them. "Fifty quid."

Aaron looked down between them until his attention settled on Elijah's arse. Suddenly freed from holding Aaron's gaze, Elijah dropped his focus to stare at the reflection of Aaron's mouth. Strong, kissable lips parted, revealing perfect white teeth. Aaron's tongue sneaked out and swiped across his bottom lip. The times Elijah had imagined that tongue and those lips…

"Yes."

For a moment Elijah thought he had said the word himself, but no, it had definitely been Aaron's voice and not his own.

Elijah blinked and looked back to Aaron's eyes. "Yes?"

Catching hold of one of the belt loops on Elijah's jeans, Aaron tugged at the denim until Elijah had no choice but to turn and face him. Eyes open very wide at the shock of actually feeling Aaron Heath's hands on his body, Elijah watched in silence as Aaron took several crisp bank notes from the back pocket of smartly tailored trousers.

Knowing that this couldn't be happening, Elijah remained perfectly still as Aaron tucked two crisp twenty pound notes, and a rather crumpled ten, into the front pocket of his jeans. Aaron's fingers lingered there as if he had a right to touch Elijah in any way he chose, as if Elijah was bought and paid for and—

"I want your mouth."

Aaron stroked his fingertips over Elijah's lips in a gentle caress and Elijah automatically opened his mouth. But, as Aaron's fingers drifted across his cheek and threaded into his hair, Elijah somehow forced himself to think logically.

This couldn't happen.

Aaron thought he was a rent boy — he thought he'd know what he was doing, that he was some sort of expert on how to go down on a guy and make him scream with pleasure.

Elijah shook his head, tugging against Aaron's fingers. He hadn't been so out of his depth since he was a teenage boy and in the back of his car with Judy Hitchings, since he first realised that half-naked and very willing girls weren't actually as interesting as he had been led to believe.

"I…"

"I want your mouth," Aaron repeated, as if that were obviously far more important than anything Elijah might have been about to say.

Elijah thought about just dropping to his knees and giving it a go. If he kept his teeth covered he couldn't do any real harm, could he? At least he'd know what it felt like to have a hard shaft slide between his lips. He'd know what another man's cum tasted like. He'd have the memory if nothing else.

Elijah closed his eyes, in a last-ditch attempt to hide from the fact it would inevitably be a bad, humiliating memory. Not because he was on his knees for money, but because he knew without any doubt that it would all go wrong and he'd have to confess his embarrassing lack of experience.

With his hand still buried in Elijah's curls, Aaron tilted Elijah's head further back. Elijah felt heat rush to his cheeks as he desperately tried to find the will to say no.

Then, without any warning, words ceased to exist inside Elijah's mind. Aaron brushed their mouths together and syllables became things that happened in other people's heads.

His lips were firm and confident as they moved over Elijah's mouth, and all Elijah wanted to do was make the moment last forever.

Finally, some sort of instinct for survival kicked in. Panic spiked inside Elijah. He put his hands on Aaron's shoulders to push him away. With an embarrassing little mew of half-hearted protest, he pressed his palms against Aaron's shirt.

Deep layers of muscle moved beneath Elijah's hands. God, Aaron felt strong. The hand buried in his hair confirmed it—easily holding Elijah in place as Aaron ran his tongue across his lips.

There was nothing Elijah could do to stop his mouth opening further. With a heartfelt moan, he gave up any attempt at a protest.

Elijah tried to lean into the kiss rather than away from it, but the hand in his hair tightened, keeping him as still as ever. Aaron's lips, soft and demanding in turn, continued their exploration of Elijah's mouth.

Fingers curling into fists, Elijah clutched helplessly at Aaron's shirt, clinging to the pale blue fabric as if it were his lifeline in a storm. He had as little control over when the kiss ended as he had regarding when it had started. Aaron pulled away far too soon, leaving Elijah's mouth naked and craving Aaron's touch.

Stroking his fingers over Elijah's lips once more, Aaron stared down at Elijah, his expression as serious as ever.

Elijah tried to swallow, tried to think. More and more panic raced through him. He'd never responded to a kiss that way. Never. Elijah tried to step away once more, but he was trapped between the sink and Aaron.

He had nowhere to go, nowhere to hide, and Aaron owned him for the rest of the night. Elijah stared up at the taller man for several long seconds, sure that he should hate at least one of those facts, not merely feel his cock grow harder at the idea of each and every damn one of them.

Chapter Three

"Sweet," Aaron whispered. His heart was racing with nerves he was determined to hide, but there was no denying that he'd never tasted a sweeter kiss in his life.

Elijah was so obviously fresh and new to everything—and he was so obviously ready to do far more than kiss a man, for all he was trying to angle his body away from Aaron in a not very subtle attempt to hide his hard-on.

"I…"

Aaron stared down at Elijah, wondering if he was going to get past that one tiny word at any point.

The boy looked frantically around the room, his eyes darting towards the tiles on the wall over Aaron's shoulder, then to the door, and finally to the condom dispenser. Elijah turned his attention away from the latter so quickly, he risked giving his eyeballs whiplash.

"Apple juice," he finally blurted out. "The sweetness. I…um…before I came in here, I was drinking apple juice."

Aaron stroked his thumb back and forth over Elijah's lips as he studied them very carefully; they were slightly darker and fuller after the kiss. So much blood had rushed there to feel another man's mouth against them for the first time. "It wasn't just the juice."

Knowing that he was the first man to ever kiss Elijah sent a huge wave of adrenaline racing through Aaron's veins, but instead of making his heart beat faster, it seemed to calm him down. For the first time in months, Aaron knew that he was in complete control of the man standing before him, and the thought didn't scare him in the least.

Elijah blushed, a soft pink tint spreading across his cheeks as he glanced up at Aaron through his lashes.

"You are sweet," Aaron informed him, with the complete authority of a man who had no doubt the guy he addressed was just as inclined to submission as he was inclined to dominance. "And you're beautiful."

He wasn't quite sure where those last few words came from. They were certainly true, but Aaron hadn't actually intended to share them with Elijah that way.

Aaron tensed. He was acting like even more of a novice than the damn virgin. But, as Elijah swallowed rapidly, setting his Adam's apple bobbing in his throat, Aaron found it hard to regret his moment of weakness. Dipping his head, he whispered his next words very softly in Elijah's ear. "It takes some doing to continue to appear beautiful when you're this close to hyperventilating, Elijah."

If nothing else, the words shocked the boy into tilting his head back and looking up at Aaron properly. The use of his given name seemed to pull the situation together in Elijah's mind—just as Aaron had known it would.

As endearing as the panic-stricken look on Elijah's face had been, Aaron squared his stance and forced himself to end the charade once and for all. "Do you really think Louisa would put you in a situation where you could get hurt?"

"Yes," Elijah replied, without any apparent hesitation. "She would."

Aaron raised an eyebrow at the expression of long-suffering, slow-burning anger that flashed across Elijah's face.

"I fell off our school roof and broke my leg on one of her dares. And I got a black eye from the captain of the school rugby team. And I almost got arrested—on three separate occasions. But, this time, I really am going to kill her for putting me in this position." There wasn't a trace of submission in his tone as he said it.

Elijah tried to move away from the sink and step past Aaron. Calmly pretending not to notice, Aaron stayed exactly where he was. There was no way Elijah could push past him without pressing their bodies together, and he was unlikely to do that while he still seemed to believe there was a chance Aaron hadn't noticed how turned on he was.

"What position is that?" Aaron asked, folding his arms across his chest.

Elijah took a deep breath. They stood so close together, his T-shirt brushed against Aaron's forearms.

"I don't know what Louisa told you, but..." But what? Elijah obviously hadn't thought ahead to how he'd finish that sentence.

It was impossible not to rescue him. "Louisa told me that you're bi-curious and might be interested in satisfying some of that curiosity with me," Aaron told him. It was close enough to the truth for that particular moment.

Elijah closed his eyes. "I am going to kill her."

"Was she lying?" Aaron asked.

"Yes—No—I mean..." He blinked up at Aaron, looking so lost, so confused.

"You mean you aren't so much openly bi-curious as in complete gay-denial?"

"Look, I don't know how Louisa talked you into this, but the joke has gone far enough," Elijah said. His voice hardened from a breathless whimper into a firm statement. The effect was spoilt by a slight tremble to his voice, but Aaron was still suitably impressed by the effort.

"Joke?"

"I'm gay. Okay. That's what she wanted you to get me to admit, right?" Elijah demanded. "Congratulations. I'm gay. Well done. I said it out loud and everything. Good bye closet—I'm no longer in denial. Yay for you!"

Aaron stared down at the younger man for several long, silent moments. "You do realise that you and your cousin share one seriously screwed up relationship?"

"Yeah," Elijah agreed with a half sigh as he slumped back against the sink. "Very screwed up. Now just back off and let me breathe. Please?"

"You think she asked me to hit on you as a joke?"

"She did much the same when she took it into her head that I had a crush on Sarah Phillips when I was six," Elijah mumbled.

Aaron stroked the back of his fingers down Elijah's cheek without really thinking about the gesture. Elijah made no complaint. He didn't try to pull away. If he wasn't gay, then he was a straight man who was very comfortable with having a gay man inside his personal space.

Aaron relaxed slightly. There was something very reassuring about knowing that Elijah was actually the man who was coping with the strange situation more easily. "And what am I supposed to get out of that arrangement?"

"Louisa on her back more than likely," Elijah snapped. "Although you shouldn't have bothered — she's an easy lay anyway. Half the guys in the office will tell you that."

The look in Elijah's eyes confirmed to Aaron that the boy regretted saying it the moment the words left his lips. But, if Elijah thought that he was after Louisa he was further in denial than Aaron could have ever guessed.

"I'm gay, sweet. Louisa is hardly my type, but you certainly are."

"Me!" Elijah squeaked, as if that was the most preposterous thing he'd ever heard.

"Is that so unlikely?" Aaron asked, raising an eyebrow at him.

"Yes." Elijah sounded very sure about that if not about anything else.

"Why?"

"Because you're... Because I'm..."

Aaron stroked Elijah's cheek again. Big blue eyes dropped closed, dark lashes fanned out on his cheeks.

"Louisa told you that I…" he trailed off, apparently unable to bring himself to actually say it.

"She mentioned that you might have a slight crush on me," Aaron admitted. And to think, Aaron hadn't been sure if *he* was the one being set up as the fall guy for a practical joke until he'd walked in and seen the look on Elijah's face. No-one was a good enough actor to pull off that sort of panic.

Silence fell over them.

"What happens now?" Elijah finally asked.

He could do this. Aaron took a deep breath, determined not to make a fool out of himself. "That depends on what you want, sweet." The words came out level and emotionless.

Elijah's blush deepened at the impromptu nicknaming.

Aaron's confidence grew. "You can go back to Louisa at the bar. Or you can kill off a bit of your curiosity."

"How?" Eyes open very wide again, Elijah looked expectantly up at Aaron, as if he had no doubt he'd have all the answers.

"One night with no strings, to try out anything you're curious about," Aaron offered.

"With you?" Elijah checked.

"Yes, sweet, with me," Aaron promised, more than willing to be damned before he'd hand over an opportunity like Elijah March to another man, and not just because his lack of experience might be the solution he was looking for himself.

"One night?"

"Yes," Aaron said. "One night. I'm not suggesting anything more than that." As much as he wished things were different, he knew he wasn't in a position to offer anything else.

"And you'll...?"

"And I'll bring you face to face with all the things you've been daydreaming about and show you how pleasurable they can be in reality. Being gay can be a lot of fun if you know what you're doing." Aaron looked down for a moment. *And incredibly painful if a man didn't know what he was doing.* Somehow he kept those words back.

"And what do you get out of all this?" Elijah asked.

Aaron smiled slightly at the pure innocence of the boy. "I get one night, too. I get you."

Elijah shuffled his feet. "It, um...doesn't bother you that I might not um...have had that much experience with other guys?"

For the first time in a long time, Aaron had to fight against an urge to grin. "I get one night," he repeated, seriously. "I get you. And I get to be the first man who kisses you, the first man who touches you, the first man who hears you gasp and whimper, and moan his name. Why would I wish any of that away?"

Elijah cleared his throat, as if weighing his options. But Aaron knew the decision had already been made—it had been made the moment Elijah didn't say no right away.

Very carefully, Elijah reached into his jeans pocket and extracted the money Aaron had given him.

Taking it from him with one hand, Aaron stroked Elijah's hair away from his face with the other, coaxing the shorter man to tilt his head back for another kiss.

At the first touch of their lips Aaron sensed the same shot of alarm racing through Elijah's body as before. The younger man tensed and pressed his hands against Aaron's chest in an instinctive effort to keep their torsos apart.

Aaron paid no attention to that, he just kept it all nice and slow, giving Elijah plenty of time to work out what was going on. The instinctive denial only lasted a second before Elijah's lips parted and welcomed him.

Aaron allowed their lips to linger together for several minutes as he thoroughly explored the Elijah mouth. Gradually, Elijah began to kiss him back and lean into Aaron's touch. But the gents' room wasn't the place for more than that.

A few brief kisses so Elijah could remember his first time started as a fantasy were one thing. But good memories were best built somewhere else—and Aaron was so determined that there would only be good memories for Elijah, everything else became secondary to that.

Finally, Aaron forced himself to break the kiss. Elijah tried to lean up and recapture the contact but Aaron held him easily in check.

"Come home with me," he whispered, trailing his lips back to Elijah's ear.

"No, I…"

Elijah gasped. His grip on Aaron's shirt tightened as Elijah pulled him closer, even while Aaron was sure Elijah's mind was desperate to push him away.

Aaron smiled and brushed their lips together. It wasn't even a real kiss, just a brief contact to tease Elijah with the promise of more. "I don't kiss and tell. There are only two people who will know what we do—you and me."

Elijah swallowed, licked his lips and blinked up at Aaron. A second passed and he bowed his head, until his temple came to rest on Aaron's shoulder. "This is a bad idea."

Aaron waited to find out what possible reason he could have for thinking that.

"Louisa is still waiting for me at the bar."

Stroking his hair, Aaron just let the boy lean against him while he made his decision.

"If I leave with you, she'll nag me into telling her everything."

Aaron continued to wait, calling on every bit of patience he had at his disposal. There was nothing left for him to say now.

"Unless she didn't know?" Elijah mused. He lifted his head.

"You could simply tell her you're leaving," Aaron allowed, making sure his expression remained blank. "It's your business where you go after that."

Elijah's tongue flickered out to taste his lips again, as if something of Aaron's kiss still lingered there and he couldn't stop tasting it again and again.

All of a sudden, the door leading into the bathroom swung open. Elijah turned his eyes up to Aaron, as if he could somehow fix the interruption with a simple click of his fingers.

A moment passed before Elijah seemed to remember that he was still standing in Aaron's loose embrace. Fear flooded his eyes. Aaron reluctantly stepped back so Elijah could move away from the sink.

The spell between them broken, Aaron doubted that tonight was going to get any more interesting than it already had, but walking away from Elijah was still unthinkable. The submissive was like a newborn colt who hadn't quite got his hooves beneath him. Aaron was still responsible for whatever happened to him next—even if he wasn't destined to get off on it.

"Where?" Elijah asked.

Or maybe the interesting part of the night was just starting…

Aaron stared down at his new friend for a second. "My place," he decided. "It's not far. We can walk there from here."

Elijah took a deep breath and nodded. "I'll…" He looked down at the money in his grasp, then at the guy who'd finished at the row of urinals and was already washing his hands.

The man wasn't making the least effort not to eavesdrop and the conclusions he'd already drawn were obvious. So was the fresh panic swirling in Elijah's eyes.

Stepping straight into the boy's space, Aaron wiped the embarrassment away with a soft, slow kiss that would immediately mark out Elijah as his lover rather than his whore. Pushing past the second of tense resistance, Aaron let Elijah relax into the kiss before he stepped back once more.

Elijah blinked up at him.

Aaron had never seen any man look less like a jaded rent boy in his life. "Go and speak to your cousin, sweet. I'll see you outside in five minutes."

Nodding, blushing vividly, Elijah fled.

Aaron slid the money into his pocket, turned around and folded his arms across his chest, completely unwilling to be chased out of any room so easily.

Elijah was his. Perhaps only for the night, but still, while Elijah was his, Aaron felt more than entitled to warn other guys away from him.

"Pretty," the other guy observed.

"Yes," Aaron agreed.

"A pity he isn't trade. He'd make a fortune!"

Aaron let his expression speak for him.

The guy smiled at first, but he quickly seemed to turn nervous. Clearing his throat, he edged crabwise out of the room, apparently not inclined to turn his back with a man who looked ready to swing at him.

Aaron shook his head and rubbed the bridge of his nose with thumb and forefinger as he was left alone in the room. This was...against all the odds, it actually seemed like this was going to work.

While Aaron waited for a minute or two, giving Elijah time to speak to his cousin, he pressed the heel of his right hand to his straining fly. Apparently there were still submissives out there who could call to both his dominant side and his cock.

When Aaron walked out of the gents, he made a point of not looking towards the bar, where he remembered seeing Louisa and Elijah sitting after they first arrived. Aaron headed straight for the coat check and the door.

Stepping out into the cold night air a moment or two later, Aaron shrugged on his suit jacket and found an appropriate place to lean against the wall on the opposite side of the narrow street. The chances of Elijah getting away from his cousin in five minutes were miniscule. Aaron settled down to wait.

The unfamiliar bulk of something in his jacket pocket reminded him that his tie was still rolled up in there. But it had certainly been worth rushing to the club straight from the office after working late that evening.

Smiling at the empty street, Aaron let the anticipation gradually build inside him. There was something magical about a man's first time with another man when it went right. When it went wrong...

Aaron shook his head and pushed his own memories away as they threatened to overwhelm him. Tonight was going to be about the memories Elijah would build, not old memories that Aaron had shoved into a back corner of his mind a long time ago.

Tonight would be all about good first-time memories—ones that Elijah would look back on in a few years' time and smile about, or maybe even blush over. Aaron's quiet little smile became somewhat lopsided. Make that *certainly* blush over. It would take a long time for a man like Elijah to grow out of the sweetness Aaron saw in him.

In a flurry of flailing limbs, Elijah rushed out of the club, looking for all the world as if the demons of hell were on his heels. Aaron somehow managed to keep a straight face.

Elijah finally spotted Aaron and, pushing his hands deep into his pockets, quickly crossed the road to stand in front of him. He obviously hadn't planned any further than that. Stopping a few feet away, he looked up at Aaron, glanced away, then brought his gaze back to Aaron's feet and kept it there.

Chapter Four

"I wasn't sure if you'd still be here," Elijah whispered.

Aaron smiled slightly. As if any man with taste could have left after only five minutes. "Ready to go?" he asked, pushing himself away from the wall.

Elijah nodded. His hands were shoved in his jeans pockets, his shoulders hunched. Aaron wasn't sure if he was trying to stop any inclination towards nervous fidgeting or if he was trying to disguise the tent in his jeans. Either way, with nothing more than his long-sleeved T-shirt to protect him from the late evening's chill, his posture just made him appear all the closer to freezing to death.

Automatically shrugging off his suit jacket, Aaron casually dropped it around Elijah's shoulders.

Elijah jerked away as if he'd thought Aaron was going to hit him — or maybe as if he was scared he was going to try to jump him right there in the street.

He looked up at Aaron, then down at the jacket. "You don't have to... I mean, now *you'll* be cold."

Aaron completely ignored his protests. When he turned to walk towards his flat, Elijah fell into step beside him without any further objection. They made their journey in silence. Elijah already had more than enough to think about. It seemed to Aaron that asking him to make polite conversation would have been cruel. Of course, the hush had absolutely nothing to do with Aaron's complete inability to think of a damn thing to say.

By the time they reached the door to his flat and Aaron stepped politely back to let Elijah in first, nervous energy poured off him so thickly, he might as well have been climbing a scaffold towards a noose.

Aaron took a deep breath, hoping his own nerves weren't so obvious.

"You've got a nice place," Elijah offered as Aaron directed him towards the living room. "Somehow Louisa convinced me it would be a great idea for us to share a place, since we moved into the city at the same time." He seemed to be completely fascinated by one of the buttons on the borrowed jacket. He didn't once look up from it.

"She stayed at the club?" Aaron checked, slowly closing the gap between them.

"Yeah, she found some new friends." Elijah smiled as he shook his head and glanced up at Aaron through his lashes. "It takes a woman like Louisa to walk into a gay bar and find enough bi-guys for a party."

Aaron took another step forward. He now stood so close, Elijah had to tilt his head back to look him in the eye.

"Your jacket," Elijah suddenly remembered. He removed it and handed it over.

Aaron took it from him and tossed it over the back of the sofa, without ever breaking eye contact.

"Sweet?" he asked as he stepped closer still, until they were almost touching.

"Yes?"

Mentally nodding his approval at Elijah's easy acceptance of the nickname, Aaron leaned in until his lips almost brushed against the boy's ear and whispered, "You'll have a lot more fun tonight if you don't hyperventilate."

Elijah blushed, but he smiled too, some of the tension drained out of him.

"Good boy. Now, pick a safe word," Aaron ordered.

"What? I thought… I mean… You didn't…"

Aaron placed a fingertip across Elijah's lips, unwilling to listen to another half-finished sentence. "I'm not suggesting we get up to anything kinky, sweet. But I'm pretty sure you're going to say no to a lot of things tonight—not because you really don't like the idea of them, but because you're used to telling the whole world that you don't like men. We both need to know when you're saying no out of habit and when you really mean it."

Elijah listened to the explanation very carefully. Finally, he nodded.

That was it.

Aaron waited, but eventually it was obvious Elijah wasn't going to be the one to speak first. "After you pick the word, you might want to tell me what it is, sweet."

Blinking those big blue eyes up at him, Elijah made his decision. "Tabitha."

Aaron nodded his acceptance as a matter of form. "Any particular reason?"

"It's Louisa's middle name. Whenever anyone in the family uses it, everyone knows things have turned really serious."

"Then if you say Tabitha everything will stop," Aaron said.

"And if I say no?" Elijah asked.

Aaron brushed their lips together, very gently. He wasn't entirely sure who he was trying to reassure with the move. "Everything might stop. Or we might just change direction. Or I might give you a little nudge to see if you're telling me the truth. I'm not out to hurt you, sweet." *Not more than you'd enjoy anyway…*

"I believe you."

So damn trusting…

Another touch of the lips and Aaron slowly deepened the kiss until he eventually coaxed Elijah to reciprocate. As the minutes passed and their tongues danced together, Elijah lifted his hands and tentatively threaded them into Aaron's hair. Time went on. His touch became more demanding as he tried to take control of the kiss.

That wasn't going to happen. Easing back regardless of Elijah's murmured protests, Aaron stared down into his eyes.

"Do you like kissing men, sweet?" he whispered.

As if he hadn't actually realised Aaron was a man until those words hit in the air between them, Elijah hesitated, pulling away from Aaron's loose embrace.

Aaron stroked his fingers through Elijah's hair again. Even as he leaned into the contact with him, Elijah frowned.

It would have been so easy to make Elijah forget everything and let the younger man simply lose himself in the pleasure and friction between their bodies. Aaron touched their lips together.

But, no. That wouldn't make a happy memory in the long run. Taking a slightly shaky breath, Aaron let the kiss linger on.

Elijah's lips had no trouble telling him how much he liked feeling another man's mouth moving against his. It was only his voice which seemed to be stubbornly closeted.

Aaron wanted the words. The need for them was like an ache deep inside him. But his needs weren't the important ones. If he couldn't say it, then Aaron was sure Elijah would be just as well served by *any* step he took on his own, anything that proved to them both that he was something more than driftwood being carried along, bobbing helplessly on a fast current.

"Are you turned on?" Aaron asked.

Elijah subtly tried to angle his body away from Aaron in an effort to disguise his arousal—even as he leaned in, hoping for another kiss.

Aaron took half a step back. "Show me."

Elijah swayed towards him, only to stop short. A frown gathered on his brow. "What?"

Aaron held out his hand, palm forward, fingers as relaxed as he could make them. "Take hold of my wrist, press my palm against your fly and show me if you're turned on."

Elijah looked at Aaron's hand as if he had never seen that particular arrangement of fingers and thumbs before. "I…"

Aaron simply waited him out.

Biting his lip, blushing furiously, Elijah seemed to decide that Aaron was right about it being easier to show rather than tell. Or maybe he just wanted to be touched as much as Aaron wanted to touch him. Whatever the reason, Elijah took hold of Aaron's hand

and put it on his crotch. There was no force behind Elijah's fingers as they pressed lightly upon the back of his hand. The contact was barely there.

Aaron could only just feel the heat from Elijah's body though the denim, he could barely make out the fact he was hard. "No," he corrected gently. "Hold my hand against your cock properly, sweet."

Elijah, flushing vividly, still avoiding looking at Aaron's hand or his face, covered Aaron's hand with his own, carefully lining up their fingers in the process.

"That's right, sweet," Aaron whispered, leaning forward and kissing Elijah softly, reassuringly.

Even as he spoke, Aaron felt himself grow more confident too. The world wasn't such a different place to the one he remembered after all. "Now, press yourself into my hand. That's right, just lean into it."

Elijah did as he was told, rubbing his erection on Aaron's gently cupped hand. His eyeslids dropped closed at the first touch firm enough to be felt past the denim. He gasped, pure awe flooding the shocked little intake of breath.

Aaron smiled down at him and began to stroke Elijah's cock. Elijah bit down on his bottom lip but he couldn't keep back the whimper. Still holding Aaron's hand in place, he thrust helplessly into his first real contact with a man.

Even while he was still hidden away, Aaron was easily able to tell Elijah was well hung, but that wasn't nearly enough information. He wanted to see him. Aaron wanted everything. Pushing down his own impatient arousal as best he could, he allowed himself nothing more than the minor release of one real kiss.

The teasing, promising brushes of lips were temporarily forgotten. This kiss was all about having complete possession of another person's mouth. Just for a few moments, Aaron let himself forget that he'd spend the rest of the night going slow and being patient, he pushed aside the pleasure he'd take in awakening Elijah's inner submissive and took what he wanted for himself.

Keeping his hand where it was, continuing to massage Elijah's cock, Aaron tightened his grip on Elijah's hair with his other hand and tipped Elijah's head back. The boy's mouth was so sweet and he tried so hard to keep up.

He couldn't, of course. He wasn't used to big hands holding him in place, he wasn't used to having to tilt his head back to reach a taller lover's lips. He wasn't used to kissing someone he actually wanted to kiss.

Gasping out his pleasure, Elijah clung to Aaron's body, his hands sliding into his hair, across his shoulders, exploring what had to be very unfamiliar layers of muscle on his partner.

Walking him backwards, Aaron pushed Elijah against the living room wall. The only sign he gave of noticing that he was trapped between plaster and Aaron was the use Elijah tried to make of the sudden leverage at his disposal. Pressing his back on the wall, he pushed his erection harder into Aaron's hand.

It would have been so easy to tumble Elijah onto the floor. Aaron knew the boy wouldn't say his safe word. He wouldn't say no, wouldn't push him away. Elijah was way past the point where any man could reasonably be expected to think of anything except the ache in his balls and the need in his cock.

But Aaron couldn't let that happen. He'd never be able to look Elijah in the eye again if he did. Hell, he wouldn't be able to look *himself* in the eye.

Pushing himself away from both Elijah and the wall, Aaron settled his hands on the wall on either side of Elijah's head and stared down at the younger man. Elijah was lost and the confusion in his eyes told Aaron just how desperate he was for direction. Damn it! Aaron was supposed to be the calm rational one. He wasn't supposed to feel as out of control as a teenager in the back seat of his father's car.

"I want to see you," Aaron announced. His voice was rough with arousal and he didn't have quite enough control to make the demand sound like a request.

Blinking up at him, Elijah nodded his acceptance of the idea in principle, but he didn't go so far as to move a single muscle in an effort to make it a reality.

"Now," Aaron specified.

Taking Elijah's hand, he led him along the hallway and into the master bedroom. Closing the door behind him, Aaron looked over the space laid out before him. It was a good-sized bedroom, half filled by a huge king-sized bed.

It was a *real* bed, not a fold out, put-up, lumpy mattress with springs that dug in your back or a frame that rattled while you screwed or got screwed. It was a real bed where two men could enjoy each other's bodies without worrying that one would fall off.

It was somewhere one man could introduce another to the pleasures that could be found in his arms without rushing him, or hurting him. It was a space where there would be room for patience as well as sex, for care and concern as well as lube and condoms.

Aaron nodded to himself. Everything was okay. He could do this.

Elijah barely spared more than a glance at the room Aaron led him into. It had four walls, a ceiling, a carpet and a bed—big deal. He could see a room any time he wanted.

All of Elijah's attention remained focused entirely on Aaron himself. He stared up at him as they stood just inside the bedroom doorway, unable to drag his eyes away.

There was over a yard of carpet between them. That was wrong. A voice in the back of Elijah's head screamed that even a millimetre of space was completely unacceptable. Wasting what could easily be his only chance to be close to Aaron was damn near criminal.

This was it—Aaron was it.

Suddenly Elijah knew with complete and utter certainty that Aaron was the spark that had been missing from all his previous attempts at wanting to get past anything more intimate than a polite handshake with another person.

"Let me see you, sweet," Aaron said as he finally turned to face Elijah. His voice was deep and gentle.

The calmness Elijah heard in him, spread slowly into Elijah's mind.

His pulse gradually slowed, his breaths came more easily. Elijah looked down at where he was fidgeting with the hem of his T-shirt. Taking a firmer grip on the material, he pulled the thin cotton over his head.

Standing in front of Aaron, and now stripped to the waist, he suddenly felt like a little boy looking up to a real man. The memory of Aaron's muscles under his hands made him greedy to reach out and touch again, but he hesitated, twisting his shirt in his hands, unsure about everything in the world.

Aaron quickly solved that problem. Taking the shirt from Elijah, he tossed it on the chair in the corner and pulled Elijah closer by his belt loops. Stroking his knuckles along those lines of muscle visible across Elijah's abs, Aaron studied him with what looked like complete approval.

Elijah relaxed a fraction—enough to force a full breath into his lungs, at least. If Aaron was pleased with him, that was all that mattered.

Aaron's hands didn't miss an inch of Elijah's skin as they casually explored his body. His touch was warm, his fingertips far rougher than Elijah would have expected a fellow office worker's hands to be. Elijah's skin ached for more. He needed to feel Aaron's entirely naked body move against his. He needed…

Elijah closed his eyes. He needed more than he knew how to put into words. The only thing he was really sure about was that Aaron would be able to provide whatever it was.

Aaron didn't once hesitate or apologise for his actions. His palms slid over Elijah's skin, moving across his chest in broad strokes before he teasingly turned his attention to tracing the line of pale brown hair that led from Elijah's belly button down to the waistband of his jeans. Without any warning, Aaron's fingers moved back up to circle one of Elijah's nipples, teasing the taut nub between strong fingers as it plead for his attention.

"You're stunning, sweet," Aaron whispered.

Elijah didn't agree, but there were more important things to say than that. "You?" he asked, tracing the line between Aaron's shirt and his waistband with his fingertips.

"Go ahead," Aaron allowed.

Elijah couldn't make his fingers work properly, especially when Aaron apparently saw no need to cease his caresses just because Elijah was trying to remember how to make buttons slide through the impossibly tiny holes in the fabric.

Finally, he was done. Elijah moved his hands over Aaron's shoulders, carefully pushing the material back out of the way. The fabric slipped down his arms and drifted down to the floor, but Elijah barely spared it a glance.

Aaron had to live in the gym. There was no other explanation for a body that perfect. Each muscle was flawlessly defined for Elijah's inspection and he soon became enthralled with examining them. Perhaps if some of his old girlfriends had looked more like body builders than fashion models he'd have had more fun with them.

Stepping closer, working entirely on instinct, Elijah pressed a kiss to Aaron's shoulder. The temptation to taste him became impossible to resist, and Elijah lapped against his skin as he ran his lips along Aaron's collar bone.

The texture was addictive. Elijah mouthed and nuzzled his way down Aaron's chest with his tongue, relishing each inch of flesh that passed beneath his lips. Wiry blond hairs teased his lips until, bending his knees, Elijah dipped his head further and captured one dark pink nipple between his lips. Working entirely on instinct, he sucked gently around it.

Nothing could have been less like kissing a woman that way. The hard, flat plane of the muscle lying just under the skin, the dusting of hairs that encircled the nub, it was all so perfect.

If Aaron had any objection to anything Elijah did, he didn't mention it. Finally sure in his own mind that there were lots of things he really did want to do with another person, that the problem had always lain with his partner's gender rather than him, lack of chastisement was all the encouragement Elijah needed.

He continued to kiss his way down Aaron's body, savouring each taste on his tongue, until he suddenly found himself on his knees before Aaron, with no accurate idea of how he got there.

Even he wasn't so inexperienced he didn't know what a man would expect to happen next when someone knelt in front of him. A line of kisses down a man's body could only have one logical destination. Elijah hesitated, just for a moment.

He considered the line of Aaron's erection through his trousers. Aaron was turned on. That was a good start.

Elijah lifted one hand to undo Aaron's fly, but his split second of hesitation must have been too long. Aaron caught hold of Elijah's hand and tugged him back up onto his feet.

Not giving Elijah time to explain that he really did want to try—that he wanted to taste Aaron's cock so badly that his head was spinning with the need to feel how Aaron's shaft slid deep into his mouth—Aaron pulled him close.

The height difference between them wasn't so great that they couldn't line up perfectly. Lips to lips. Bare chest to chest. Cock to cock.

Aaron's hands gripped Elijah's arse, dragging him closer so they could thrust against each other. All the overpowering sensations the kiss in the other room had inspired inside Elijah, returned. He gasped into Aaron's mouth, and rubbed himself blatantly against the larger man's body.

Wave after wave of pure bliss raced through Elijah's veins, every one of them heading straight for his cock. Suddenly, fear joined Elijah's pleasure. He pushed at

Aaron's shoulders, desperately trying to put some distance between them.

He was not going to ruin everything by coming in his boxers, he couldn't let that happen. Without any warning, Elijah found himself standing a full yard away from Aaron. He stared across at him, barely able to catch his breath.

Aaron studied him in return. Several moments passed before he stepped closer and silently offered Elijah an impossibly gentle little kiss. It was chaste and sweet, and obviously designed to calm someone Aaron thought was on the verge of a panic attack.

Elijah blushed.

Getting up and staying up had taken a lot of hard work and surreptitious fantasising on his part when he had tried to mess around with women. Trust his luck, if the only way he could have sex with women was to think about men, and the only way he could last long enough to have sex with a man was to think about women.

Elijah knew he had to say something, explain why he had pushed Aaron away. He had to somehow manage to not look like an idiot. "I was afraid I was going to..." He waved his hand around vaguely as words failed him.

Aaron smiled slightly. He stroked Elijah's fly with the back of his fingers. There was nothing vague about how his hands moved. "These need to go," Aaron said, tugging lightly at the top button.

Elijah couldn't agree more. He was so hard within the tight confines, they were practically castrating him.

"Take them off."

Elijah was more than willing to be obedient if all the orders Aaron intended to give him were like that.

With more enthusiasm than coordination, he pushed the denim down his legs, dragging his boxers with them. He kicked them off, along with his shoes and socks, all in one messy bundle.

He wasn't going to think about the fact that he was naked in a room with a man who was still half-dressed. Elijah knew that would just make him more nervous than ever. No, he was going to focus on getting Aaron just as naked as he was as quickly as possible. That was a much better plan.

Elijah trailed his fingers across Aaron's belt and the skin just above it at the same time.

Aaron nodded his permission before quickly bringing their lips together once more. The kiss didn't help Elijah's coordination at all. A lifetime seemed to pass before he was eventually able to undo Aaron's trousers and push the fabric out of his way. He tried to blindly catch Aaron's underwear so he could push that away too, but his fingers only found bare skin. Commando. Elijah slid his arms around Aaron's body. Pulling the larger man closer, Elijah gathered enough confidence to move his hands over Aaron's buttocks and palm his arse.

Somehow Aaron was able to kick off his shoes and his trousers without breaking the kiss. Then, all at once, full-frontal naked body contact!

Elijah frantically ran his hands over Aaron's skin, helplessly trying to explore all of him at the same time, too desperate to get a bit of everything to savour anything properly.

As they thrust, their cocks rubbed against each other's bodies and smeared pre-cum over each other's skin. Elijah's mind whirled faster and faster, unable to process anything in its confusion.

Aaron pulled away. Elijah frowned and shook his head. He understood that well enough. Any air between them was a bad thing. Then, Aaron slipped a hand into the gap between their bodies and wrapped a strong hand around Elijah's erection. Elijah cut his protest short.

Whimpering, stretching up on tiptoes, Elijah desperately tried to thrust into the inviting channel of palm and fingers. But Aaron simply lifted his hand in time with Elijah's thrusts. He still received nothing more than Aaron seemed inclined to provide.

Breaking the kiss, Elijah looked up into Aaron's eyes trying to work out what Aaron wanted from him, what he needed do to convince Aaron to let him come. As he stilled, Aaron looked down between their bodies as he whispered.

"Watch, I want you to be able remember how your cock looks in my hand."

Elijah quickly followed both his lover's gaze and his order. Aaron's hand was so big, so strong, as it wrapped around Elijah's shaft, stroking him properly now that he was frozen in position and willingly giving all control over to Aaron.

Elijah watched as Aaron's hand closed around the head on the up stroke, twisting slightly to provide a moment of perfect friction. Elijah fought to keep his eyes open. As they fluttered closed in spite of his eager attention, Aaron whispered to him again.

"Watch."

Taking half a step forward, Aaron altered his grip and enclosed both of their erections at the same time. Two achingly hard cocks, flushed dark with arousal, and the paler skin of Aaron's hand circling them, pressing sensitive flesh against sensitive flesh. Elijah had never seen anything more magnificent.

He gasped, completely enthralled by the soft, silkiness of cock against cock and the rougher skin of Aaron's hand.

"Give me your hand," Aaron demanded.

Mesmerised, Elijah added his hand to the mix. It was smaller than Aaron's, the fingers a shade or two paler. Matching his movements to Aaron's, Elijah helplessly watched their combined movements push him closer and closer to his orgasm.

It was too soon, it was too much, but he still couldn't stop. If this was all he managed to do tonight, it would still be the best sexual experience he ever had. It would still be—

No. Elijah shook his head and managed to pull away. Aaron grunted his frustration at him, but Elijah wasn't going far. He dropped to his knees again. He had to at least try. If nothing else, he had to give Aaron more than his hand, he had to make it something his lover could take pleasure from too. He deserved so much more than a hand-job.

Encircling Aaron's swollen shaft with his fingers, Elijah leaned in, mouth open. Reaching out to Aaron with his tongue, he lapped at the head, tasting the pre-cum, as it began to leak onto his tongue.

Strong, musky and so undeniably male—Elijah closed his eyes and savoured the taste. Flattening his tongue, Elijah tried to swirl it around the head of Aaron's cock and coax more taste from him. But his tongue didn't seem to belong to him. Years' worth of talking and eating apparently hadn't prepared him to do far more interesting things with it.

Moaning with an addictive combination of frustration and delight, Elijah ran his fingers up and down Aaron's shaft until he finally built up the courage to take more than the head. Sure he was never going to fit the whole shaft in his mouth, but still desperate to take as much as he could, Elijah pushed his head forward until Aaron's glans touched the back of his throat.

His body protested to the unfamiliar sensation. His throat threatened to close up. Elijah whimpered his frustration and pushed forward again. His gag reflex kicked in full force, making him pull back once more.

Damn it, this shouldn't be so complicated. Cock. Mouth. You had to be a special kind of idiot to screw that up—even on a first attempt.

Aaron's hands came to rest lightly on Elijah's shoulders, his thumbs stroking up and down the curve of his neck. Elijah couldn't bring himself to look up and see the expression on Aaron's face. Aaron's disappointment would be unbearable.

Elijah dipped his head again. Damn it! He still couldn't make his mouth and throat do what he wanted them to do. His lips barely kissed his fist before his throat gained complete control of his brain and made him retreat.

Suddenly, Aaron tried to pull Elijah to his feet. Elijah murmured his protest, lips still wrapped around Aaron's cock, his tongue still struggling to work out what to do as he fought to stay on his knees.

"Up," Aaron demanded.

Heat raced to Elijah's cheeks as he realised that his fumbling had already worn out the more experienced man's patience. He saw little choice but to let Aaron make him to stand.

"Teach me?" Elijah whispered, before Aaron had a chance to say anything.

Aaron frowned as if he had no idea what Elijah was talking about.

One hand resting on Aaron's chest, Elijah forced himself to meet Aaron's eyes and hold his gaze for several long moments. In that second, he knew what he really wanted. There was one thing that was even more important than finding out what he enjoyed for himself, what gave him the pleasure he'd been unable to find with any female lover.

"Teach me how to make it good for you?" Elijah asked.

Chapter Five

Teaching… After being celibate for so long since Charles' departure from his life, Aaron wasn't sure he had the restraint to do anything that required so much higher brain function.

The memory of Charles and their last encounter rushed to the front of Aaron's mind. Every muscle in his body tensed. For a moment, Aaron thought that the sudden recollection would soften his cock, the same way it had with all the other men he'd tried to screw after their break-up.

Aaron stared down into Elijah's eyes for several long moments. There was no guile in the boy at all. What a man saw was what he got with Elijah. There was nothing to fear in being with him, nothing to stop him remaining as hard as a rock.

Aaron shook his head at himself, trying to bring his mind completely back on line.

The moment he saw Elijah's expression change, Aaron knew Elijah had misinterpreted the gesture. He caught hold of Elijah's arm and stopped his retreat before he had the chance to develop any kind of momentum.

"There'll be no teaching," Aaron told him, as he scrambled for a way to cover his slip. "No essays. No presentations in front of a blackboard."

Elijah blinked up at him.

Aaron gave his best shot at looking like someone who was considering the possibilities very carefully. "But perhaps a few practical lessons never hurt anyone..."

Elijah smiled slightly and immediately nodded his willingness to be an incredibly eager student.

Aaron closed the gap between them. The kiss was sweet and gentle. Aaron drew out the tender touch of lips while he guided Elijah to walk slowly backwards.

Elijah jumped when he hit the edge of the bed. He jerked away from Aaron to look over his shoulder as if he thought another man might have crept into the room, as if Aaron would let that happen.

Aaron didn't say a word. He just nudged Elijah to sit on the bed. The younger man quickly shuffled backwards to the middle of the mattress, making plenty of room for Aaron to join him. Ignoring the wide expanse of empty bed, Aaron slowly crawled up and over the smaller man's body. Elijah had little choice but to lie back as Aaron supported his larger frame above him.

Aaron pressed another brief peck against Elijah's lips.

Pulling back, he placed another kiss upon the younger man's collar bone, in much the same way Elijah had when he'd begun to explore him with his mouth just a few minutes before.

Copying Elijah's exact route, Aaron trailed his lips down to the younger man's nipple. Elijah arched off the bed, pressing his chest towards Aaron's mouth. Either he was naturally very sensitive, or Elijah was suffering from the sheer overload of new stimuli that had rained down on him that day.

When Aaron sucked around the tiny peak, Elijah let out a half cry. His hand came to rest on the back of Aaron's head. There could be no doubt how much he loved what Aaron was doing. Elijah made no attempt to hide anything at all from his lover. He let out a disappointed whimper when Aaron continued the journey down his body.

There was little hair to get in the way of Aaron's lips. It was as if Elijah had purposely decided to grow as few strands as possible, just to make sure a dominant had all the access to him that he might ever want.

As he moved passed Elijah's abs, Aaron smiled against the boy's stomach, enjoying the relative novelty of the fine strands that made up a sweet little happy trail. He followed them like bread crumbs until he reached Elijah's cock.

The younger man had lifted himself up onto his elbows at some point, and as Aaron glanced up along his body, Elijah stared back at him in wonder. Their eyes met. Elijah's hands clawed at the bed sheets, as he desperately sort for self-control while Aaron wrapped one hand around Elijah's erection and steadied it with his fist.

The sheet came away from one corner of the bed when Aaron dipped his head and deftly circled the tip of Elijah's cock with his tongue. Aaron found his lips quirking into a smile, even while his head remained bowed over his lover's lap. No, he'd truly never need to worry there was more going on in Elijah's head than what showed on his face.

Elijah barely seemed able to breathe as Aaron took his cock into his mouth for the first time. It was hard for Aaron to remember back to a time when he had been as inexperienced as the man before him, when so many things had been fresh and everything a new sensation to be cherished. But, when he looked up into Elijah's eyes, Aaron felt a little bit of that wonder at the world come back to him.

The simple fact that there was no possibility of any half-forgotten booby traps being along the path before him allowed Aaron to relax for the first time in months. Nothing he did could drag up bad memories of the way another man had screwed Elijah over in the past. All Aaron had to do was make sure the memories he created with Elijah were good ones, and he could do that.

Bobbing his head lower, Aaron took Elijah's shaft deep into his mouth again and again. Pre-cum danced on his tongue. Elijah gasped and tried to thrust his cock even further between Aaron's lips.

Taking the submissive by the hand, Aaron effectively led him slowly forward and let him peek over the edge of current boundaries, into the possibilities that were waiting for him when he was finally allowed to come. Then he straightened up. Elijah's cock curved back towards his stomach, slicked with saliva and still freely leaking pre-cum.

"Wait, please?" Elijah's hand darted forward and tugged frantically at Aaron's hand, trying to drag him back.

Aaron shook his head. There was no way in hell Elijah would stop himself coming if he did that. "Roll over for me."

For several long seconds, Elijah looked up at him with so much confusion, Aaron was almost prepared to believe that Elijah really didn't know why any gay man would ask another guy to turn his arse towards him. Suddenly, Elijah's mind seemed to catch up with events. His eyes opened wide. He scrambled to turn over, limbs losing any illusion of co-ordination in his haste.

Aaron grinned down at the back of Elijah's head as Elijah arranged himself on his stomach before him. Elijah's legs were stretched out on opposite sides of where Aaron's knees rested further down the mattress, and he doubted that Elijah had even realised that he was effectively spreading himself in rampant invitation.

Setting his hands on the mattress to either side of Elijah's body, Aaron leant forward and pressed a kiss between his shoulder blades. Somehow he resisted the desire to rub his cock along the cleft of Elijah's buttocks in the process.

Elijah twisted around as if trying to look behind him, but he stopped as soon as Aaron put a hand on his shoulder and nudged him to lie back down.

"Just relax. If I am teaching any part of you right now, it's your body not your brain. Don't overthink it. Just let yourself feel it all." Aaron whispered the last words against the small of Elijah's back, before adding another kiss there.

A moment later, he placed a third kiss on the skin right at the base of Elijah's spine. A gentle nudge to the inside of his knees convinced Elijah to spread his legs wider than ever. At the same time, Elijah arched his back, as if pure instinct was telling him exactly how to offer his arse to another man, without him needing to say a word.

Aaron dipped his head again. His lips brushed very gently across the tight ring of muscle around Elijah's hole. The boy gasped. His buttocks tensed. But he didn't pull away.

Another gentle nudge to the inside of Elijah's thighs, prompting Elijah to wriggle on the mattress until he finally got his knees under him. Lifting himself off the mattress, he rushed to make his hole much more easily accessible.

Aaron gave Elijah a few moments to find a position he could maintain comfortably before he reached out to him again. With one hand settled on the curve of each of Elijah's buttocks, coaxing the cheeks slightly apart, Aaron bowed his head once more.

As far as Elijah was concerned, breathing was now something that happened to other people. His body was no longer his to command. His thoughts whirled in a dozen different directions as far too many nerve endings desperately fought to get his attention and relay their garbled messages.

Aaron could breathe, though, Elijah had no doubt about that. His breath caressed the sensitive strip of skin between Elijah's buttocks.

Elijah murmured his approval into the mattress as his arms trembled beneath him and he helplessly lowered himself onto his elbows and brought his cheek to rest on the bed sheet.

A lifetime seemed to pass before Aaron's lips caressed him again. Elijah whimpered. He bit down on his bottom lip, but there was no way in hell he could stop the stream of pleasure-filled sounds leaving his mouth.

Aaron's tongue circled around the very edge of Elijah's hole, sending waves of pure bliss rushing through his body. Apparently everyone on the planet had simply forgotten to tell him that his arse was connected directly to his cock—and that even the mildest touch of a hot, wet tongue placed there could be more erotic than he'd ever thought possible — that it could be even more pleasurable than the way Aaron had kissed the tip of his cock a few moments before.

Unable to remain still, Elijah rocked his hips. He tugged at the sheet again, but for some reason the cotton wasn't providing the same kind of resistance it once had. The fabric merely bunched up in his fists.

This kiss was so much more intimate than the others they'd shared. Head down, arse up, in Aaron's bed, Elijah had never felt more vulnerable. He'd never realised that knowing he was completely at another man's mercy could be so damn hot either.

Without any warning, Aaron stopped. Worse still, he pulled away.

Elijah shook his head. He had no idea if Aaron could see his head properly while he was in that position, but he shook it anyway.

"Hush."

Something else pressed against Elijah's arse then, something even slicker and more dexterous than Aaron's tongue. Fingers! Somehow, even while his brain was completely pleasure-addled, Elijah managed to work it out.

Aaron's fingers circled his hole, coated in some kind of lube. Elijah closed his eyes and stayed very still, terrified that any movement on his part might break some sort of magical spell, might make Aaron move away again and take that new kind of touch with him.

"That's right," Aaron murmured.

Elijah nodded. It was more than right, it was the most glorious thing he had ever felt. He rocked his hips again. This time, the motion didn't make Aaron pull away. One of the Aaron's fingertips pressed harder against the tight ring of muscle, until it finally slipped past it.

At that point, Elijah's brain completely gave up on any attempt to process anything. He was aware of pleasure, mixed with occasional moments of discomfort, but his mind just floated through it all, high on adrenaline, endorphins and a few emotions that Elijah would have been too scared to confront, even if he'd been capable of analysing them.

Elijah knew without any doubt that he was high on Aaron as much as all the new possibilities Aaron was introducing his body to. Almost before he realised what was happening, Elijah felt Aaron's fingers leave him.

He rolled over, already reaching for Aaron, needing to draw him closer.

There was a packet in Aaron's hand. Elijah frowned at it as he desperately tried to focus and work out what he had done wrong.

Condom.

That wasn't wrong. That was good — it was fantastic!

Elijah nodded quickly. He desperately wanted to lean forward and take it from Aaron, but his hands were shaking as it was. There was no way in hell he could have done anything with it if he had somehow gained control of the packet.

Aaron deftly tore the wrapper open and withdrew the thin sheath of latex. He rolled it over the head of his cock, then stopped. Their eyes met as Aaron took hold of Elijah's hand.

With Aaron's guidance and steadying touch, Elijah carefully rolled the condom the remainder of the way down Aaron's shaft and helped him slick the covering with extra lube.

Then, as seamlessly as if he had been doing it his whole life, Elijah lay back on the bed and tugged at Aaron's wrist, asking him to cover his body with his larger frame—asking Aaron, as politely as he knew how, to screw him senseless at the earliest convenient opportunity.

The tip of Aaron's cock came to rest against Elijah's hole. Squirming slightly, Elijah managed to pull his knees back further. Their bodies lined up a little more flawlessly.

Most of Aaron's weight was supported on his arms rather than by Elijah's body, but still he found himself in awe of his size and strength as Aaron loomed over him. One more time Elijah was reminded just how much control Aaron had over him.

He only had Aaron's word that he'd stop if he screamed out his cousin's middle name. He was no match for Aaron physically. Elijah knew he should be scared out of his wits. The only thing he actually felt was strangely serene.

Being under Aaron's control felt…right. It was how things should be. It appealed to Elijah's cock, his brain and to a part of his subconscious he was only just beginning to become aware of.

"Look up at me."

Elijah obeyed without even thinking to question the order or Aaron's right to issue it. Their eyes met. The pressure upon Elijah's hole increased as Aaron leant forward, pressing his cock against Elijah's arse the same way he had rubbed himself across Elijah's palm an entire lifetime ago.

Elijah gasped as Aaron pushed into him, the blunt head of his shaft stretching the tight ring of muscle wide open. Without any permission from Elijah's brain, Elijah's hands clawed at Aaron's shoulders, but they clung to him rather than tried to force him away.

The pain was sharp and sudden. Aaron's cock didn't feel anything like his fingers had as they'd coaxed and cajoled their way inside him. Elijah had never imagined any man's shaft could be so big, so—

"Just breathe through it," Aaron ordered.

Elijah blinked his eyes open and looked up at him.

"You're fine. Everything will be fine."

His words made Elijah smile regardless of anything else. Yes, for the first time since that night in the back seat of a shabby old car, Elijah really believed that everything would be fine. Aaron made everything fine.

As the moments passed, Elijah eased his hold on Aaron's shoulders. Very slowly, his body seemed to adapt and accept Aaron's cock being buried inside him like that. So big, so…perfect.

Elijah stared up at Aaron. The guy still hadn't moved a muscle. He was just there, patiently supporting his weight, waiting for Elijah to catch up with him. There was no annoyance to be seen in his expression, only quiet concern for his lover.

Without thinking about it, Elijah reached out and stroked his fingers down Aaron's cheek. In that moment, he'd never felt safer or more protected in his life. He'd never wanted another man to thrust his hips so badly either.

"Please?" Elijah asked. He tentatively rocked his hips, not knowing how else to ask for what he needed. Apparently he'd stumbled on exactly the right combination of code words and actions.

All his movements very controlled, very deliberate, Aaron swayed away from Elijah, sliding a little bit of his cock out from his hole, before thrusting slowly back into him.

Elijah arched against the bed as pure bliss rushed through him and set fire to nerve endings he hadn't even realised he had.

With his legs pulled back and no way to gain any sort of leverage, there was nothing Elijah could do but accept whatever Aaron chose to offer him. He was free to simply enjoy the new and wonderful world he'd stumbled into without any feeling that his lover expected more from him.

Fireworks exploded inside Elijah every time Aaron's cock rubbed against his prostate. Lightning flashed down his spine, finding new and interesting pleasure centres to earth itself into with each thrust of Aaron's hips.

Elijah stared up at Aaron's face as Aaron's thrusts gradually speeded up. The forks of lightning stabbing at every nerve ending inside Elijah's body were joined by an ominous rumble of thunder from a previously slumbering part of Elijah's mind.

His orgasm caught him off guard. Elijah came, helpless to do anything but close his eyes and watch the pretty sparkling lights as they detonated behind his eyelids, filling his mind with colour and energy he'd never even guessed at the existence of.

By the time he was able to summon up the energy and the will to open his eyes, Elijah knew that his particular bit of the world was never going to be the same again.

For one thing, he was never going to want to spend a moment of his life doing anything that prevented Aaron's cock being buried deep inside him during every waking second of his day.

But, apparently, Aaron didn't feel the same way. He pulled back at the first opportunity, his cock leaving Elijah's body aching and empty in its wake. Elijah slowly lowered his legs back onto the bed.

For some reason he half expected Aaron to disappear in a cloud of smoke, as unreal as any figment of a rich fantasy life could be. But, as soon as he had dispensed with the condom, he lay down alongside Elijah, real and reassuringly solid as the mattress dipped beneath him. There was barely any empty air left between them. The mere fact that Elijah could feel the heat radiating off Aaron's body made him feel a little better about the world.

"So," Aaron murmured softly, the words barely a whisper against Elijah's ear. "Have you decided if you're gay or not?"

Elijah couldn't help it. He turned and buried his face in the curve of Aaron's shoulder as a burst of laughter escaped him. When he lifted his head, having gained just a tiny amount of control of himself, he looked up at Aaron once more.

He still appeared completely serious. If Elijah hadn't seen the way his eyes twinkled he might have actually believed it had been a genuine question.

"I guess… I think I've known for a long time," Elijah admitted softly. "But, you know, I genuinely thought I liked girls when I was younger. I liked the idea of them in my head. But then, reality was a bit…" He shrugged. "If being with a man only turned out to be interesting in my imagination, then I'd have to face the fact that I was really out of options."

"And?" Aaron asked. "Compared to the ideas in your head?"

Elijah lowered his gaze. "Better," he whispered.

Aaron casually rested his fingers in Elijah's hair. He wound the digits through the long strands over and over again. That sort of gave Elijah permission to touch Aaron in return, in that same lazy, relaxed way.

It was as if they had known each other forever, as if they were so comfortable in each other's space neither of them ever had to worry about it anymore. It felt completely natural to lay naked on Aaron's bed with him.

Elijah was more than content to stay there drawing patterns on Aaron's skin for as long as Aaron would let him do that, maybe even until they both fell asleep all cosy and relaxed, only to wake up and start all over again tomorrow.

One night…

Elijah tried to push the words out of his head, but they kept returning, forcing their way through all the afterglow and bliss that still sparkled in the rest of his mind.

Aaron had offered him one night, nothing more. As they continued to lie there, other thoughts rushed through Elijah's head, almost faster than he could process them. Then, finally, one particular idea caught hold of his mind by the throat and pinned it against the wall. The others faded to nothing.

Suddenly, as everything that had been said that night was replayed inside his mind, Elijah had no doubt why Aaron had been willing to take a chance on someone who had no idea what they were doing.

"You like having sex with virgins," Elijah blurted out. He stumbled slightly over the virgin word, but he pushed forward regardless. This was no time for conservative measures. "That's your kink, isn't it?"

"I wouldn't say that," Aaron countered.

"What would you say then?" Elijah asked, half sitting up. "Because I'm pretty sure you wouldn't have invited me back here if you hadn't known full well that I was a…a complete novice."

"I'd say that I have quite a few kinks, and virgin hunting isn't one of them." Aaron lifted himself up onto one elbow. "But, perhaps your lack of experience was a factor," he admitted. He sounded as if he wanted his tone of voice to convey it was no big deal.

For once, Elijah found himself completely incapable of trusting whatever view of the world Aaron wanted to present to him.

Aaron stroked Elijah's hair again, tugging gently at the strands, encouraging him to look up.

Elijah pretended not to notice. If he glanced up he knew he'd end up nodding and smiling and doing whatever Aaron suggested. Aaron was the type of guy it was easy to obey. Instead, Elijah reached out and trailed his fingers along the length of Aaron's cock. Unless he was very much mistaken, Aaron would be more than capable of regaining his erection with a little bit of encouragement.

Elijah made a decision—the first he had made that night without any assistance from Aaron. If this night was all his sex life was ever going to consist of, he'd better make the most of it.

"You said one night. Is that until the sun rises tomorrow or did you just mean until we both get off?" Elijah asked slowly, testing his way forward with each carefully selected word.

Aaron considered the matter for so long Elijah had to bite the inside of his cheek to stop himself speaking up and brushing his own question aside. He stared down at Aaron's cock, imprinting the sight of it into his memory as firmly as he could, just in case it was the last time he'd see it.

"There's no rule against you staying for another round if you want to," Aaron finally allowed, in a very similar tone of voice. "Do you have anything in particular in mind?"

"Yes," Elijah rushed out, before he lost his courage completely. "I'd like you to teach me how to suck your cock using all your favourite tricks and techniques. And, if you have no objection, I'd also like you to…to tie me up or whip me, or whatever. I'd like you to show me what all your other kinks are."

Chapter Six

Aaron couldn't have kept his chuckle back for anything. He couldn't remember the last time a man had shocked him into laughing that way either, but was sure it was long before Charles had ever made an appearance in his life.

Elijah didn't join in. His cheeks turned red, but he didn't look down. He held Aaron's gaze as if far more than just his life depended on it. He seemed so determined, so very ready to launch into a campaign speech to try to convince Aaron why his plan was a good one. As if any man in his right mind would turn down an offer like that.

Slowly, Aaron let his features settle into a more serious expression. He reached out and placed his hand on the side of Elijah's neck. There was no collar there to interrupt the simple skin-on-skin connection. He wasn't an experienced submissive. He wasn't some guy Aaron had picked up in a kinky club.

Elijah wasn't someone a guy could dominate without being very careful about it.

"You're sure that's what you want?" Aaron asked.

Elijah nodded.

"How long have you been thinking about being tied up?" Aaron asked.

Elijah looked down, suddenly fascinated by the rumpled sheets.

"Or are you just offering because you think I'd like it?"

Elijah would have shrugged. His shoulder had just stared to rise when Aaron moved his hand onto it and stopped the gesture short.

"I want a real answer, sweet."

Elijah lifted his gaze. There was so much confusion in his eyes.

Aaron barely held back a sigh. "In case you're wondering, kinky games are something that *both* the guys playing are supposed to enjoy." He'd always played that way. If someone had asked him a few months ago, he'd have said that he'd *never* done anything to a lover that the man in question hadn't thoroughly enjoyed.

"I think I would like it," Elijah whispered. "I mean, I like it when you tell me what to do."

He couldn't have come up with a more perfect answer if he'd spent a decade on the scene, learning exactly how to worm his way under a dom's skin. "Good," Aaron said. "Because I like ordering you around."

Elijah smiled hopefully, and Aaron's decision was made.

"Do you remember what your safe word is?"

The younger man nodded.

Aaron had to consciously stop himself copying the gesture. One of them had to stay verbal. "Stand up."

Elijah obediently pulled himself to his feet and stood next to the bed, waiting patiently for his next order.

"Turn around."

A touch of confusion appeared in Elijah's expression, but he did as he was told without protest.

"No," Aaron corrected. "Do it again, more slowly. Let me get a good look at you."

Elijah seemed to catch up with the idea then. He blushed, but he also followed the command.

He gradually turned around, displaying each inch of his naked body for Aaron's inspection. Every movement the boy made went straight to Aaron's cock, just because he knew each move existed only because he ordered it. His attention went to Elijah's crotch. Apparently Aaron wasn't the only one who was already getting turned on by the little game.

"Stroke your cock."

From the look on Elijah's face, he couldn't have been more surprised if Aaron had asked him to stand on his head and recite the alphabet backwards.

"I want to watch you play with yourself."

Elijah's cheeks flushed something close to crimson as his hand crept forward to do Aaron's bidding. He wrapped his fingers loosely around his cock and started to gently stroke his erection.

"Sit here," Aaron ordered. He tapped the mattress next to him. "But don't stop."

Elijah sat. Aaron reached out to him and encouraged him to lean comfortably back against the pillows. Leaving him there, trusting that the mild pleasure he was being permitted to give himself would be enough to keep Elijah entertained while his lover turned his attention to other matters, Aaron walked across to the chest of drawers on the other side of the room and opened the top one.

His heart was beating so fast, it seemed impossible for the beat to get any quicker, but somehow the rhythm kicked up another notch as he stared down into the drawer.

He wasn't doing anything wrong. There was nothing evil about anything in his toy box. Aaron couldn't let Charles' parting comments rule his world forever. All those thoughts flashed through his mind but, even with his back to Elijah, Aaron made sure no hint of his emotions appeared on his face.

A good dominant solved both his submissive's and his own problems without ever betraying the slightest hint of strain. A man like Elijah had to be able to look up at his lover with complete confidence. Aaron closed his eyes for a moment.

When he was finally ready to step out of the darkness behind his lids and open his eyes, it only took him a moment to find what he wanted. Quickly picking up a leather cuff, he selected a long piece of chain to go with it.

Aaron turned back to Elijah, without any trace of anxiety on his face. The boy's hand was still wrapped around his cock, but it wasn't moving. He was completely focused on Aaron, apparently far more interested in trying to work out what the man he'd agreed to submit to was doing, than in doing what he was told.

"If you stop again without permission, I'll have to punish you," Aaron mentioned, careful to keep his tone of voice light and conversational.

"I'm sorry, I—"

Aaron arrived at the side of the bed just in time to put a fingertip over Elijah's lips.

"There's no need to apologise." Aaron took his finger away. "Whatever happens when you're submitting to me, it's down to me, not you. I get the credit when it goes well. And I get the blame when it goes badly." He looked down at the cuffs in his hand as he tried to push away thoughts that had no business invading his mind at that moment.

"Aaron?" Elijah asked, very softly.

"The only thing you need to do while you submit is to try your very best to obey each and every order I give you. If you fail, even when you put everything you have into it, that will be because I gave the wrong order or because I haven't trained you well enough to obey it, not because you're not a good enough submissive. It's important that you understand that."

Elijah nodded.

Aaron glanced down, but not at his own hands this time. Elijah's fingers weren't moving quickly, but they weren't completely stationary either.

"Good boy."

He soaked up the praise like…like a submissive who had been starved of anything like a real dominant in his life for far too long.

Elijah continued to keep his hand moving as Aaron fastened one of the leather cuffs around his wrist, and while Aaron deftly looped the chain connected to the wrist cuff up through the rails on the headboard and took hold of the opposite end of the chain, too.

Aaron rearranged the pillows on his side of the bed and stretched out there, content to just watch the show for a while. He saw Elijah glance towards him out of the corner of his eye, obviously trying like hell to work out what was going on and failing.

"Speed up a little," Aaron ordered.

Elijah turned his attention to where his hand was still moving over his cock. He dutifully began to stroke his shaft faster, but his attention didn't seem to be on what he was doing.

"Don't forget the head," Aaron reminded him. "It feels good when you play with the tip, doesn't it?"

Elijah nodded. He stared down at his cock as if he had never seen it before. His fingertips slowly circled the glans. The breath caught in his throat. His eyes fell closed as he murmured his pleasure at his own touch, as if even that seemed new and dramatic after all the other firsts he had experienced that night.

Aaron watched, completely enthralled, until he couldn't risk putting the moment off any longer. He gave a sharp tug on the chain.

Elijah's eyes flew open as his hand was jerked roughly away from his cock. "What—?" He turned to Aaron. Confusion and annoyance warred in his eyes, battling for control of his expression.

"I didn't tell you to stop."

Elijah looked at the chain in Aaron's hand. His gaze moved towards the top of the bed as he followed the metal, link by link, towards the headboard, around the wooden rail and back down to his own wrist.

Very slowly, Elijah wrapped his fingers around his cock once more.

"That's right," Aaron murmured.

He gave the boy plenty of time to regain his rhythm. Elijah had been paying attention. He paused every so often to caress the tip of his cock, smearing his pre-cum across the head. The mere fact that Aaron had expressed enjoyment at watching him do that seemed to have been enough to lodge the requirement deep in Elijah's psyche.

"Faster now, make sure each stroke goes all the way down to the base of your shaft. Half strokes don't count," Aaron warned.

Within minutes, Elijah's eyes were closed, his head tipped back upon the pillow. He did as he was told, pumping his cock, harder and faster, making every action strong and more confident than any Aaron had seen him make.

He was obviously lost in his rush towards another orgasm. His abs tensed. His legs kicked out against the mattress.

The chain snatched Elijah's hand back, just in time to make sure he had no chance of coming.

"Why—?" Elijah sat up and pushed messy chestnut curls back out of his eyes with his free hand.

"Because I can, because I have the right to make you stop and start whenever I want," Aaron said, very calmly.

Elijah's Adam's apple bobbed as he swallowed several times in succession. Oh, yes, that idea appealed to him just as much as Aaron had guessed it would.

Aaron smiled across the bed. "I—"

He didn't even need to finish the order. Elijah seemed quite capable of picking the thought straight out of his brain.

I didn't tell you to stop.

The submissive couldn't have followed the unspoken prompt more quickly if Aaron had shouted it at the top of his lungs.

Elijah didn't close his eyes this time and Aaron held his gaze as Elijah once more moved his hand towards his cock. Very gradually, without ever looking away, Aaron increased the tension on the chain.

Elijah's attention went to the cuff wrapped around his wrist. He followed the chain back to Aaron's hand. He smiled slightly as he looked back to Aaron's face and it was impossible to tell what he loved more, the control or the connection between them.

Aaron adjusted his grip on the chain slightly. Every time he moved his hand, Elijah had to tug against the cuff and the chain, had to fight against the limits Aaron was placing on his movements to get a little more pleasure for himself.

Aaron didn't deny him completely, he just carefully rationed Elijah's freedom to please himself. There was no doubt about it. Aaron saw the way Elijah responded so instinctively to it all. The pleasure in Elijah's expression wasn't all from his cock. Far more of it seemed to flow directly from his new-found submission.

That knowledge sent more adrenaline rushing through Aaron's veins more rapidly than any hard cock or tight arse ever could. His cock ached with his own need to come, but his fist remained around the chain.

Balanced on the cusp of his submission, Elijah was an angel ready to fall. All he needed was someone to catch him when he did.

Pulling smoothly on the chain, Aaron increased the tension on it even further. Elijah whimpered, but he made no actual complaint. He didn't try to shuffle up the bed and bring his cock within easier reach of his hand. He accepted it all as if he really believed Aaron had the right to make things difficult for him purely for his own amusement.

"Good boy," Aaron murmured.

There was no embarrassment to be seen in him now. Elijah obviously had far more important things to do than blush. He squirmed against the mattress and pulled harder at the cuff as he got closer to the edge.

Aaron tightened his grip on the chain in response. Elijah's movements turned frantic, his breathing erratic. Aaron never took his eyes off him. A sharp tug on the chain each time Elijah got close to the edge easily ensured that the submissive was completely incapable of driving himself to orgasm.

A sheen of sweat broke out on the younger man's skin. He bit down on his bottom lip in frustration. "Please?"

Aaron was half willing to bet his soul that Elijah had no idea he'd said the word out loud, had no inkling of how prettily he'd begged.

Releasing the tension on the chain, just a little, Aaron finally allowed Elijah just enough freedom to get what he wanted. His hand stroked faster and faster, his hips bucked as he was finally allowed to come on what had to have been at least his eighth or ninth attempt to reach his climax.

A cry tore through the air, Elijah jerked, thrusting rapidly into his hand as semen spilled onto his stomach in long creamy ropes. Each moment was captured by Aaron as a stunning mental snapshot, each one to be filed away for future reference. Next time he jacked off, Aaron knew what he'd be thinking about. And next time he woke in the middle of the night wondering if Charles had been right, he'd think about Elijah then, too.

As the moments passed, Elijah collapsed back against the mattress and fell still.

Aaron didn't move a muscle until the boy finally blinked open his eyes. Submission — that was Elijah's main kink. Whatever else he might be into, Aaron had no doubt about his need to submit. The plea for reassurance from a more dominant man shone brightly in Elijah's eyes as he turned towards his lover.

Without the slightest hesitation, Aaron pulled him across the bed and gathered Elijah close to rest with him. Elijah instantly moulded his body into the perfect shape to fit cosily in to Aaron's side.

One of the boy's legs crept forward to hook over Aaron's shin. Elijah's arm slid around Aaron's waist. Cum smeared across Aaron's skin as Elijah's torso pressed against him, but even that didn't make the moment any less perfect.

Elijah sighed softly. His breathing quickly evened out. His eyes closed. Afterglow seamlessly gave way to a content, deep slumber.

Aaron lifted his head off his pillow and peered down at Elijah's face. If there was one thing Charles had definitely been wrong about, in Elijah's case at least, was that every submissive felt a terrible pressure to serve their dominant twenty-four-seven.

Aaron smiled down at the top of Elijah's head as he laid his head back on the pillow and the boy snuggled into him. Elijah's knee stopped just short of nudging Aaron's still untended erection. He was pretty sure the night would be a good memory for Elijah, even if he had fallen asleep before Aaron had had a chance to revisit that blow-job idea with him...

* * * *

Aaron stretched out, sleepy, content and not at all inclined to pay too much attention to the sunlight streaming into his room. His bed was warm and comfortable. Anything he needed to do that day could wait. Aaron slid his hand over the sheet alongside him, searching for the one thing that would make his morning perfect.

No slumbering form lay on the other side of the bed to interrupt his hand's journey down the sheet. A frown creased Aaron's forehead. He was more than half asleep, but some part of him knew what was wrong — more wrong than it had been on any other morning. There was supposed to be someone there...

Aaron blinked open his eyes.

Something inside him gradually relaxed as he heard water running in the en-suite. Elijah hadn't left in the middle of the night. Aaron smiled at the ceiling as he stretched out and relaxed back on the bed once more.

Wonderfully instinctive submissiveness aside, the boy still had the right to go and take a leak without having to wake his lover up to ask permission. A few minutes passed before the bathroom door finally swung open.

Aaron smiled across at him, impatient to see if Elijah really was as amazing as he remembered him being and —

Clothes.

Elijah was already fully dressed when he stepped back into the bedroom. He didn't once look in Aaron's direction as he closed the bathroom door behind him. "I guess I'd better get going."

Somehow, Aaron managed to school his expression into something more appropriate and less horror stricken before Elijah looked in his direction, but he still had to grind his teeth to stop himself inviting Elijah to stay.

Hell, who was he kidding? *Ordering* Elijah to stay would be more like it.

Pushing back the blankets, Aaron sat up, swung his legs over the side of the bed and forced himself to be practical. "Of course. I'll give you a lift home."

"There's no need to—"

"Remember what I said about obedience last night?" Aaron cut in. Still completely naked, he walked towards the fully-dressed submissive.

For just a moment, the boy glanced up and met his eyes. "Yes. I remember."

His expression hid nothing. It was obviously a good memory.

The muscles in Aaron's shoulders relaxed slightly. Perhaps he hadn't screwed everything up after all. He stared down at Elijah in silence as his mind raced.

It was a good thing that Elijah was ready to leave straight away. If he hadn't been, Aaron would have had to nudge him out the door and it would have been impossible to do that without hurting him. Yes, Aaron told himself, this was all very good. It was going exactly to plan. He wasn't in the market for a boyfriend and—

Aaron took a deep breath and made a conscious effort to slow down his thoughts.

"I'm driving you home." He held up one hand when Elijah seemed to be about to speak. "This isn't up for debate."

Elijah nodded. "Okay."

"When I get out of the bathroom, you're still going to be here," Aaron stated. He wasn't sure who he was trying to convince.

Another nod was all Aaron got for his trouble.

He slipped a knuckle under Elijah's chin and made him look up once more.

"I wouldn't leave without saying goodbye," Elijah whispered.

Of course not, he was far too polite for that. He was a nice boy, and a good sub in the making to boot. He'd keep his promise. Aaron stepped into the en-suite and closed the door.

Leaning back against the vanity unit, Aaron ran his hand down his face and tried to remain composed. It was just because Elijah was the first guy he'd been with since a painful break up. That was all. It was the residual emotion from that which made everything feel more intense—more like they were both as inexperienced as Elijah.

The boy wasn't really as special as he seemed. Yeah, Aaron told himself, nothing special at all.

Chapter Seven

The hairs on the back of Aaron's neck prickled. His shoulders tensed. Someone was watching him.

He looked up from his lunch and carefully scanned the sandwich shop near the office building, one table at a time. Part of him half expected to see Louisa March rising from her seat and heading in his direction, intent on talking him into doing something else that was completely out of character and more than a little likely to drive him completely insane.

Aaron clenched his teeth and held back a sigh as he tried to push his brain into something like working order. There was no one watching him. He was getting paranoid now, on top of everything else. Wasn't that just bloody wonderful?

He glanced up again, just for a moment. Every muscle in Aaron's body knotted as big blue eyes and messy chestnut curls suddenly appeared within his field of vision and made their way towards him.

Every ounce of survival instinct Aaron possessed screamed at him to turn sharply away, dismiss the boy from his mind and turn his attention back to his sandwich as if Elijah was nothing to him.

If he'd actually tried to take a bite of his lunch, Aaron was pretty sure he'd have choked on it. Going back to his food was impossible. That was the only reason why he didn't take his own very good advice when Elijah's steps ground to a halt near his table.

"Are you going to sit down?" All things considered, Aaron was quietly impressed with how calm he sounded as he nodded to the empty chair opposite him.

Elijah seemed more than panicked enough for both of them. He stepped forward and placed his tray on the table, but he didn't even try to look Aaron in the eye.

"How have you been?" Aaron asked — but just because that was the polite thing to ask, of course, not because he really wanted to know. Not because he'd been thinking about Elijah non-stop for the last week, desperate to find out if he was okay, hating himself for having left the boy on his doorstep and simply driven away, even when he knew damn well it had been the right thing to do.

"I'm fine," Elijah said, his words just a fraction too brittle to be believable. "Are you?"

Aaron kept the smile he'd forced onto his lips in place through sheer force of will. "You don't need to worry about me."

Elijah prodded at his sandwich. "I've been —"

Aaron interrupted him with a chuckle. "There's no need to tell me, I can guess what you've been doing."

Elijah blinked at him, eyes full of surprise. "You can?"

"Of course!" Aaron ground out, leaning back in the uncomfortable wooden chair and doing his best to look relaxed and at ease, while he felt anything but. "I'll bet that you've been doing exactly what damn near every gay man who steps out of the closet does — screwing pretty much every other willing guy in sight."

Aaron had been wrong. Hearing himself talk about Elijah getting laid by another man wasn't any easier than hearing Elijah talk about it himself after all. The words turned to ash in his mouth.

The boy stared at his plate for several seconds as colour raced to his cheeks. Finally, he looked up. "You don't mind?"

Aaron managed to force out another chuckle. "Why would I?" It was the same question he'd been asking himself for the last week. Why should he care who a one-night stand screwed around with after they'd said their farewells? "Neither of us was under any illusions, right? One night, no strings, no second date. That was the deal."

Elijah nodded. "Yeah." His plate seemed to fascinate him.

To Aaron's intense relief, several other men from the office chose that moment to join them at their table. Any possibility of a private conversation ended. The requirement to have any kind of conversation faded away.

Aaron pretended to listen to the chatter about the new deal everyone was working on, but his eyes never truly left Elijah. The boy had obviously been partying hard. Not that anyone could blame him, Aaron was quick to add inside his own head. But that didn't mean he had to like the dark circles that were appearing under Elijah's eyes or approve of the way his shoulders seemed to sag as if far too many uncertainties were pressing down on him.

Aaron took a bite of his sandwich and forced himself to swallow it, even though it tasted like cardboard. Perhaps...

He took a deep breath, but there was no way to get rid of the idea now it was in his head.

Perhaps it was time for him to hit the clubs again too. Not because he wanted to check up on what Elijah was getting up to, though. If that happened, it would just be a complete coincidence.

* * * *

"I wouldn't waste your time if I was you."

Aaron glanced over his shoulder. The bartender had that particular look of bartenders everywhere — as if he'd heard it all, seen it all, and cleaned up after guys who had done it all in the middle of the dance floor, too.

God, if that was the first thing he thought when a cute bartender smiled at him, Aaron really knew he was getting too old and cynical for this sort of club! A frown flitted across Aaron's forehead as the barman's words slowly sunk in. "What?"

"Pretty-boy over there," the bartender drawled, idly wiping a cloth over the bar. "You know, the guy you've been staring at for the last half an hour? I'm just saying that, if you're after some action, you'd be better off turning your attention elsewhere."

Aaron tightened his fist around his practically untouched bottle of beer. The teenage boy that he hadn't even realised still lived inside him desperately tried to push its way to the surface and deny staring at anyone. Luckily, the more mature side of him was far too desperate for any news to put off a gossip by having a temper tantrum. "You know him?"

The bartender shrugged. "He's been in here most nights the last week or so. Never lets anyone pick him up, though. There's a betting pool going in the back room if you can't resist taking a shot at him," he added.

Aaron didn't throw his beer bottle at the guy, but it was a touch and go decision. Elijah deserved far better than—

Suddenly, an even more important bit of information pushed its way to the front of Aaron's mind. "*No one's* had any luck with him?" he asked, as nonchalantly as possible.

The bartender grinned and shook his head. "No bugger at all. There's getting to be quite a bit of money in the pot if you're inclined to play for it."

Behind the serious expression Aaron kept pinned to his face, something inside him grinned its relief.

"He is pretty, isn't he?" the bartender mused, almost as if he were contemplating trying to get Elijah for himself.

"Sweet," Aaron murmured. Elijah wasn't pretty—or at least that wasn't the part of him that was the most important, most appealing thing. He was sweet—like apple juice.

Aaron could damn near taste the stuff on his lips. When he took a deep breath, the stale smell of beer faded away and the scent of Elijah's arousal flooded his senses. Half hard ever since he set eyes on Elijah earlier that evening, Aaron's cock rose to full mast.

The part of Aaron that was still trying to be sensible, and remember all the reasons why he was staying firmly on the other side of the club to Elijah, waved a white flag.

Pushing himself away from the bar, Aaron quickly strode to where Elijah sat at one of the high tables on the other side of the room.

Almost as soon as he stepped forward, Aaron realised that another man was sauntering across to Elijah too. Like hell! Speeding up, Aaron overtook on the inside lane and blatantly cut the guy off just one table away from where Elijah was perched.

"What the hell do you think you're—?" The guy closed his mouth when Aaron glared over his shoulder at him. Apparently it was quite obvious how violent he felt towards anyone who was going to try and screw his submissive for a bet.

As his would-be competitor raised his hands in surrender and slinked away, Aaron turned back to Elijah. He lifted himself up onto the high seat next to him and put his beer on the table as he played for time, but he still had no idea what to say to Elijah. "Made any more good memories yet?" The question was out before he could stop it.

All Elijah could do was stare at Aaron as if he had never seen him before.

"Elijah?" Aaron prompted, a frown already starting to spread across his normally smooth brow.

Elijah lowered his attention, to his drink. He knew what the answer was supposed to be and dutifully filled in his end of the script. "Yeah, lots!"

He glanced up at Aaron a moment later, and knew without any shadow of a doubt that he was still a bloody awful liar, despite all of Louisa's attempts to coach him over the years.

"Any bad memories?" Aaron asked, a little more slowly. "I won't bother to ask you to tell the truth, since it's always so obvious when you lie."

Elijah smiled slightly. "No bad ones," he said. It took a little effort, but he managed to hold Aaron's gaze as he said it.

Aaron nodded his acceptance of the truth.

"You?" Elijah asked.

Aaron raised an eyebrow at him. "I'm long past the point where you need to worry about me, sweet."

Elijah bit down on his bottom lip. "I don't know, your interests are so…um, specific, I'd have thought you might have trouble finding a suitable, um…"

He couldn't force the V word past his lips.

Aaron looked confused for a moment. "A virgin?" He shook his head. "It's not as simple as that."

"So you sometimes screw people who aren't, I mean guys who have already…?"

Aaron's lips twitched but it was impossible to tell if he was holding back laughter or the inclination to tell Elijah to sod off and stop asking stupid questions. "It has been known." Aaron took a sip of his beer.

Elijah stared, completely fascinated, at the way Aaron's lips caressed the neck of the bottle. His cock turned rock hard as he remembered the way Aaron's mouth had felt against his cock. So warm and wet, so glorious, and so wasted on the glass rim of an inanimate beer bottle.

Dropping his gaze, Elijah turned his attention away from Aaron's mouth before he ended up coming right there at the table. It would have probably been easier to do that if his eyes hadn't just moved from admiring Aaron's lips to admiring the rest of his body.

The dark green T-shirt was the most casual thing he'd ever seen Aaron wear. The fabric clung to Aaron, hinting at all the muscles beneath the garment. Black jeans did much the same for the lower half of Aaron's body.

Elijah's breath caught in his throat as he realised that he wasn't the only one sitting at the table with a hard-on

"I'll do anything you want." Elijah knew it was a stupid thing to say, he knew he was making an idiot out of himself, but he still couldn't stop the words leaving his mouth.

Aaron was silent for several seconds. "Either you've suddenly become a very good liar, or you really mean that…"

"I can't lie worth a damn," Elijah whispered. "You know that."

"I know lots of other guys have hit on you whenever you've visited this club. Did you say that to them?"

"No." Elijah stared down at his glass. "I didn't want to obey them." He frowned as he turned the glass around and around in his hands. "I thought I'd want to. I figured it would be easy to find another guy I wanted to do all sorts of things with, but it's not…"

His glass was empty. That was a bad thing. Looking up, Elijah caught the barman's gaze and pointed to his glass.

"How many of those have you had?"

Elijah paused to pay for his drink before answering. How many had he had? It was a good question. He had no idea of the exact answer. "Enough to be tipsy enough to blurt out how much I want you, but not enough that I'm so drunk I want to do anything with anyone else?" he suggested.

He tried to lift his glass to his lips, but Aaron's hand came to rest on his arm and stopped him.

"Getting drunk and tumbling into a stranger's bed is a bad idea. You'll only get hurt if you start doing that."

Elijah stared down at Aaron's hand. Even that chaste little bit of contact with him was something to be cherished. "It hurts that you don't want anything to do with me anymore," he found himself admitting.

"We said one night," Aaron reminded him.

"I know."

"I'm not in the market for more than that, sweet. I'm not in a position to be anyone's boyfriend, and even less in a position to take control of another man."

Elijah closed his eyes at the unexpected return of that nickname. He nodded his understanding even if he had no idea what sort of position Aaron was talking about. All he really knew was that if he stayed there, he'd just embarrass them both by begging Aaron to reconsider. "I should probably…" He began to slide off his barstool.

Aaron caught hold of his other arm too. Elijah suddenly found himself standing directly in front of his former lover, with nowhere to hide and no way to retreat. "Do you remember agreeing to obey me last time we were together?"

"Yes," Elijah whispered. He'd barely been able to think about anything ever since.

"I haven't given you permission to leave this table." His tone was just as serious as his expression.

Aaron let go of Elijah's arms. It felt suspiciously like he was giving Elijah a choice over if he wanted to accept that Aaron still had the right to order him about or not.

He could walk away and there would be no repercussions. But there was no real choice to make. Elijah silently resumed his seat, more confused, but also more hopeful, than ever.

Aaron didn't speak for a long time. It was almost as if he didn't know what to say. For the first time, it occurred to Elijah that maybe Aaron didn't always have all the answers. Confidence didn't make him omnipotent. Dominance didn't mean this was all easy for him.

As Elijah silently stared across at Aaron, he realised that there could well be things going on in Aaron's life and inside Aaron's head that he couldn't even guess at.

Finally, Aaron broke his statue impersonation and downed whatever was left in his bottle of beer. This time, he was the one who caught the bartender's attention. He pointed to Elijah's glass. "I'll have the same."

A moment later, a glass was placed in front of Aaron. "Don't go away," he ordered the barman. He tossed the drink back and paid for both that one and the next one to be delivered at the same time.

"In the long run, I'd hurt you more if I tried to keep hold of you," he announced, as soon as they were alone once more.

Elijah frowned slightly. He couldn't imagine anything hurting that much. "I—"

Aaron's fingers covered Elijah's mouth. The older man went to say something, but stopped himself short too. He looked around the room.

"We can't talk here."

"We could go back to your place?" Elijah offered, quickly. "Pick up a bottle on the way and finish the conversation there?"

Aaron nodded slowly. "You understand that we're just going to talk?"

Elijah nodded too, but he didn't try to meet Aaron's eyes. If a conversation was all he could get, he'd take it, but he was damned if he wouldn't even hope for a hell of a lot more than that.

Chapter Eight

"Damn, I can't even remember the last time I drank this much," Aaron mumbled as he leant back against the high cushions of the huge leather sofa that almost completely filled his living room. "You're half my size—how the hell are you still standing...or sitting for that matter?"

Elijah smiled slightly from his place on the chair to his right. "It's hard not to develop a high alcohol tolerance when you grow up with Louisa."

Aaron chuckled. He seemed to find smiling a lot easier now that he was tipsy. "I had a boyfriend like that, once," he mused.

Elijah glanced up at Aaron through his lashes. "You did?"

Aaron nodded and knocked back the remainder of his drink. Elijah helpfully topped up his glass again.

"Thanks," Aaron said. "You're a good guy, you know that?"

Elijah pinned his smile to his lips as firmly as he could, but even then it felt like it might slip away. If

Aaron was going to confess drunken love for him, he wasn't sure he could handle it. Not when he was already half terrified that he was starting to fall into the kind of love that didn't fade away when a guy stopped being under the influence.

Aaron dropped his head back, rested it against the top of the sofa and closed his eyes.

Elijah, sitting on the very edge of his seat, took the opportunity to stare unobserved. "What was he like?"

"Who?"

"Your ex," Elijah reminded him. "The one who was a big drinker."

Aaron opened his eyes and frowned at the ceiling, as if he was struggling to remember which one of his many boyfriends that was. "Charles," he said. "He was…" Aaron took a sip of his drink.

Elijah remained very still, cradling his barely touched drink in his hands while sneaking covert glances at Aaron.

"He was bratty and obnoxious. A complete prick, to be honest. He didn't give a damn about anyone or anything. He was a bloody good actor, though—I didn't realise any of that until I'd already accepted his submission and taken him under my protection. By then, it was far too late to simply walk away."

Elijah goggled at him as images of a whole host of kinky arrangements flooded his mind. Not just a guy who was tied up now and again, a submissive. His cock ached at the thought. It was impossible to stop picturing himself in that kind of arrangement with Aaron.

"And he had this way of knowing exactly where to put the boot in during an argument," Aaron added.

"Oh?" Elijah was damned if he had any idea what else he could say to that.

"Never should have argued with the little bastard," Aaron muttered, obviously more to himself than anything else. "Sometimes life is a hell of a lot more fun when you don't know certain things—when certain possibilities have never occurred to you."

"It is?" Elijah prompted.

"When ignorance is bliss," Aaron told his drink. "Wisdom is a complete pain in the arse."

When Aaron looked up, there was so much sadness in his eyes, Elijah couldn't help himself. Scrambling forward, he dropped to his knees on the floor in front of Aaron's chair and reached out to put his hand on Aaron's arm.

Aaron blinked at him, as if he'd forgotten there was anyone else in the room and thought he was only talking to himself.

"I'm sorry," Elijah whispered.

Aaron frowned. "What for?"

"For whatever he said that hurt you so badly," Elijah said, very simply.

Aaron stroked down Elijah's check with his thumb. "Such a sweet boy."

Elijah said nothing. He merely stared into Aaron's eyes, suddenly wishing that he'd been as much of a slut as Louisa had always been. Maybe then he'd have some clue how to help Aaron. If nothing else, he was pretty sure he'd have known how to take his lover's mind off whatever was worrying him and let him lose himself in pleasure for a while.

Without any experience to fall back on, all Elijah could do was bite down on his bottom lip and desperately try to keep back an offer he had no business making.

Aaron's thumb rubbed against Elijah's chin until he got the hint and released his lip from between his teeth.

"Are they good memories?" Aaron suddenly asked.

Elijah frantically tried to put the pieces of the offered puzzle together, but it was no use. He had to admit yet another failing to his lover. "I don't understand what you're asking me."

"Your memories of your first time," Aaron specified. "Are they good ones?"

Elijah nodded so quickly, Aaron's hand fell away from his face. "Of course they are!" Sudden realisation struck like lightning. A shiver ran down Elijah's spine as the current fought its way towards the ground in an effort to earth itself. "Yours weren't…"

Aaron shrugged, as if it didn't matter.

"No! It does matter," Elijah argued, shuffling forward, wanting nothing more than to be closer to Aaron.

"I'm fine, sweet," Aaron said as he pushed Elijah's hair back from his face.

Elijah shook his head. He'd been worrying about his own stupid problems, and Aaron wasn't fine at all. All at once that much was obvious.

Aaron's hand slid behind Elijah's head and settled in the shorter strands of hair just above his nape. A tug forward pulled Elijah even closer, until he was off the floor and onto the sofa, half curled up next to Aaron's side and half sitting on his lap. Aaron's strong arms wrapped around Elijah and encouraged him to rest against his chest. "Hush."

"Shouldn't I be the one trying to make you feel better?" Elijah whispered, after a few moments.

Aaron chuckled. The vibrations echoed through his chest and into Elijah's body. "There's no need for that."

Elijah closed his eyes. The need for it couldn't have been clearer if it had been painted on banners and people had marched down the main street waving them high in the air. Elijah's inability to fill the need was just as blatant.

"Whatever you're imagining, stop it," Aaron ordered. "There was nothing dramatic or tragic about my first time. So you can stop conjuring up any terrible scenarios for me."

"But it's still a bad memory?" Elijah asked.

Aaron shrugged. Something in the gesture just made room for Elijah to snuggle even closer. "We were both clueless eighteen-year-olds," Aaron said. "The only difference was, I admitted as much, while he pretended he knew what he was doing. As it turned out, his acting ability far outweighed either his practical skills, or his patience. Maybe if he'd lost the coin toss and ended up bottoming instead of me, it would have been different. As it was..." He shrugged again.

"That's why it was so important to you that my first time was amazing," Elijah whispered into Aaron's chest.

The older man pressed a kiss to the top of his head in response.

"It was. I'm not just saying that," Elijah added. "It was perfect."

He felt Aaron's lips twist into a smile against his scalp.

"You must really hate him," Elijah murmured.

"Tommy?" Aaron asked. "My first lover? No, not really. Somehow I ended up being more angry at the guys I went with after him—I could never forgive them when they did anything that reminded me of that night."

Elijah glanced up at him.

"Were you telling the truth?" Aaron suddenly asked. "When you said that you haven't done anything with anyone else since the night we spent together?"

Heat rushed to Elijah's cheeks, but there was no way he could hide the truth. "I haven't found anyone else I wanted to do anything with," he admitted. He was just about to add that he wasn't actually so much of an idiot as that made him look, when the ability to speak was stolen from him.

Aaron's lips covered Elijah's mouth. Every thought vanished from his head as Aaron deepened the kiss. Suddenly, Aaron's hands were everywhere. Elijah desperately tried to keep up, to pull Aaron's clothes off as quickly as his own disappeared, but he was far too fuddled with lust to make any real use of his fingers.

Elijah was vaguely aware of them both sliding onto the floor alongside the sofa. The carpet was rough, but Aaron's hands were soon sliding over Elijah's bare skin, taking his mind off that. Elijah arched into his touch, unable to retain any sort of control over his body. That didn't matter, though, because Elijah had no doubt that Aaron had more than enough control in him for both of them.

When strong hands pinned Elijah's wrists to the carpet on either side of his head, the world became an even more idyllic place. Elijah rocked his hips up, rubbing himself against Aaron's body, thriving on the strength and confidence that radiated off the dominant.

Without any warning, Aaron pulled away just as suddenly as he'd pounced on him.

Elijah groped blindly at Aaron's arm, trying to catch hold of him and tug him back. "Where are you going?"

"I'm drunk," Aaron announced, pushing a hand through his hair.

For the first time Elijah could remember, Aaron failed to look entirely confident with his ability to handle the situation.

"So are you," Aaron added. "We're both drunk and—"

There was more than a touch of panic in his eyes. Elijah scrambled forward and settled his hand on Aaron's cheek. "It's okay."

Aaron shook his head, irritably pushing Elijah's hand away. "No, it's not."

"I... Oh!" Elijah's eyes opened very wide as he realised what the problem had to be. "It's okay," he said again, stumbling over his words in his rush to get them out. "We don't have to. I don't mind."

Aaron frowned at him as if he didn't have a clue what Elijah was talking about.

"If you can't because we've had too much to—"

Aaron shook his head, pushing the whole idea aside with a wave of his hand. "It has nothing to do with the drink stopping me getting it up."

"Oh..." If it wasn't that, then it had to be him. Aaron had made it clear that he wouldn't want to have anything to do with him after that first time, and now it was obvious why. Elijah half pulled himself to his feet, suddenly knowing he had to get out of there.

Aaron's hand caught hold of Elijah's arm and stopped him before he even reached his full height.

"I'm sorry," Elijah whispered, not looking back to meet Aaron's eyes.

"For what?"

A gentle tug on his arm brought Elijah to his knees, but he resisted Aaron's attempts to turn him to face him. "For everything?"

Aaron's tone grew more serious than ever. "I said we should stop because I want all your memories to be good. A drunken fumble just doesn't cut it."

Elijah turned to face Aaron then. The dominant still wanted him. Relief rushed through him fast enough to make him lightheaded with it. "Maybe I like drunken fumbles?" he suggested.

Aaron glared down at him, so stern, so severe. It was hard to keep his nerve in the face of the more dominant man's disapproval, but Elijah forced himself not to back down.

"I won't risk hurting you by playing with you while we're drunk," Aaron snapped.

"I'm not scared of you," Elijah said.

"Well, maybe you should be."

Elijah shook his head. The idea of Aaron ever being anything less than amazing was ridiculous.

"I don't play drunk," Aaron repeated. "I've always had more sense than that."

Something in his tone made Elijah wonder what sort of things Aaron didn't believe he'd always had sense about, but he couldn't let himself be side-tracked. "I'm not suggesting you get out the whips and string me up from the ceiling." He stared down at where his hand rested on his knee. His fist was clenched so tight, his knuckles were white. "Is that what you're trying to tell me, that the idea of screwing me loses its appeal if you can't—?"

Aaron covered his mouth.

At any other time Elijah would have loved being gagged by the older man's skin. But this was too important for him to allow his kinky side to screw it up for the rest of him. Elijah wrapped his fingers around Aaron's wrist and pulled Aaron's hand away from his lips. "Guys have sex drunk all the time. There's no reason why I couldn't look back on it as a good memory. If you're going to make excuses, you'll need to make better ones because…" His words faded away as Elijah's strength slowly drained out of him.

Begging was one thing. Demanding anything off Aaron was something else entirely.

Aaron stared at him so seriously for such a long time, Elijah became sure that he wasn't going to give him any sort of answer, let alone a positive one. He shifted positions, about to try and pull himself to his feet once more.

"I want you to do exactly as I say," Aaron suddenly announced.

Elijah nodded, quickly subsiding back to his knees.

"I'm serious about this," Aaron added, catching Elijah's chin between his thumb and forefinger and making Elijah meet his gaze. "If you disobey me, not only will everything stop tonight, but I'll never lay a hand on you again. Understand?"

Elijah nodded again and pushed away any references to the future, desperately trying to clear his mind of everything but the present. "I understand."

Aaron stood. Reaching down, he offered Elijah his hand. A second later, Elijah stood in front of his lover. He hadn't thought it was possible for him to feel more nervous than he had been when he was an honest-to-God virgin, but somehow he managed it then.

Two weeks ago, Elijah was pretty sure there was nothing he could have done that would have counted as screwing up seriously enough to put Aaron off. He was *supposed* to have been clueless then. But now…

Every part of Elijah's body tingled as he frantically sought for control of each muscle he possessed. He had to obey perfectly and, in turn, his body needed to follow the orders Elijah passed on to it, just this once.

Seconds ticked on. Elijah realised that there were several inches of empty air between them, and Aaron was doing nothing to close that gap. He looked up.

As their eyes met, Aaron stepped forward. His thumb brushed against Elijah's cheek as Aaron guided him to tilt back his head. The kiss was slow and sweet, and nothing like the kind of kiss Elijah wanted to receive from Aaron that night.

Lifting one hand, Elijah tried to drag Aaron down. He tugged at his rumpled T-shirt. Aaron swayed back and glared at Elijah's hand as if he thought Elijah was likely to get dirty paw marks on the nice clean fabric.

"I'm—"

Aaron shook his head. Elijah fell silent without finishing his apology.

"I'll tell you when I want you to speak. Do you remember what your safe word is?"

Elijah nodded.

"You're allowed to say that whenever you want to, but nothing else."

"Okay."

Aaron took hold of his wrist and turned away from him without another word. Leading the way into the bedroom, he tugged Elijah along behind him like a little tiny trailer being towed behind a huge truck.

Elijah half smiled as Aaron closed the door behind them, sealing them into his bedroom for the night. He was pretty sure the world would always be a better place once they were closed in there together. His memories of his last visit there weren't just good, they were bloody brilliant.

Once more, Aaron found himself staring at his bedroom and frantically trying to work out if he was making the biggest mistake of both their lives. His hand was still wrapped tightly around Elijah's wrist, but not too tightly. Aaron lifted Elijah's arm and inspected the hold he had taken on the submissive. The skin beneath his fingers wasn't turning white. He wasn't hurting him.

Everything was fine.

Aaron repeated that fact one more time, just to make sure it had sunk into his brain. Everything was fine. And everything would stay fine, because he wasn't going to let it become anything else.

"Stay there."

Leaving Elijah by the door, Aaron strode across to the chest of drawers on the far side of the room and opened one of them. All his toys stared back at him, in nice neat rows.

It had been so long since he'd used most them, Aaron found himself staring down at the collection as if he had forgotten what he was supposed to do with half of the items there.

For a moment, he came close to slamming the drawer closed and simply calling the whole thing off. Just in time, he caught sight of two pieces of innocent-looking fabric in the back row of toys.

Aaron picked up the lengths of silk. He nodded to himself as he looked back towards Elijah. The boy was still standing by the door, watching him with obvious curiosity, but no sign of anything that could be fear.

Aaron had his back to Elijah as he tied the lengths of silk to the bed frame, on each side of the bed. His hands remembered everything his brain had been afraid it might have forgotten. Knots appeared almost without him needing to think about them. Within seconds, Aaron was done. He straightened up and turned to Elijah.

"Come here."

The submissive stepped forward.

Aaron reached out to remove Elijah's T-shirt. The boy automatically lifted his hands to help, but Aaron gently swatted them aside.

"You don't do *anything* without my permission," he reminded him. "That includes moving."

Elijah began to nod his understanding, only to still his head.

Despite retaining the sure and certain knowledge that he was drunk out of his mind, Aaron was pleased to note that his co-ordination was still reasonably good. It took him hardly any time at all to have what was left of Elijah's clothes tossed onto the floor and the submissive stripped down to his bare skin.

"Lay down in the middle of the bed."

Aaron watched Elijah get into position before quickly securing each of his wrists with the free ends of the scarves. They wouldn't hold up to any real struggling — Aaron still knew his knots well enough to be sure of that, but that just made them all the more suitable for the occasion in his mind.

He joined Elijah on the bed and knelt between the younger man's feet. Elijah's ankles weren't tied and he bent his knees to put his soles flat on the bed sheet to make more room for his lover between them. In the process, he spread his legs.

Aaron took a moment to just enjoy the sight. "You have no idea how gorgeous you are, do you?"

Elijah managed to blush. Naked and spread, he still succeeded in blushing at a simple little compliment.

Aaron leant forward. The alcohol seemed to be fading away as he focused on the man before him. He wasn't even sure if he was capable of playing drunk after all. The dom inside him seemed to have sobered up fast as soon as the bondage came out to play.

In complete control of his every movement, he pressed a gentle kiss to the tip of Elijah's cock. "You asked me to teach you how to go down on someone last time you were here," he remembered. "Then you fell asleep before we had the chance to do that."

Elijah nibbled at his bottom lip, but he didn't say a word.

Aaron's lips quirked into a smile, and this time he didn't feel the least need to force back the expression and offer a solemn glare in order to let his lover know he was taking his responsibilities seriously.

It was time to give Elijah the lesson of his life. Reaching out with his tongue, he licked a line from the base of Elijah's cock all the way to the tip. The taste of Elijah's shaft rushed through Aaron's senses. He immediately repeated the action, eager for more of the same.

Elijah pulled at the scarves. Aaron smiled as Elijah's hips moved, doing their best to thrust Elijah's cock up between his lips.

There was plenty of time. No need to rush. Aaron flattened his tongue and swirled it around the head, collecting up all the pre-cum that had gathered there and swallowing it.

Sweet… His first impression of Elijah had been right in so many ways.

Swaying back, Aaron pressed another kiss to the tip of his cock. There was no need to worry about driving Elijah over the edge too quickly this time. There was no need to keep him on edge, no need to keep him ready and eager to be screwed. There would be no screwing tonight.

As drunken thoughts repeated themselves over and over in his mind, Aaron lowered his head and let Elijah's cock slip further into his mouth. Whimpers and mews of pleasure filled the air above him. Elijah's legs kicked out to either side of Aaron's body but he didn't take him too deep. He needed to start off with things that Elijah would be able to copy when he wanted to go down on someone and finish sucking another guy off for the first time.

Aaron brought his hands to rest on Elijah's hips, holding him firmly against the mattress, keeping him still and making it impossible for the younger man to thrust up into his mouth and get anything that Aaron didn't want to give him.

Aaron had no doubt that he was in complete control of everything that happened between them. Even if he was drunk out of his mind, he was still able to look after the submissive and make sure his memories of their time together would be happy. He was also completely capable of showing him what a bloody good blow-job felt like.

Elijah let out a half-scream as Aaron gave in to the temptation to up the ante and let the tip of Elijah's cock slip into his throat. Holding him there, Aaron hummed a random little tune in the back of his throat, calmly educating Elijah on just how wonderful those vibrations could be.

Looking up along Elijah's body, Aaron watched the way his torso shook with ragged breaths. The boy's arms pulled at the restraints, but there was no doubt in Aaron's mind that the only reason Elijah wanted to move was so he could put his hands on the back of his head and push his mouth down even further on his cock.

It was impossible to smile when his lips were stretched around Elijah's shaft, keeping his teeth covered and creating a snug little seal around him. But still, for the first time in a long time, Aaron felt himself wanting to smile when he had a submissive in his bed.

There was no pressure, no fear. Aaron's cock remained rock hard as he continued to lap and suckle around the submissive's erection.

Elijah was his and Aaron had no reason to question his ability to look after him and give him anything and everything he needed. Aaron dipped his head again.

As Elijah's hips pressed up against Aaron's hands, the skin beneath his fingers turned white. Aaron just sucked harder around his shaft. Another cry filled the air, and Elijah's cock jerked as he came, hard and fast, flooding Aaron's mouth with his semen.

Swallowing rapidly, Aaron took everything Elijah had to give him, showing him the proper way to react to that, as well as everything else. By the time Elijah fell still, gasping for breath, success was flying through Aaron's veins, carried high by adrenaline-fuelled wings.

It took all the control Aaron had left in him to pull back and let Elijah's rapidly softening cock slip delicately from between his lips. Aaron sat back on his heels and stared down at the boy, simply enjoying the sight of a sated submissive.

"Screw me?"

"What?" Aaron blinked. "No." There was a bloody good reason why he had decided he wasn't going to do that. Aaron couldn't recall what it was, but he certainly remembered making the decision and a good dominant didn't change his mind on a whim.

"Please?"

"You're not supposed to speak without permission," Aaron reminded him.

"Please?" Elijah repeated.

Aaron frowned. "I told you not to—"

"I know, but you can't refuse to let me come if I talk now, can you?" Elijah asked.

Aaron glared down at him in silence. The sheer honesty in the boy took his breath away. The fact that he was so innocent he actually believed that was the harshest way a dominant could ever punish his lover made Aaron unsure if he'd ever be able to breathe again. "Say your piece," he finally allowed.

"Screw me?" Elijah asked once more.

Aaron gaze didn't waver as he studied the younger man.

It would be a mistake. Aaron knew that, but at the same time, it was hard to believe that anything that happened between them could actually be a bad thing. He needed Elijah so much, and from the expression in the boy's eyes, Elijah needed him just as desperately.

Suddenly Aaron knew, deep down in his soul, that it would be far more cruel to deny Elijah what he needed just because his lover was afraid to screw up, than it would be to do anything else. A good dominant didn't cling to a decision even after he'd realised it was wrong.

Whatever Elijah needed, it was Aaron's job to provide it. That was what being a dominant meant.

Leaning forward, Aaron released Elijah's wrists. He saw the crestfallen expression on the boy's face as he dropped the lengths of silk over the side of the bed. "I'm not saying no," Aaron corrected, taking hold of the younger man's chin and making him look up.

Elijah offered him a small, hopeful smile.

"But you need to understand that it won't be the same for you, now that you've come," Aaron warned. "I'll be the only one who really gets to enjoy it."

Elijah really was a true submissive at heart. He didn't even blink at the idea of it being all about his lover rather than him.

Aaron felt himself fall a little further under Elijah's spell as he reached for the lube. "We're going to go slow."

"Okay."

Aaron was pretty sure Elijah would have said the same thing if he'd announced they were going to hang upside down from the ceiling. But, that was fine. Elijah didn't need a sense of self-preservation. Aaron would look after him.

The minutes slid past as Aaron worked his slicked fingers carefully inside his lover. Time didn't matter. He might have been half drunk on alcohol, but he was high as a kite on the relief of finally being able to reconnect to the dominance he'd been pushing down for so long.

Eventually, Aaron was sure that Elijah was as ready as he could ever be. Condom quickly rolled down over his cock, Aaron silently arranged Elijah neatly on the bed and spooned behind him. Wrapping the younger man completely in his embrace, Aaron rocked his hips and gradually sheathed his cock within his lover's body.

Elijah wasn't truly ready for another round. His cock was still soft, but that didn't seem to bother the boy in the least. He pressed back against Aaron's body as enthusiastically as ever, just as many pleasure-filled murmurs left his mouth.

Aaron rocked his hips at a snail's pace, keeping everything very gentle, knowing that he wouldn't need anything more than that to take him over the edge. As his senses became more heightened, he was aware of every nuance of Elijah's body language. The simple fact was, Elijah didn't seem to have it in him to lie about his emotions. He really did enjoy having Aaron buried deep inside him.

Elijah let out a contented little sigh as Aaron tipped over the edge and came inside him with several deep, purposeful thrusts. For a few seconds, he remained perfectly still, unwilling to pull away.

Even after Aaron finally separated their bodies and cleaned them up, Elijah remained sleepy and snuggly in the aftermath of his own pleasure and his un-told number of drinks. He was soon in Aaron's arms again, arching against him like a kitten, purring as Aaron stroked his hand down his back and held him close as they both drifted off to sleep.

Chapter Nine

"Has anyone ever told you that it's rude to pry into another man's toy drawer without his permission?"

Elijah jumped. He jerked his head up and looked over his shoulder. The simple fact he was able to do that without wishing someone would decapitate him, just to save him from a hangover, confirmed that he hadn't drunk as much as he thought he had the previous night.

It was impossible for Elijah to tell how long Aaron had been awake. The older man didn't seem the least bit foggy from sleep. He could easily have woken when Elijah first slipped out of the warm cocoon they had created under the blankets. He may well have watched Elijah creep all the way across the room.

Aaron raised an eyebrow. Elijah remembered that there was still a question outstanding. He shook his head in answer.

Aaron's lips twitched. "You're allowed to speak now."

Elijah cleared his throat. "No one could have told me anything like that," he whispered. "I've never seen another man's toy drawer."

Aaron smiled properly then. "I know." The smile suited him. As hot as his serious expression was, the fact that he was the one who'd made Aaron smile was even more erotic.

Elijah lowered his gaze, only to look up at Aaron through his lashes a moment later. Elijah made his way cautiously back to Aaron's side. If he was going to make his move, it had to be now. There was no way he was going to run away as he had last time he'd spent the night with Aaron. Suddenly, showing that he knew the score and wasn't a love-sick novice wasn't important.

Elijah took a deep breath. It was time to prove that he wasn't completely clueless about the kinky side of the world, and that he had the balls to fight for what he wanted. Rather than join Aaron in the bed, Elijah knelt on the rug by the side of it.

"Tell me about him?" he asked.

"Him?" Aaron echoed.

"Charles—you mentioned him last night."

Aaron's chest swelled as he took a deep breath and let it out very slowly. He didn't say anything.

Elijah clenched his fists as he fought against every instinct that screamed at him to simply let it go. Aaron obviously wasn't pleased with him for mentioning the other man's name, and he wanted Aaron to be pleased with him so badly…

"Are you still in love with him?" Elijah forced himself to ask.

"Charles?" Aaron asked, as if it was the craziest suggestion he'd ever heard. "No, sweet. I never was."

Elijah nodded his understanding.

Aaron was silent for a few moments before he continued. "There's only one man I've ever taken to my bed who I thought there was any chance that I could fall in love with, and it certainly wasn't Charles."

Elijah looked beseechingly up at Aaron, but he couldn't bring the question to his lips. It was stupid to even hope that after knowing each other for such a short time, they could *both* be —

"Yes, sweet, you're right to think I'm talking about you."

Elijah closed his eyes for a moment, just relishing the words.

"Sweet?" Aaron asked, after a while.

Elijah opened his eyes, but he didn't lift his gaze from the carpet. "He was your submissive." Elijah didn't bother to make it a question.

"Who?"

"Charles," Elijah said. The calmness he heard in his own voice shocked the hell out of him.

"If you insist on talking about him all the time, I'm going to start thinking that *you* are the one who might be in love with him." The blanket moved as Aaron sat up.

Elijah couldn't even manage a smile for the teasing. "Tell me what that means?" he asked, looking up at Aaron's face.

"Submission?" Aaron's forehead creased into a frown. "There's no one answer. It means lots of different things to lots of different —"

The dominant's frown deepened as Elijah reached up and brought his fingers to rest on Aaron's mouth, silencing him the way Aaron had so often silenced him in the past. Their eyes met.

"I only care what it means to *you*. I think…" Elijah looked down for a moment. "I think, if you had a choice, you'd want the man you fell for to be a submissive. And, I don't think I could have fallen for you if you weren't a dominant so…tell me what it means to you?" He dropped his fingers to rest on the edge of the bed. "What it might mean to us?"

Aaron didn't move a muscle. His gaze homed in on Elijah's eyes and didn't waver. "A submissive is someone who likes to be tied up the way I tied you up last night, but that's not all he is. He's also a man who doesn't just obey his lover because he'd afraid that he'll be punished if he disobeys. He does it because he enjoys being obedient, because he takes pleasure in taking orders from a man he can trust to always give him the right orders."

Elijah didn't say anything, he didn't even nod. Whatever his answer was, he was sure Aaron would see it in his eyes.

"It means a man who thrives on being under someone else's protection," Aaron added.

"Someone who likes knowing that his lover is watching over him, making sure that he only has good memories to look back on?" Elijah suggested.

"Yes."

"I do like knowing that," Elijah whispered.

Aaron tensed. "But…?"

It took every scrap of mental strength Elijah possessed to push on and say what he knew needed to be said. "Maybe there's a difference between good memories and perfect memories?" The words came out so quietly, Elijah half expected Aaron to ask him to repeat himself in a louder voice.

"That difference being?" Aaron asked, his voice as strong and serious as ever.

Elijah cleared his throat. "Maybe the phone rings at the worse possible moment, maybe we lose our balance and fall off the bed, maybe we drop the lube or get cramp or" — he shrugged — "maybe needing anything or anyone to be perfect all the time puts so much pressure on them, it's bound to make something buckle sooner or later?"

"Oh?"

"Maybe we could enjoy looking back at some moments and laughing at them. People screw up. I sure as hell know that *I'll* screw up. But that doesn't mean the memories won't still be good, that we couldn't be good together." Elijah stared down at where the edge of the blanket draped over the side of the bed, too scared to meet Aaron's gaze. "I mean, if you're willing to give us both a chance?"

Silence was now Elijah's least favourite thing in the universe.

"Where did all the courage come from?" Aaron asked.

Elijah relaxed the moment he registered Aaron's tone of voice. "Maybe it's your influence?" Elijah suggested. "Maybe it's being under the influence of someone who could be just the sort of dominant I need?"

He was pushing his luck, taking it too far, Elijah knew that, but he couldn't seem to keep anything back from Aaron. If he wanted him to believe he was capable of offering Aaron real submission, he was pretty sure that meant not hiding anything from him.

"And do I get the same excuse?" Aaron asked. "Shall I put down everything that I've done since we met to my coming under your influence?"

Elijah looked down. "I'm not saying it works both ways."

"Then you're wrong," Aaron cut in. He reached out and tugged at Elijah's wrist until he finally gave in and joined Aaron on the bed.

Aaron guided him to curl up against his side with his head on his shoulder. As much as Elijah had found it surprisingly erotic to kneel at the side of his bed, he couldn't help but realise that this position was very good too. If nothing else, it eliminated any need to meet Aaron's gaze.

Aaron's arm looped around him, holding him safe and secure. Under his protection... In that moment, Elijah knew exactly what Aaron had meant when he said it.

"I mentioned last night that not all my first memories of being with another man were happy ones," Aaron said, out of the blue.

Elijah nodded, afraid to speak in case he should say something that might stop Aaron continuing with whatever it was he was about to say.

"The thing is, everyone always talks about the same things when they talk about kink. It's always about that a sub should do this or that, that he should always obey his dominant."

"I can —" Elijah begun.

"Hush."

Elijah glanced up at Aaron. The older man seemed to be almost entirely in a world of his own. His gaze was fixed on some point far beyond the wall on the other side of the room.

"What they forget to talk about is what a dom should be able to do for his submissive." Aaron altered his position slightly, and pulled Elijah a little more closely into his arms at the same time. "They forget that a dom is responsible for anything that happens between them. He's the one who is ultimately responsible for whatever memories they create together."

Elijah said nothing. He almost felt like Aaron wasn't saying it to him anyway, it was just something he needed to say, so that it would have been said and he could move past it.

It was only when Aaron fell silent that Elijah risked speaking up. "Charles said something to you about that, didn't he?"

"He pointed out that I wasn't immune from making the same mistakes I hated some of my early lovers for making. What made me think that I never reminded one of my boyfriends of a time they would much rather forget? How many times had I given one of my submissives a bad memory in a scene and never even noticed?"

Elijah lifted his head and looked up at Aaron. He saw the pain in his eyes for all he was sure that Aaron was doing his damndest to hide it.

"You can't remind me of anything bad," he whispered.

"I know."

"And I'm a crap liar. You'd always realise if I wasn't enjoying every single second I spent with you."

"I know."

"And Charles was a prick."

Aaron smiled then. "Yes, I know that too."

Elijah thought for a moment. "What I said about making good memories, even when they aren't perfect…"

Aaron stroked his fingers through Elijah's hair. "Yes, I know you were right about that as well."

Something inside Elijah relaxed as the need to be perfect faded away. A smile came to his lips. "Do you also know that, just last night, I received a really wonderful lesson in how to give someone a truly fantastic blow-job?"

"Oh?" Aaron prompted. A little of the sadness was already leaving his eyes.

It wasn't a cure as such, but Elijah was still pretty damn pleased with himself. He nodded enthusiastically. "And I think the best way to make sure the lesson sinks in properly is to practice everything I was taught right away."

"Is it really?" Aaron slid his hand through Elijah's hair, pushing it back off his face. "You're not responsible for cheering me up, sweet. I thought I made it clear that doms look after subs, not the other way around."

Elijah caught hold of Aaron's hand and pressed a kiss to one of the fingertips. "I think everyone is responsible for trying to be a good influence on whoever they are with. Charles was a really bad influence on you."

He wrapped his lips around Aaron's index finger. Slowly sucking the digit into his mouth, he attempted to cradle it with his tongue, just as Aaron had worked his cock the night before.

Lifting his gaze, he risked looking Aaron in the eye. He still seemed so serious. Elijah had no idea what words would leave Aaron's mouth when he finally spoke up.

"I think..." Aaron announced, very slowly. "A mouth like that could be very...influential, in the best possible way."

Elijah smiled around the finger, but even as Aaron said it, he knew that there was only so much even the best blow-job on the planet could do to influence his lover.

There would only ever be one of them who made the decisions, one of them who truly dominated the relationship. And Elijah wouldn't have had it any other way. Holding Aaron's palm with both his hands, he pulled back to tease the very tip of his finger with his tongue.

A faint trace of salt was the only taste he received for his trouble, but he sensed that he was pleasing his lover in some way, and that was ambrosia to a different kind of taste bud.

Aaron shifted slightly on the bed. The blanket fell back. If he had hadn't woken up hard, he was now fully erect. Elijah carefully removed Aaron's fingertip from his mouth.

Before he could lower his head towards Aaron's crotch, Aaron's hand slid into his hair and pulled him forward. "You asked me what real submission is like?"

Elijah nodded, enjoying the way Aaron's fingers tugged lightly at his hair in the process.

"You. It's a man like you."

Their foreheads rested together for a moment.

A gentle brush of the lips and Elijah was freed to resume his descent. Aaron chuckled as he apparently realised that he was following the same path they had traced out on each other's bodies a lifetime ago. Only, this time, Elijah was finally allowed to achieve his objective.

Elijah smiled. There was little comparison to be made between Aaron's finger and his erection. Elijah licked his lips, moistening them before he wrapped them around the very tip of Aaron's cock.

Salty and sweet in equal measure, the flavour of Aaron's pre-cum exploded across Elijah's tongue. He instantly murmured his approval and lapped at the slit to gain more of it.

"That's right."

Elijah stared up Aaron's body. He remembered what it had felt like when Aaron had hummed around him. Their eyes met. For a second, Elijah remained completely motionless, trapped by Aaron's gaze.

The dominant's fingertips stroked down his cheek and broke the spell, allowing Elijah to go back to his somewhat clumsy attempts to try to remember and replicate everything that Aaron had done for him before.

He settled his hands on the dominant's hips, just as Aaron had held him in place, only to realise that there was no need for him to do anything of the sort. Aaron had more than enough control to remain still if he wanted to.

Elijah slid his hands over Aaron's sides and down his legs instead, simply relishing the feel of another man's body beneath his. If Aaron had a problem with anything he was doing, he didn't mention it.

Elijah didn't seek out his corrections. There would be time enough to learn everything he could about the exact things Aaron liked. For now, all he needed was to try, and to know that Aaron had seen him try. If Aaron knew that he was doing this because he wanted to please him then all was right with the world.

The part of Elijah that he was already starting to think of as the submissive side of himself grew a little stronger, a little more confident. His mouth ungainly, but that didn't matter.

Elijah swirled his tongue around Aaron's cock, encouraged on by Aaron's occasional words of praise and the strong hand that had settled on the back of his head very early on in the proceedings. There was no pressure behind Aaron's touch, just acceptance, just possession.

In those moments, Elijah had no question that he belonged to Aaron, and that all his memories past and present were going to be influenced by the man he was going down on.

Elijah whimpered again, as he fell a little further for his lover.

The need to please his dominant bubbled up inside Elijah, making him ever more desperate to drag Aaron over the edge into his pleasure. He dipped his head lower, suckled more vehemently, whimpering his plea to be allowed to swallow Aaron's cum.

Aaron's fingers tightened on his hair every time he got close to trying to take too much, got close to making the same mistakes he'd made that first time — back before he'd realised the benefits to be found in following a more dominant man's lead.

Finally, Aaron's hips bucked. Cum flooded past Elijah's lips. It was too much for him. Some leaked from the corners of his mouth, but that didn't matter, it wasn't going to make the memory of it any less perfect in Elijah's eyes. He knew now what the real flavour of a completed blow-job was. It tasted like success.

When Aaron caught hold of Elijah's arm and pulled him up the bed, the kiss they shared tasted suspiciously like the beginnings of love.

About the Author

Kim Dare is a twenty-seven year old full time writer from Wales (UK). First published in December 2008, Kim has since released over thirty BDSM erotic romances.

While the stories range over male/male, male/female and all kinds of ménage relationships and have included vampires, time travellers, shape-shifters and fairytale re-tellings, they all have three things in common—kink, love and a happy ending.

Kim Dare loves to hear from readers.

You can find her contact information, website details and author profile page at http://www.total-e-bound.com.

Total-E-Bound Publishing

www.total-e-bound.com

Take a look at our exciting range of literagasmic™
erotic romance titles and discover pure quality
at Total-E-Bound.